The Legend of Safehaven

The Legend *of* Safehaven

R. A. Comunale, M.D.

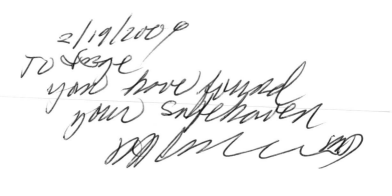

2/19/2009
To [name]
you have found
your safehaven

MOUNTAIN LAKE PRESS

MOUNTAIN LAKE PARK, MARYLAND

ALSO BY R.A. COMUNALE

Requiem for the Bone Man
Berto's World

LIBRARY OF CONGRESS
CONTROL NUMBER: 2008908391

ISBN: 978-0-9814773-3-6

ISBN-10: 0-9814773-3-X

COPYRIGHT © 2008 R.A. COMUNALE

ALL RIGHTS RESERVED

PRINTED IN THE UNITED STATES OF AMERICA

MOUNTAIN LAKE PRESS
24 D STREET
MOUNTAIN LAKE PARK, MD 21550

FIRST EDITION, NOVEMBER 2008

BOOK AND COVER DESIGN BY MICHAEL HENTGES

To Nancy and Bob K., the true legends of Safehaven

Recollection

Mama and Papa died for us.

Sandoval and Felicita Hidalgo sacrificed themselves one night on a storm-tossed ocean so that my brother, my sister, and I, Antonio Galen Hidalgo, might live.

Federico Edison and Carmelita Nancy do not believe that I remember, but I do.

God help me, my son, I remember it as clearly as I see you now: Papa held Mama tightly, whispering his words of love, as the waves overwhelmed them in a never-ending echo within my soul.

I remember the first time I saw the bear-sized man—my Tio Galen—and his friends, Tio Edison and Tia Nancy. I remember the night of the second hurricane. It was on Bald Head Island. The three of them carried us to safety in the old lighthouse, as the fierce storm raged around us. They fought for us, when the government sought to take us away and return us to Cuba, even though our dear parents had perished to bring us to a safe land. And they brought us to the mountain in Pennsylvania, which became our home and the place where we grew to adulthood.

Now, my son, I hold you in my arms. One day, when you are old enough to understand, I will teach you these things about myself and about your grandparents. Then you must remember my words, for you are my immortality. When I am gone, you must carry them. You must remember the three Old Ones, your Abuelo Edison and your Abuela Nancy, and especially your Abuelo Galen.

Someday I will tell you this again, my son—my beloved Galen Antonio Sandoval Hidalgo. I will tell you...

CHAPTER I

Genesis One

"He's seeing ghosts again."

He heard them whispering from the kitchen doorway.

You don't know how right you are, my friends.

He continued to stare, as the procession of wraiths filed past him: Papa, Mama, Leni, Cathy, June, his schoolmate Dave, all his friends—and all gone now.

Galen lay slumped in the big easy chair in the living room overlooking the mountain vista. It was a cool August evening, and the flames licked the inside of the fireplace glass door like undersized tigers, as he stared blankly out the large picture window.

Edison and Nancy had often seen him sitting there, reliving a past only he could perceive. It had been three years since he and the children had moved in with them—three years in which they had tried their best to understand what continued to plunge him into darkness.

Far removed from his longtime home and medical practice in Northern Virginia, Galen now sat perched high and isolated in the hills of north-central Pennsylvania, Everything he had agonized over and sacrificed to achieve during the last forty years—all had symbolically gone up in smoke along with his past dreams of wife, family, and children of his own.

Ashes where once hope and dreams had been.

He sensed his friends watching him, though they went to great lengths not to disturb him or broach the subject of his fitful sadness. They did not realize this was how he had always managed to drag himself out of the past—by embracing it before letting go.

Could he do it now?

The philosophers had it wrong. The only true immortality is in the hearts and minds of those who follow you in life. They carry your memory forward in time and remind the world of who you were, what you were, and why your life really mattered.

He knew Nancy and Edison felt the same way. Both had accomplished so much during their lives. But now, all three of them had found renewed meaning for their existence in children who weren't remotely or genetically their own. Maybe the kids were meant to be surrogates, tossed up by the Fates to confuse, confound, and perhaps fulfill their remaining years.

For the children, for their future, Galen quickly sold the house that had served as his home and workplace for four decades. He would miss the sounds of the nighttime creaking, so resembling his own joints, and the distinctive groans of the plumbing, which like his own, would need replacement to restore full function.

Most of the furniture, the knickknacks, the framed photos on the walls, the objects of value only to him, the books and magazines, went to new homes. His patient files were either reassigned or incinerated. His part-time secretaries—his lifelines and support system—finally entered retirement, satisfied that their charge was delivered into a life that did not require their constant attention and protection.

What he treasured—those holy relics of his loves and friendships—were the only possessions he carried to his new home in his ancient red Jeep Wagoneer.

Now, all that remained was what he and Cathy had called their secret hideaway.

He had joked many times with his beloved second wife that he really needed a Fortress of Solitude, just like the one Superman used as a refuge whenever he wanted to restore himself. And Cathy, dear Cathy, had taken him at his word.

.   .   .

"Tony, look, it's in today's paper. This could be what you're looking for."

She laid the Sunday Real Estate section in front of him and pointed to a small ad:

FOR SALE BY OWNER: MOUNTAINTOP ACREAGE

He phoned the seller that very day and drove immediately with Cathy to the outskirts of Front Royal, Virginia, near the northern terminus of Skyline Drive. Nestled in one of the valleys of the Blue Ridge Mountains, watered by the north and south forks of the fabled Shenandoah River, the Civil War town overflowed with history.

The property owner, a retired pharmacist, met them at the local roadhouse/cafe renowned for its sweet apple cider and fresh donuts. Over servings of both he showed them the plat for almost 60 acres he had decided to sell.

They followed his red pickup truck, climbing the winding dirt road, past the apple orchards, to the very top of Blue Mountain. They saw POSTED signs of the Virginia Fish and Wildlife Service, as they approached the crest along a rutted dirt road almost impassible except for trucks and jeeps, and stopped in front of a gigantic oak at least six feet in diameter. They got out and walked toward the owner, who was lovingly patting the big tree.

"See, here it is folks, untouched since the last logging crew came by about twenty years ago. I made sure they didn't take old Ollie.

He's been here since colonial times according to the tree experts.

"By the way, did you folks know the road we took for the last half mile is part of the Appalachian Trail?"

He walked them through the upper level, the long-unused logging trail winding its way across the slope of the mountain, its ruts filled with bushes and small trees.

The old man made a sudden motion to keep quiet then pointed to his right. Galen and Cathy saw two deer peacefully drinking from the free-flowing spring that bubbled up between two glacier-strewn boulders. No doubt, like the rest of the area, the mountain was honeycombed with limestone caverns that served as subterranean rain cisterns, until the water found an escape route.

She took his hand and whispered "a buck and a doe," and he understood.

He immediately fell in love with the place, and when he looked at Cathy he knew she had instantly read his mind in that way of all women.

"Yes, Tony."

That was all she needed to say.

In short order they signed the papers, paid the deposit, and arranged for the bank loan. It was all theirs now.

"Cathy, I don't think we should build anything on it. Let's leave the animals to their home. We can always come to visit, maybe even camp out or stay at a local motel. I don't want to spoil the beauty of this place.

"Besides, Mr. and Mrs. Deer were here first."

Once more she answered him, as he knew she would.

"Yes, Tony."

Then came that fateful dinner and his nervous question: "What's the matter, honey?"

An MRI followed, sketching his beloved wife's fate in glowing electrons on the monitor screen: metastasized pancreatic cancer. Like Leni before her, and like nearly everything else that had mattered in his life, Cathy was soon taken from him.

Afterward he had made the pilgrimage to their special place every chance he could, walking the trails, pretending that Cathy and Leni were by his side, rushing to be the first to name the plants and animals each had spotted. He felt thankful for the isolation. Not that it mattered, but anyone watching him as he talked to himself surely would have considered him crazy and fled down the mountain. Yet alone, he said what he wanted—his heart exposing its deepest feelings—and even talked to the animals. They didn't mind.

．　　．　　．

He hadn't returned to the hideaway for quite a while. His relentless workload had acted as a diversion. Truth be told, as the years passed, he had built up a reluctance to go. The relief and exhilaration he originally felt had been replaced by creeping sadness. And now the children had become the focal point in his life.

Maybe it was time.

Alone in his room he sat at his desk and mapped out the logistics of the trip in his mind before approaching the others.

"How would you all like to take a quick trip to my Fortress of Solitude?"

Edison and Nancy responded with looks of puzzlement. This was the most energetic their friend had sounded since he had moved in.

Even Galen realized the incongruity, so he tried to lighten the mood.

"I figure we might have to hide out there if the government ever decides to avenge their man Thornton, after we dissed him so badly. I still can't believe we got away with becoming guardians of the kids."

They immediately relaxed.

"It needed to be done," Nancy replied. "People shouldn't just be pawns for the powerful to play with. I still think if Thornton hadn't been convicted on federal charges the children would have been sent back to Cuba."

Edison quipped, "Yeah, imagine, a federal official lying. Who would have thought it possible?"

The three burst into spontaneous laughter.

"Besides," Edison continued, "they wouldn't blame us, they'd blame Judge Todwell. She's the one who went to bat for us and made it easy for us to adopt the kids."

Galen interjected, "*Mirabile dictu*, an honest public figure. Amazing!"

Edison paused.

"I wonder if she and that lawyer ... what's his name ... Comer are still ... uh ... friendly."

Nancy shot him a quick conspiratorial look, and he blushed. Then she turned to Galen.

"When would you want to go?"

"How about tomorrow?" Edison piped up.

Now Galen paused.

"Hmm, that way, if the black helicopters come for us, we'll be gone."

That did it. Once more the three shared a burst of laughter.

The children, who had witnessed the exchange, studied their guardians, and then nine-year-old Freddie turned to his sister.

"*Que loco!*"

Carmelita, who had just celebrated her tenth birthday, promptly smacked the top of his head and told him to stop being so disrespectful.

"*Si, mamacita Carmelita!*" he replied, mocking her.

She smacked him again.

Eight-year-old Antonio kept his mouth shut.

Edison drove them in his "kidmobile," as he now called his minivan, down Interstate 81 through Harrisburg. There they picked up U.S. Route 15 and followed it south to Frederick, Maryland, where it joined I-270 into the Washington, D.C., area. Edison surprised Galen by veering from the plan and taking Route 340 west for a few miles before resuming on Route 15.

"I really hate the Beltway," he grumped, but Nancy understood. They knew that even a brief approach to Galen's old home would sink their friend's mood, and though they had dealt with him patiently since he had moved to the mountaintop, both were becoming a little weary of it all. And they knew the visit to his former refuge would be emotional enough.

As it turned out, the detour provided some scenic benefit, meandering as it did through some gorgeous countryside before widening through the now-sprawling outskirts of Leesburg, Virginia, then shooting straight down to join I-66 west near Manassas.

Nancy took in the gigantic outlet malls and sea of townhouse clusters lining both sides of the wide highway. She wondered what the many men who had fought and died in this area in the Civil War nearly 150 years ago would think of it all.

The interstate began a detectable rise, as the surroundings gradually changed to horse and dairy farms, and they could see the first row of the Blue Ridge Mountains in the distance, their tops appearing volcanic in the heavy mist. They were part of the vast Appalachians, which run more than a thousand miles from Georgia to Maine and are among the oldest ranges on Earth.

They rode through a cleft in the hills near Delaplane then descended into a valley outside the small community of Linden.

"Here's our exit," Galen called out.

They pulled off the highway and stopped at the roadhouse where he and Cathy had closed the deal so many years ago. It had changed a bit, not quite as rural or folksy, but it still featured cider and donuts.

"Okay, guys and gals, pit stop and eats," Edison called out. He knew Galen needed the break as badly as he did.

Ah, the pleasures of senior-citizen bladders!

Newly relieved, they reconvened at one of the tables that reminded the three adults of the old diners populating every rural roadside after World War II: chrome-trimmed, Formica counters and the long soda bar with red vinyl, mushroom-pedestal seats that stretched the length of the room.

After wolfing down donuts with apple juice—an act for which Edison's dyspepsia would punish him later—they wandered through the adjoining crafts shop, which was loaded with hand-made quilts, wooden lawn ornaments and signs, and stuffed animals. The kids were fascinated by all the toys made of wood. Edison, ever the master carpenter, made mental notes on how he would duplicate them in his shop.

Nancy and Carmelita browsed the dry goods and quilts, while the boys pulled at the two men, pleading for the specialty of the house: raccoon-tail fur hats.

Edison grabbed a hat and put it on.

Galen did likewise.

"Fess Parker," he said.

"Buddy Ebsen," Edison replied, grinning.

A beat, and then suddenly as if on cue the two sang, in unison, "Davey, Davey Crockett, king of the wild frontier!"

Those younger than sixty just stared in confusion.

Galen bought hats for each of the boys and offered to get one for Edison and Carmelita as well. Edison was tempted but noticed Nancy's disapproving look and declined.

Carmelita also declined but did ask for something else: a framed needlepoint. It was in the style of an 1830s-vintage sampler, done by young girls in the distant past to demonstrate their home skills. She didn't know that, of course. She only knew it somehow attracted her, its border of birds and good-luck signs double-framing its message, which she read in her now-flawless English:

"Bless the children of this house and those who love them so."

Edison, faster than Galen at pulling out his wallet, took the framed art to the counter.

"How about one last bathroom break?" Galen asked. He and Edison took the boys, and Nancy took Carmelita. Apple cider makes a very effective diuretic.

They headed briefly along state route 55 then turned at the old general store. The former dirt road, now paved, twisted and turned up Blue Mountain.

Not just the pavement had changed. The apple orchards had fallen victim to the lure of developers' money. Where once row after row of carefully pruned trees blossomed in the spring and appeared laden with Christmas-ornament-colored apple globes in the fall, new houses were sprouting.

The three adults sighed wordlessly, as older people often do when confronted by the inevitability of change.

As they climbed higher, Galen saw the reason why the old gravel road had been replaced by asphalt: two giant microwave-relay towers at the mountain crest, joined by an even more recent cell phone tower. He missed the rumble-bumps of the old road—but his kidneys didn't.

"Look at that," Edison said almost giddily. "I helped design those beasties!"

Sometimes, change is not so hard to take.

Nancy looked admiringly at her husband. She knew all the great things he had accomplished in his long career, for many of which others had claimed credit. She leaned over and kissed his cheek.

They reached a crossroads at the top, and the pavement ran out.

"Behold the Fortress of Solitude," Galen announced.

The kids had no idea what he was talking about, but they perked up and looked out the windows, as Edison drove onto the tree-haloed, narrow dirt road, still posted with the wildlife-service signs, that ended at the giant oak. Old Ollie still cast its mighty shadow over the entrance.

As the children unfastened their seatbelts, Nancy took charge.

"Now listen carefully, kids. You stay here with us. Don't go running off to play yet, understand?"

All three nodded.

Nancy knew the boys wanted to race around like the wind, but until everyone got their bearings on this mountain, she didn't want to take any chances. Sure enough, Tonio and Freddie quickly disappeared. She looked around nervously, until she saw Freddie tagging along with Edison and Tonio heading after Galen.

Well, as long as the men don't get lost, the boys won't, either.

Galen walked slowly down the logging path. He wanted to visit the spring once more. He heard footsteps running up behind him and turned to see Tonio. Though he had relished the thought of being alone for a while, he realized it would be good to share this with the boy. So he put on a smile.

"Come, Tonio, let's go to a very special place, a place where the animals come to drink. You and I will be the first to see it, okay? Then we can bring your brother and sister with Tia Nancy and Tio Edison."

He walked even more slowly now that Tonio was with him. Yes, it was better to have company, to share observations, to give of one's self by teaching another.

"Look, Tonio, see that? It's a pileated woodpecker. And over there, Trifolium plants."

Each new site brought forth burbles of delight from the boy.

As they neared the spring, Galen gestured to Tonio to keep very, very quiet. They moved as silently as a young boy and an old man could. Luck was with them. They saw two raccoons drinking from the pool that the dam of glacial rock had formed below the spring. Tonio tugged on his coonskin hat, as he watched the animals wash their faces in the clear-flowing water.

Suddenly Galen heard Edison shouting.

"Freddie, Freddie! Where are you? Come on now, get back here!"

Galen motioned for Tonio to follow, and they headed as fast as they could up the mountainside. They found Edison, Nancy, and Carmelita in a panic.

"What happened?"

"I don't know. Freddie and I were walking over that crest. I sat down to tie my shoelaces, and when I stood up he was gone! Nancy and Carmelita didn't see him, either."

Galen's mind raced. Little boys do foolish things. He spoke quietly to conceal his own nervousness.

"First, everybody should stay together. We'll all go back to the place where Freddie disappeared. Then we'll plan our search."

The five moved slowly toward the crest, turning their heads left and right, trying to catch a glimpse of the missing boy. As they mounted the hillside, Nancy spotted something.

"Look, his cap! He must have come this way!"

They moved toward the fur hat caught on one of the ever-present, wild-raspberry canes.

"Slow down." Galen spoke quietly. "And pipe down. Watch the ground for any sign of his tracks, and listen for him."

As they proceeded, Nancy noticed a depression in the moss and forest-plant ground cover. Then they all saw it: a hole, who knows how deep, but just wide enough to swallow a young and maybe overly curious boy. Was it an animal burrow or a surface communication to the vast, underlying limestone honeycombs in the mountain? The three adults silently prayed for the shallow-burrow alternative.

They moved ahead slowly and carefully, not wanting to disturb any dirt by their vibrations. Edison gently squatted down next to the hole and tried to peer inside, but the cover was too dense to reveal anything.

"Freddie, Freddie," he called. "It's Tio Eddie. Can you hear me?"

All five strained their ears and waited.

He tried again. "Freddie, its okay, you didn't do anything wrong. We just want to help you."

Then they all heard the soft whimpering. From the sound of it, Freddie hadn't dropped in very far. Nancy spread apart the cover and stuck her face in the opening.

"Its okay, Freddie, we're all here—me, Carmie, Tonio, your tios. We want to get you out. *Queremos ayudarle.* Tio Eddie will get some rope and a flashlight from the car."

At that, Edison took off through the forest.

"*Escuche cuidadosamente.* Listen carefully, Freddie. We know you're a big boy. When Tio Eddie returns, he's going to lower the flashlight with the rope. When you get it, I want you to shine the light to where you hear us and tug on the rope. Okay? *¿Usted entiende?*"

She heard him snuffle then say "yes."

Soon Edison charged back carrying a coil of heavy tacking rope, flashlight, car shovel, and a bag of chocolate candies—as usual, he traveled prepared. He lay flat on the ground next to the hole, while Galen tied one end of the rope around a nearby tree. Edison tied a smaller string to the rope, attached the flashlight to it, and then spoke as calmly as he could.

"Freddie. I'm going to lower the flashlight to you. It will be on, so you should see the light. When you get it, hold onto it very tightly. Shine the light back up, so we can see where you are."

Nancy piped in.

"*¿Todo a la derecha? All right? ¿Usted entendía?* Do you understand?"

She had made it a habit to mix English and Spanish when speaking to the children.

"Yes," was the sheepish reply.

Edison lowered the rope slowly. About six feet played out before he felt a tug on it.

Good! He's not too deep.

He stuck his head as far in as he could and saw the light beam.

"Good boy, Freddie!" Edison said. "Now turn the flashlight around toward you so I can see where you are."

"*Brille la linterna en se,*" Nancy added.

The light moved and Freddie's face appeared. Edison saw the frightened boy sitting in a small, natural, cave-like formation with his knees drawn up to his chin.

"Freddie, remember when you and Tonio and I played cowboys, and I made a lasso out of the big electrical cable, and we practiced making loops with it?"

He didn't wait for a reply.

"Make the same loop with the rope then put the lasso under your arms."

"*¿Usted entendía?*" Nancy asked again.

Edison called down, "Did you do that, Freddie?"

"Yes."

"Shine the light on yourself again, so I can see what a good job you've done."

The light moved erratically then outlined the boy. He had done it right, just like when they were playing.

"Freddie, I want you to raise your arms up high and grab the rope. It's going to feel very tight across your chest. Tio Galen and I will pull you up, so hang on."

He felt the rope moving. Galen stood behind him, wrapping the cord around his powerful forearm for traction.

"Edison, keep lying there to help guide the rope, while Nancy and I do the pulling. Keep your flashlight trained on it to make sure nothing sharp is in the way."

Edison nodded. Galen and Nancy began a slow, steady, backward motion. They felt the weight increase, as they pulled the boy toward the opening.

Edison held the light in his teeth, while he used both hands to prevent the rope from rubbing the sidewall of the tunnel. The other two children stood wide-eyed, watching the determination of the three adults to save their brother.

Little hands clutching the rope appeared first, and then Freddie's head, torso, rump, and legs slid through the opening.

Galen experienced a strange thought: *Good Lord! The forest just gave birth to Edison's new son!*

Nancy removed the "umbilical cord" from Freddie, who was blinking at the sudden burst of leaf-dappled sunlight hitting his dark-acclimated eyes.

Carmelita and Tonio moved toward him with the bag of candy, and Tonio put the coonskin cap back on his brother's head. He examined Freddie, dirt-streaked all over, and made the remark that broke the tension-filled moment.

"Freddie, you smell like dog poo!"

Galen's face creased in a rare smile.

"Congratulations, Edison, you have a bouncing new son!"

Nancy cleaned up Freddie as best she could and wrapped him in one of the car blankets. Edison carried him at the head of a triumphant procession back to the vehicle. By the time they reached it, Freddie had scarfed down most of the candy and was falling asleep in Edison's arms.

"It must have been a fox den at one time," Nancy guessed.

"Most likely, since Freddie got covered in their refuse," Galen replied.

"I think we need to get him washed up at a gas station," Edison chimed in. "Otherwise this car will be uninhabitable."

Galen couldn't resist. "Better learn how to change diapers, little brother."

As they headed back down the mountain, they once again passed the wildlife-service signs, and then and there Galen decided his mountain refuge would forever remain a safe haven for its animal inhabitants. He would donate the land to the Commonwealth of Virginia, and it would become part of the preserve.

Cathy would like that, he mused, and the wind blowing through the open car window seemed to whisper, *"Yes, Tony."*

The water-hose-improvised shower at the gas station sufficiently deodorized Freddie to allow the rest of the passengers to breathe through their noses again.

As they drove away, Galen noticed that Edison was exhibiting signs of post-traumatic anxiety letdown, which he had seen so often in new parents.

Nancy also seemed a little disconcerted, sitting in the back with the three kids, who by now were sufficiently sugar-loaded that they bounced between buzz and somnolence.

"Why don't we salvage the day, Edison," Galen said softly. "I know a campground and portage site along the river not too far from here. We brought the kids' swimsuits, and you and Nancy could do a bit of canoeing—just like in the old days, eh?"

He nudged his friend gently, and Edison laughed.

"What about you? You can't just sit in the car and pretend you're Buddha."

"No problem," Galen replied. "There's a bunch of trails along the Shenandoah. I'll commune with nature while the rest of you get wet."

Twenty minutes later they pulled into the campground.

"Bob, why don't you and Galen go rent the canoe?" Nancy said, as she guided Carmelita, Freddie, and Tonio toward the bathhouse.

The two men headed to the rental desk, and Edison picked out what he called a "nice shell." When Galen paid for the rental, Edison seemed surprised by the gesture.

"Hey, this was my idea," Galen quipped.

They turned back toward the bathhouse and saw Nancy emerging with only two of the children in swimsuits. Tonio stood apart, still in his day clothes, looking pouty.

"He doesn't want to go in the canoe," Nancy said in exasperation.

Galen walked over to the boy.

"What's wrong, Tonio?"

He lowered his eyes then looked up at Galen.

"No tengo gusto del agua."

Galen's Spanish was minimal, but he understood.

Strange, he understands and speaks English fluently now but reverts to his early childhood tongue when upset.

"That's okay, Tonio. You can walk with me through the woods instead."

He turned to Edison, who had been watching the exchange.

"Why don't you and Nancy show the kids some of your old-style canoeing? I'll rent a second shell. Nancy and Carmelita can go in one, and you and Freddie can take the other. You could make it a race between the guys and the gals."

Edison opened his mouth, but before he could speak Galen had taken out his wallet and turned toward the desk, where he rented another canoe. When he rejoined his friend, he said with a feinted grumble: "This better not lead to any canoodling later on, you old goat!"

Edison grinned and winked.

Galen turned to Nancy and the children.

"Tonio and I will follow the trail along the river up to the bend that looks over the abandoned Civil War railroad crossing. We'll act as judges to see which team gets there first. Okay?"

The quartet nodded.

Galen and Tonio headed for the trail, while Nancy and Edison slid the canoes to the edge of the river. They made sure Carmelita and Freddie's life jackets were secured, helped the children into their respective shells, and then carefully climbed aboard.

"Nancy, let's use that large Jackson Oak tree on the bank as the starting point. Freddie, I want you to watch how I hold the paddle and how I bring it down into the water to get the most force behind it. Carmelita, watch how your tia does the paddling. After a while, we'll let you join in."

Whatever trepidation the children might have felt about being on the water quickly dissipated. This was a calm, shallow stream, not a vast, raging ocean, and the pleasantness of the day captivated them all.

Memory inevitably slipped Edison and Nancy back to the first day they met—only now they sat in separate canoes. Under their controlled paddling, they moved the boats to the middle of the river and held their position.

"We'll start on the count of three," Nancy said.

The children shouted, in unison, "ONE, TWO, THREE!" and Nancy and Edison began energetically stroking, as the canoes shot forward, one and all laughing loudly.

"Tio Galen, are you angry that I didn't want to go in the water?"

"No, Tonio. I know you must have a very good reason. Do you want to talk about it?"

Tonio meekly shook his head, so Galen continued walking but moving slowly enough for him to keep up.

Then Tonio stopped, and Galen stopped as well, turning to him.

"What's wrong?"

"Tio, do you love me as much as you love Freddie and Carm?"

He saw that the boy was serious.

"Of course, Tonio! Why do you ask?"

"Would you have saved me like Tio Eddie saved Freddie today?"

Galen squatted down to look him in the eye.

"Yes, Tonio. Tio Eddie, Tia Nancy, and I would have worked just as hard, maybe even harder, to save you if you had been in trouble."

Then he reached over, swept the boy up on his shoulders, and resumed the tour of the trail. In minutes he was pointing out and naming the birds, small animals, and plants they encountered, and Tonio grew giddy at the new experiences.

Galen's eyes misted, as he realized how much the boy's moods were like his own, and he wondered if having a son would have been like this.

The two canoes swept forward, bows neck and neck, as they rounded one river bend then another. The water grew a little darker now, almost channel depth. Soon the old railroad crossing trestle appeared in the distance, as well as something else among the glacier-strewn boulders.

Just then Freddie yelled, "What's that?"

Nancy and Edison saw the problem immediately: An overturned canoe abutted one of the large stones, a young girl clinging to the side.

Both adults paddled toward the trouble spot, with Edison's canoe getting there first. He caught water to bring the boat to a stop, reached over carefully to avoid tipping, and with Freddie's help lifted the girl aboard.

"Nancy, I'm going to take this child to the rendezvous point with Galen. She doesn't appear hurt, just in shock. Will you show Carmelita how to salvage an overturned canoe and follow us to the bridge crossing?"

"Sure," she replied. "We'll be right behind you."

The girl was conscious but moaning softly.

"My sister, where is she?"

Edison bent toward her.

"Was someone else in the canoe with you?"

She started to cry.

"We got into an argument, and somehow the boat tipped over."

"There she is!" Freddie yelled and pointed toward a second rock farther on.

Edison paddled hard toward the other girl, who appeared unconscious. Suddenly Freddie leaped out of the boat. Before Edison could stop him, he swam toward her. He reached her quickly and instinctively threw his arms around her to raise her up. Edison arrived a few moments later, positioned the canoe, and slowly lifted the child into it.

Then Freddie spotted his brother and Galen, but before he could call out, Edison had reached over and wrenched him into the canoe by his shorts.

"Freddie, I could..." he started to say but thought better of his words. He quickly paddled to the river bank, where Galen and Tonio were now standing. Nancy and Carmelita were not far behind, with the girls' canoe in tow. All the boats ran up the sloping bank together.

Galen reached out and pulled both canoes farther onto the sandy soil then scanned the two new occupants of Edison's canoe. The older girl, about twelve, was still crying. The younger one was breathing but not moving. He gently picked her up, placed her on the riverbank, and examined her for injuries.

"Tio Galen, will she live?" Freddie whispered.

"Oh yes," Galen said, smiling, as the girl opened her eyes and saw the wet boy standing next to the big man.

At nine years old going on sixteen, Freddie couldn't take his eyes off her. Her hazel eyes seemed to penetrate his water-soaked skin. Wet, blonde hair closely framed her baby-round face.

"What happened?" he asked.

The older sister answered first.

"We were visiting Grandpa Alex and Grandma Debbie here in Front Royal. Our daddy is with the Air Force—Colonel Luke Daumier. He's being transferred to a post in Pennsylvania next week, so we thought we'd do one last canoe trip. But then she started to act like a brat, and the canoe overturned."

Freddie moved closer to the younger girl. He had never seen anyone so pretty.

She looked up at him.

"Did you save me?"

Freddie didn't know what to say, so Edison said it for him.

"Yes, my dear, he did."

"What's your name?"

"Freddie Hidalgo," he stammered. "Wha ... what's yours?"

"Lilly Daumier."

Before he could jump back, she sprang from the ground and threw her arms around him.

"Okay, let's get the girls back to their folks and the boats back to rental," Nancy said. She and Carmelita helped the two girls along the path, accompanied by Freddie, who wanted "to keep them safe." Galen and Tonio brought up the rear, while Edison alone powered the armada of rope-linked canoes back up the river.

"Tia Nancy, why did Freddie do that ... I mean ... jump into the river?"

"Because he's a boy, Carm. Because he's impulsive, impetuous, and..."

She thought back to the day that a certain scrawny, cross-eyed young man had climbed into her canoe despite her protests. She sighed.

"Tio Galen, why did Freddie turn all red when the girl hugged him?"

"There are several answers to that, Tonio. The scientific one has to do with dilated blood vessels just under the skin. The human one has to do with feelings. Unfortunately, we can't control either one. Let's head back now."

Bear and cub moved in unison along the trail.

CHAPTER 2

Moonsingers

"Bob, where's Galen? Didn't the two of you come home together?"

The men had headed out at the crack of the autumn dawn, her Bob to play with his beloved old locomotives at Steamtown National Historic Site in Scranton, and Galen to one of the city's free clinics where he "kept his hand in," as he called it, by volunteering medical care for the indigent locals. The work had helped to lift the dark clouds that still seemed to take hold of him periodically in the six years since he had joined his friends on the mountain. He felt useful again. With the three kids progressing so well in school now, Nancy also kept busy volunteering for the Red Cross.

"He's somewhere in the woods," Edison said. "He asked to get out of the kidmobile on the way up. Said he was carrying out some observational experiment with the forest animals. I gave him one of the phones, so we can call him when the school bus drops the kids off. Better he keeps his mind active. I don't want to see him slip into another depression."

Nancy nodded and returned to the kitchen and her dinner preparations. Three adults and three preteens could scarf down a lot of food.

Galen sat in the blind he had set up as his observation post, quietly waiting and watching. He had trained his binoculars on an opening in the rocky hillside, upwind from the blind, and he mentally reviewed his notes. He still couldn't believe it—*Canis lupus*, the gray wolf! Actually two of them, male and female. What were they doing this far south? He had always thought them to be northern predators.

Must be the ever-encroaching developments forcing wildlife closer to the cities and suburbs.

He had read that even his beloved Northern Virginia was seeing an influx of coyotes. Deer were overwhelming the subdivisions, and traffic incidents involving the animals had become near-daily occurrences. One poor black bear paid with his life for wandering into a hospital.

There! He saw the movement. The male, must be a good eighty to ninety pounds, carrying a dead rabbit in its mouth to the den opening. Then he saw the reason why: The smaller female was limping—she couldn't hunt. He adjusted the binoculars and saw the healing wounds of buckshot.

Oh, no, Mrs. Wolf. You don't want to fall into the sights of any of our local brave hunters!

The male put the dead rabbit down and sat on his haunches, while the female hobbled to the prey and ate her meal.

Slowly, slowly, Mrs. Wolf, don't wolf it down.

He chuckled softly to himself at the absurdity of the thought.

The male nuzzled the female, and they both entered the den. It was still a bit early for mating. That would happen in a few months, probably sometime in January, and the cycle of life would start over.

Galen sighed as he watched the lupine couple.

Leni, Cathy, June. You all shared my life so briefly, only to be snatched from me, leaving me no family, no one to share my later years.

He felt the clouds gathering and caught himself.

Yet, here I am living on a mountain in the middle of Pennsylvania caring for three orphans.

He noticed a blurred reflection of his likeness in a rain puddle at his feet.

No, old wolf, your time isn't quite past. You still have pups to raise.

He glanced at his watch then quietly slipped out of the blind and walked the half-mile down to the bus stop to wait for the kids, thinking about how at dinner he would tell Carmelita, Freddie, and Tonio about the new guests on the mountain.

The dog felt the pain from the kick radiate up his abdomen to his back. It was not the first time the two-legged one had done this. Usually he would just slink away to a corner of the yard at the end of his run, tail between his legs, to show the big one he understood who was dominant.

Not this time.

Maybe it was because he was old now. Or maybe in his dog's soul he felt the urge to try at least once for dominance. So instead of retreating, he turned his head toward the large one, mouth muscles pulled back along his long jaw line in a snarl. He felt the satisfying penetration in his teeth, as they pierced the large one's pain-making leg. His tall pointed ears heard the cry of agony that only he had vocalized in the past. Now his attacker felt the pain.

"You damned sonofabitch, I'm gonna blow yer brains out!"

Lem Caddler clutched his right leg to staunch the flow of blood. He backed away slowly from Clyde, or as he usually called the big, German Shepherd-Labrador mix, his "good ol' huntin' dawg." This had never happened before. For one thing, he had been raised believing a dog was an animal, not a member of the family. For another, he had learned from his father that you gotta show a dog who's boss, which was what he had done—often. And now the bastard had turned on him. He held his hand on the wound as he hobbled toward the farmhouse to grab his shotgun. No way he'd let that dog get away with this.

"'Bout time to break in that new dog, anyway," he muttered to himself. "This one's got wuthless for huntin'."

Clyde trembled as he watched his master enter the house. Instinctively, he knew: Escape now or die!

He looked around the yard and spotted the chain holding the new dog, like himself but younger and sleeker, cowering behind the large maple tree. He loped over to the animal and they faced muzzle to muzzle. The smaller dog, possibly sensing its own future fate with Caddler, rolled over onto his back, exposing his underbelly to Clyde. Then he rose and followed him in a run to the full extent of their restraints. Clyde had expected the usual sharp snap against his neck, as he had felt so many times, but now the leather collar, grown weak and cracked over the years, gave way easily.

Not so with the young dog. He let out a painful yelp, as the stretched chain yanked him back on his rear end.

Just then Caddler emerged from the farmhouse, shoving shells into his gun's twin barrels.

With all his strength, Clyde bit into the dog's collar.

"What the...?" Caddler cried out. "I'll shoot ya! I'll shoot ya both! Dumb bastards!"

He raised the shotgun and fired. The rain of buckshot struck the two animals like the simultaneous stings of a hundred hornets.

Pumped with fear and pain, Clyde bit through the collar, and he and the other dog lit out for the woods. Before Caddler could load up and get off another round they were gone.

The three children helped clear away the dishes from dinner—a nightly custom—then sat back down at the table. The next activity, also a custom imposed by Nancy, was inviolable. Each evening, they were required to report the happenings of the day at school. What lessons had they learned? What were their homework assignments? Were they having any problems with the schoolwork, the teachers, or their classmates?

The after-dinner time became like a family conference. It was an opportunity for everyone to share newly learned lessons, to vent emotions, to ask questions or receive explanations, to admit lapses in judgment or behavior and, in some cases, for the children to accept the stern words of their elders. The three guardians took their parental role very seriously, and they involved themselves as much as possible in their charges' lives. Only when they grew older did the children fully appreciate how different their tios and tia were from the modern-day, average American family.

Sometimes, what the adults talked about actually interested the thirteen-year-old girl and the twelve- and eleven-year-old boys—and tonight was just such an occasion.

"Guess what I saw today!"

Galen actually grinned as he looked at the others seated around the table.

"We have some surprise guests on our mountain!"

Freddie rolled his eyes.

Probably another bird, he thought.

Always perceptive, Carmelita caught the unusual degree of excitement in her tio's voice. Tonio, the youngest, spoke directly to Galen.

"Did you see something from that blind we helped you put up in the woods, Tio?"

"Yes, Tonio. Ladies and gentlemen, we have a strange and wonderful new family living nearby: Mr. and Mrs. *Canis lupus!*"

"Can us loop us?" Freddie asked, stifling a yawn.

Galen sighed to himself.

Puberty isn't far off for this one. Hope the three of us can handle it.

Nancy and Edison caught on immediately. Nancy's voice registered worry.

"Will they be dangerous to us? Don't they attack people, especially children?"

With that comment, Freddie suddenly became all eyes and ears.

"Shouldn't we get the game warden to remove them, Galen? I know we agreed to keep the mountain undeveloped as a Nature Conservancy project, but this might be a bit more than we can handle."

"The wolves are a classic case of 'don't bother us and we won't bother you,'" Galen replied. "I don't think we need to worry. All they want is shelter and food."

The after-dinner session ended on a rollicking note, as Edison leered wickedly at the kids.

"Lions and tigers and wolves, oh my!"

He began growling, baring his teeth, and raising his claws like the Big Bad Wolf, and the children responded with giggles and squeals of delight.

He had to find food for his mate. The biological imperative had driven the dark-gray beast farther than usual from the den. It was nighttime now, but his powerful olfactory sense detected the smell of small game. There—over there, the place where the great beasts roamed at running speed over the hard not-grass. He would have to cross it, even though he feared the noise and the strange odors. No sooner had he started across than one of the monsters bore down on him. He felt the terrible pain radiate throughout his body as he was thrown into the air by the impact. He landed in the ditch by the side of the road. His legs twitched briefly, and then his life force departed to run and hunt forever in the Elysian Fields.

The SUV driver had felt the impact, as he rounded the bend on the tortuous mountain road.

"Can't stop now," he said, out loud. "Have to be in Pittsburgh by mid-morning."

She grew weaker. Powerful hunger stirred her, but her injuries kept her from roaming outside the den. Where was her mate?

"Tio Galen, something must be wrong. We haven't seen the male wolf in three days."

"Yes, Tonio, I agree. That's not like him. I have a bad feeling he's been injured or killed. Around here, it's either hunters or cars. And the female can't travel to hunt. She must be starving."

He stroked his jaw line a moment, pondering the dilemma.

"Go up to the house and ask Tia Nancy if she has any raw meat we could leave near the den opening."

As Tonio raced back to the house, the old man marveled at the boy's speed and agility. He felt … proud.

Tonio returned about ten minutes later carrying a paper bag. Then man and boy quietly approached within a few steps of the den and placed the chopped beef, which Nancy had provided, on the ground, being careful to hold only the wax paper wrapping to avoid scenting the meat with their hands.

They retreated as quietly as they had come, waiting and watching from the blind, until the female caught the smell and dragged herself to the opening. She saw the meat then looked around for her mate. Who else could have brought it? But his scent was not there. Something else was—something she had not experienced before. Her hunger quickly overpowered her fear, and she grabbed as much of the food as she could in one bite and slipped back into the den.

They had bonded, the old dog and the younger one. They had escaped from the two-legged pain-giver, and now they roamed the countryside as their distant ancestors once did, living off small game and the occasional, unsealed garbage can.

Slowly, the wounds of that day had healed, as little by little the buckshot fell from the pits it had made in their bodies. They would not have comprehended it, but when Caddler had let loose with both barrels, he was standing outside the shotgun's effective range. He had injured both animals, but their fear-driven adrenaline was enough to power their flight to safety, and now they had regained their full strength. The big tan dog and the smaller-but-swifter, gray-brown mixed breed made a good team, as they hunted and wandered.

They had begun to feel the change in season, as the temperatures slowly dropped day to day. By instinct they knew they would need shelter soon.

Their roaming carried them higher and higher up in the mountains, and the rocky outcroppings became more clustered, some forming good protection from the rain—but nothing enclosed enough to ward off the impending cold.

The younger dog sensed it first: a strange mixture of messenger scents—food, female, two-legged ones—coming from the same direction. He ran ahead of the older dog and approached a large stone ledge. As they moved closer, the scent grew stronger: female. They reached the den opening and found food remnants scattered about.

The older dog felt a stirring within, and for the first time in his life he let out a howl, his ancestral memory taking over. The younger dog watched his pack leader and let out his own, piercing warble. Then, from within the stone cave, came an even higher-pitched, solitary reply.

"Tio Galen, are those more wolves?"

The three children crowded the blind with the bear-sized man.

"No, those are dogs, but from the looks of them, they must be wilding. I bet they ran away from wherever they lived and now roam free. Let's see what Mrs. Wolf does. The food we've been leaving seems to have given her strength, but she's still listless. She must miss her mate."

Galen stood mute as the impact of his own words struck him.

Her muzzle twitched, as the male scent hit her olfactory system. No, this was not her mate, and so she felt the tensing of the fight-or-flight reflex building in her muscles. She inched toward the den opening, and then she saw them: two males, sitting there, watching her, not moving. She let out a warning snarl, but they didn't respond. She moved out farther, tail stiff in the aggressive posture, front legs apart, ready to run or lunge.

Now the big male edged forward, a four-legged chess piece whose movements were choreographed by Nature. She prepared to lunge for his neck when he stopped and sat on his haunches again. She sensed no fear or aggression.

Casting wary eyes on both of the dogs, she sat likewise. Canine Kabuki.

"It looks like Mrs. Wolf is confused by our two Lotharios, kids. If this had been a wolf-to-wolf confrontation, one of them would be lying on the ground, maybe with its throat ripped out."

Galen felt excited. He thought this might be the beginning of a fascinating interplay of wild-versus-domestic response. Could the female accept the other two? The humans watched the big dog crouch down and inch forward on all fours toward the seated wolf.

Finally their muzzles touched. The female let out a quiet snarl then stopped, as the big dog nuzzled her. She stood up, turned, and calmly moved back into the den. The two dogs followed her.

"It's working!" Galen exclaimed.

He noticed the three kids were casting wondering looks his way, so he smiled at them.

"Nature always finds a way!"

They did not understand his cryptic reply.

Winter struck with a vengeance. The wind pierced the mountain retreat with banshee shrieks, the tympani of cracking, ice-laden tree limbs a percussive accompaniment. Galen had anticipated the hard winter from the comments in the "Old Farmer's Almanac," so he and Edison had made some advance preparations.

Edison was not a naturalist, but he enthusiastically designed remote monitoring units—self-contained and weatherproof audio and visual sensors to transmit data from the territory surrounding the canine den. Nancy, more practical than either of the two men, had stocked a separate freezer with meat byproducts, which the frequent observers would leave near the den in case the three animals were unsuccessful in their daily hunts.

The kids' contribution was to assist in the observations and sensor placement. They also named their "doggies." As they shinnied up trees and reached sensor sites inaccessible to the two duffer scientists, Freddie would tease Carmelita by asking her who the female wolf loved more: Zeus, the big mixed shepherd, or Mercury, the younger, grey-brown dog. But Carmelita wouldn't be baited. She was thirteen now, and her Tia Nancy had instructed her well in the ways of womanly wisdom.

"Athena will make up her own mind, Freddie," she replied curtly.

"Tio Eddie, flip to infrared. Maybe we can watch them during their night hunt."

Freddie was the first to suggest multi-spectrum sensors, and now he played the controls like a pro, as he cycled through the different sensor sites and panned and tilted the cameras with his thumbstick looking for his quarry. Edison, beaming with pride at his remarkably young protégé, sat at the keyboard in support of Freddie, while the others watched the shifting scenes on the big, central video monitor. The darkness took on the moonscape color of the night sensors, and then they saw them: three canines, two dogs and one wolf, beginning their nocturnal prowl. The big shepherd had assumed the role of alpha male, and the female wolf stayed side by side with the younger dog, as they proceeded to flush out their evening dinner: a large jackrabbit.

Eating their fill—the alpha first, then the female, then the lowly dog—they suddenly turned simultaneously toward the camera and stared at it, as though the three pairs of canine eyes were trying to bridge the divide between themselves and those who watched.

Tonio reached over his brother's shoulder and hit the transmit button. Slowly, he spoke into the microphone.

"Good dogs! Good Athena, good Zeus, good Mercury!"

The animals perked up their ears then responded in trio voice, their harmony a salute to their unseen benefactors.

Now it was mid-March, still cold and snowing as expected in the central highlands of Pennsylvania. Warm and comfortable inside the house, Galen had tuned his computer to WBJC on Internet radio, and the haunting tones of Borodin's "In the Steppes of Asia" permeated his small room. A knock on the door snapped him out of his reverie.

It opened, and Edison and Nancy stood there, smiling.

"Come on, Grandpa, we just got us a litter of grandkids!" Edison laughed, as he took his friend's arm, and the three hustled back to the monitor station. The children already were watching in front of the screen and listening to the faint yips of the newly arrived litter on the audio speaker.

"Good girl, Athena," Carmelita whispered to herself.

Spring weather did not arrive until early May. The three adult canines guided the seven, newly weaned pups out into the forest. Schoolmarm Athena herded them, directing their attention to the actions of Zeus and Mercury during a hunt. They sat and watched in fascination as the younger dog flushed out the prey—a young, white-tailed fawn—into the path of the alpha, which seized its neck in his powerful jaws and administered the coup de grace.

After the pack had completed its meal, the adults again herded the littermates to the site of the camera and made them sit in a semicircle facing it. Tonio and Freddie took turns with the microphone, calling them all good dogs and laughing as the young pups' ears pricked up at the boys' voices.

Carmelita snatched the microphone away from her brothers and softly spoke the names of the adults. Their ears stiffened in apparent understanding. She began to sing a Cuban lullaby, long buried in her memory, and even the boys became quiet. As she finished, Athena began a soft moaning howl and a choir of ten erupted in doggy vocalization.

Freddie opened his mouth in an attempt to imitate the pack, when he felt his younger brother's grip on his shoulder and heard his sibling's whispered "Don't!" He remained quiet.

Summer sunlight filtered through the leafy canopy of the forest, and time continued its growth work on both kids and pups. Carmelita, now fourteen, had reached that precarious age between childishness and self-awareness. Freddie, on the verge of thirteen, was all legs, and the feral look of incipient manhood had begun to lengthen his face. Even Tonio, soon to turn twelve, was more serious and focused. Meanwhile, the pups were engaging in the full activity of the hunt.

Nancy, Edison, and Galen were feeling the passage of time, too, but for them it was the encroachment of morning aches, difficulties with bowel regulation, and increasing awareness of entropy. They knew what awaited them at the end of life's corridor, so they savored the warm breezes of summer even more.

"Tonio, look, the pack is reforming its social structure."

Galen sat in the blind with his faithful shadow, though it had become unnecessary now. All the canines were aware of their presence, and they treated the two-legged ones as part of the pack posing no harm.

Amity or not, Galen was trying to avoid interfering in the wolf-dog social evolution. He kept his distance and insisted the children do the same.

"There, see that, boy? There's already an alpha male in the litter."

They watched, as one of the pups, under the vigilant eyes of Zeus, appeared to guide the others. But Galen was surprised to see something else happening as well. The young alpha, bigger than his littermates and easily able to beat them at games, selected two others to pair off with him: a lighter-weight, dark-grey male and a reddish-brown female. It was like a high school clique with the three calling the shots for the other four. This was not typical wolf behavior.

Even stranger was what happened next: The clique members approached the blind together, sat down, and stared at it. Tonio stood up, even as Galen tried to stop him, and stepped out of the shelter to face the three directly. He crouched down and looked into the three pairs of green eyes, softly whispering "good dogs" over and over.

The alpha pup stood up, cautiously approached the boy, and sniffed at him. Slowly the other two followed suit. Tonio remained still except for his continued whispering, until the trio turned and trotted back to the others. Only once did they turn and look back, when Galen stepped from the blind. They stared intently at him for a few seconds then walked away.

"That could have gotten you hurt, boy."

Galen stared at Tonio intently.

"No, Tio, they're my friends."

Man and boy turned and began their ascent to the mountain house, side by side, bear and cub.

It was an apple-butter fall. The air was laden with the tart-sweet smell of multicolored leaves, their shades of red, yellow, and brown replacing the verdant greens of summer. Another school year was underway, and the children, the boys a little taller and all entering the emotionally wrenching teen years, were as busy as humanly possible with homework and school activities.

Edison and Nancy sat in the picture-windowed living room during their afternoon tea break. Edison took a long sip of his favorite Jasmine tea, now served hot to ward off the change in temperature. Nancy had been thinking quietly. When she spoke, her voice, gentle as always, eased her husband out of his own reverie.

"Bob, hunting season starts in two weeks. How are we going to protect the pack from all those Nimrods who think killing animals makes them manly?"

Edison savored his tea a moment longer before setting the cup on the side table.

"Galen and I have been talking about that. The ground is posted, but that won't stop the clowns who think they're Daniel Boone and have the right of passage anywhere. A few of them in town are just itching to come up here. They know it's untouched territory, and they imagine it's crawling with game. They keep asking permission to hunt. I keep telling them it's out of our hands, that the property belongs to the Nature Conservancy trust, and that even I couldn't hunt on it, God forbid I'd ever want to."

Nancy smiled at her man. Instinctively she knew that the only time her Bob would consider hurting another living creature would be if she or the kids or Galen were threatened. But they had to do something—and soon.

Galen sat in the blind, dictating his observations of the wolf pack into a small digital recorder Edison had given him. He, too, worried about their safety.

"Will that be all, Mr. Caddler?"

The clerk handed him his change and stepped back from the wave of alcohol-laden breath emanating from the broken-blood-vesseled face that stared back across the counter.

"Ya sure ya put what I wanted in there?"

Caddler pointed at the box on the counter.

"Yes, sir, four boxes of double-ought-eight shells and two boxes of ammo for your rifle. Anything else?"

The weather-beaten man grunted, picked up the box, and walked out grinning to himself.

Got some unfinished business to settle. Ain't no one keepin' me offa huntin' land. Been huntin' there since I 'as a boy. Let's see what them damn city folks think 'bout stoppin' a load o' buckshot!

School had let out early for a teacher workday, so when the bus dropped the kids off, instead of walking up the lane to the mountain house, as they normally would, the three ran to the blind to watch their canine friends. Only they didn't stay inside the blind anymore—something they hadn't told the elders. They had been accepted by the pack and could stand openly and marvel at how the young ones played at being adults, while the adults patiently watched and corrected only when a pup grew too aggressive.

Today, Athena minded the pups alone.

"Zeus and Mercury must be out hunting prey," Freddie said.

Carmelita winced at the word "prey." Nancy had taught her that predators such as wolves played a necessary part in Nature's cycle of life, but even so she didn't like the idea. She tried not to think about it, as she watched Athena boxing a wayward pup now bigger than herself.

She's so much like Tia Nancy—gentle yet firm.

Suddenly the quiet of the forest was shattered by the echo of double-barrel shotgun blasts, which startled both canines and children. The three elders up at the house also heard the shots, just when they were discussing how to keep the hunters at bay. Edison and Galen rose immediately and headed out the front door.

"Nancy," Edison yelled back. "Call the state police. Tell them we have poachers on the mountain!"

He ran to catch up with Galen, who was moving like a locomotive toward the blind area.

The kids heard thrashing approaching them in the underbrush, and soon Zeus rushed into the small clearing in front of the den, closely followed by Mercury. Trailing them, still some distance away, was the sound of unsteady human feet, accompanied by an angry but barely discernable voice.

"Don't remember this path. Damned rocks and branches! Ain't no one been here. Better huntin' fer me!"

He paused, staring through alcohol-clouded eyes.

"Wha' the hell's that? Don' remember no damned cave!"

Carmelita moved to the pack and shooed them toward the den. The adult animals obeyed, herding their young ones inside then standing guard near the opening.

A few moments later the children saw the shotgun-carrying man enter the clearing, attempting to reload while moving—a dangerous practice.

"So this is where them goddamn varmints 'a' been hidin'. Well, they ain't gonna hide no more!"

Caddler shouted at the two boys and girl standing a few yards from the den opening, "Get outta my way! I'm gonna shoot those sons o' bitches!"

Finally reloaded, he snapped shut the twin barrels and had the gun pointed in the general direction of the kids just as Galen and Edison arrived.

"Caddler, didn't I tell you that this is a no-hunting area?" Edison yelled.

As he turned to face Edison, Galen stepped in on his flank and served up a roundhouse right directly to the man's jaw. He moaned and promptly collapsed, his shotgun falling away to the ground.

"Sergeant, why are we driving up here? It's hunting season, for crying out loud. We gonna chase down every dumb sonofabitch who strays onto posted land?"

Pennsylvania State Police Sergeant Ben Castle looked at the younger man sitting in the passenger seat of the patrol car and let out a snort. He was what they called a newbie, fresh out of police academy, so he had been paired up with the experienced older man to learn what couldn't be taught in a classroom.

God! This kid hardly has more than peach fuzz on his face!

"Douglass, every state cop, no matter where he or she is assigned..."

Castle mentally sighed at the thought that females actually were state troopers now—but some of them were damned good ones!

"Every cop should be acquainted with the neighborhood he—or she—patrols and the people in it. Sometimes the routine calls can be the most dangerous."

Just as he spoke, he spotted Caddler's old pickup truck parked by the road near the entrance to the lane up to the top of the mountain.

"Shoulda known," Castle muttered.

Just then the radio squawked out, "Sixteen-oh-eight, sixteen-oh-eight."

Ben grabbed the microphone.

"Central, sixteen-oh-eight. Go ahead."

"We have a ten-fifty-seven, vicinity of Mountain Vista Lane. See Mrs. Edison."

"Central, sixteen-oh-eight, approaching scene," Ben replied and gunned the big Ford's motor as they shot up the driveway.

"What's the story, Sarge?"

Douglass was fully alert now—nervous even.

Castle kept his eyes on the winding road, as they approached the summit.

"Here's a classic example, Lachlan."

The younger man relaxed at his superior's use of his first name.

"See, down at the bottom of the road I spotted Lem Caddler's truck. He's a born troublemaker and a drunk to boot. Gets mean when he's had a few. Now, some pretty good people live up here, three retired folks, a doctor and an electronics guru and his wife who's big on Red Cross work. Got three adopted children, too."

"So, Private Lachlan Douglass, you understand now why Caddler's truck at the bottom of their driveway spells trouble? Add to that the gunshots report and we're maybe walking into a real problem!"

The younger man nodded sheepishly, as they slid to a stop in front of the house. Nancy ran out to meet them.

Galen's face was flushed with anger. He stood over the man he had flattened, who still lay spread-eagled on the ground.

"This is protected property, Caddler," Edison said. "No hunting allowed. It never will be on this mountain!"

"Remember that the next time you get drunk," Galen added. "This is a safe haven for animals."

Before the man could mutter a response, Nancy appeared in the clearing leading the two state troopers. They promptly stood Caddler upright, searched and handcuffed him, read him his rights, and led him back to the car.

The three children remained silent, stunned by the suddenness and violence of the event. When the troopers and their prisoner disappeared from sight, Zeus poked his head out of the den and crept toward the three adults, followed by Mercury and Athena. The canines faced the humans. Zeus stepped up to Galen and licked his hand. Mercury followed suit with Edison. Athena, wild by birth, hesitated at first then approached Nancy and rested her head against the woman.

Then the young dog-wolves ventured out and, seeing their elders with the adults, ran toward the children, who took turns stroking their heads and muzzles.

"I think that's enough excitement for one day," Galen quipped, and Edison and Nancy let out sighs of relief in agreement.

Freddie was rolling on the ground, rough-housing with one of the pups, when he sat up suddenly and yelled, "Yeah, I guess it's old man Caddler who's in the dog house now!"

The others laughed at the attempted pun, and the wolf-dogs yipped and barked even louder.

"Carmelita, would you hand me the serving tray?"

Nancy had just taken a fresh batch of brownies from the oven, and the aroma was beginning to circulate through the house. She knew everyone would soon be gravitating to the living room for their share of the treats. Carmelita retrieved the tray from its place leaning on the countertop against the refrigerator.

"Tia Nancy, do you think the wolves really understand what we did? They seem so tame, so attached to us now."

Nancy stacked the brownies on the tray and glanced at Carmelita.

Is this how my daughter would have been?

"I don't know for sure, Carmelita, but the adult animals seem to have bonded with us. Only time will tell if the next generation follows their lead."

The weather turned mountain-cold again. Gusts of the north wind swept the remaining leaves from their branches, presaging the first snow of the season. Galen's arthritic right knee, which had been worsening since the summer, drove him to spend more time in the living room in front of the fireplace. Books and diagrams and photos crowded the coffee table, where he went over and over his notes about the wolf pack. The social structure fit no known pattern of prior observations by researchers in the field. Zeus, the alpha, was actually teaching his heir apparent. Mercury and Athena were instructing the younger grey male and red-brown female. It seemed like an ordained succession was being established, but it would take another wolf generation or two to see if the pattern held true.

Galen looked up as Tonio entered the room and peered over his shoulder at the pages of graphs and notes in his lap.

"What's this about, Tio?"

Galen motioned him to sit, and he explained his conclusions to his eager protégé.

"Tio Eddie, can I come in?"

Freddie had heard the cutting and grinding noises coming from Edison's wood shop.

"Sure, Freddie. Here, take a look at this."

"What is it, Tio?"

"It's a gift, a gift for the mountain. Something Tio Galen said to Mr. Caddler that day struck me as appropriate. Think the old goat will like it?"

He held up a three-foot-long wooden sign. On it, in large letters deeply engraved into the heavy solid oak wood, he had fashioned one word: SAFEHAVEN.

They sat on their haunches, facing the house in the distance and the two-legged pack inside it that was of them and not of them. Their eyes reflected the amber, winter-solstice moonlight in luminescent green.

The three in front kept ears and muzzles on full alert. The alpha male, a full one-hundred pounds, let out a solitary howl of unwavering tone. The male next to him, not as large but sleeker and more streamlined, joined in, their canine bodies taking in large, gasping breaths to produce the contrapuntal vibrations of their vocal chords. The female, smaller but even more alert, added the second harmonic. The younger members of the pack sat in quiet respect, observing the ways that would govern their future lives and those of their pups.

They were the Moonsingers of the mountain.

CHAPTER 3

Choices

He closed his eyes, feeling the music, feeling the flow of mind to hand, as his fingers spread over the cracked and yellowed ivory keys.

He was small for his age, wiry with the black hair and piercing brown eyes of countless generations of nomadic tribes. Olive-brown skin delineated a nose carried forward from some long-dead European Crusader seeking solace from the distant memories of his home country. And, maybe, the genes of that ancient warrior conveyed the message of something else.

"Ibni Faisal, taala ila huna wa aazif lena alhanen alal piano."

Faisal, my son, come, play the piano for us.

He was a simple man, his father, a baker of breads and honey cakes, as his own father before him had been. Short with powerful arms, hairless and darkened even more by the ever-present heat of the great ovens, he marveled at what Allah had granted him: a son blessed with the gift of music. His arm encircled his wife, as they sat in the little room above the bakery shop, and he nodded with pleasure at his son, who sat down before the old, French upright piano.

The yeasty scents of baked goods interwoven with the aromas of spices and honey used in the special pastries all mingled together in the hot, evening air of the little town.

The boy took his seat, feeling the coolness defeating the searing heat of the day. He turned to his parents and his little yellow-brown dog, Fez, all waiting expectantly for him to work his magic on the keyboard.

He would surprise them with a Chopin polonaise. He had heard it on the shortwave broadcast, and his mind processed the twisted helices of notes, until he could play it for real.

"Sir, everything is secure. We've just done a full sweep. I think we've got a quiet one tonight."

Captain Lachlan Douglass nodded to his sergeant, an old man at twenty-four, one year younger than himself.

What the hell am I doing here?

Douglass had just been married and completed his training at the Pennsylvania State Police Academy, when he got the word: His Army Reserve unit had been called to active duty. Now, here he was in hell, experiencing the joys of one-hundred-thirty-degree days and ninety-degree nights in the Middle Eastern battle zone. His six-foot, three-inch, one-hundred-seventy-five-pound body protested the extremes.

Ben, you wouldn't know me now.

He missed his gruff patrol-car partner, Ben Castle, in the same way a son misses his father.

The beard would throw you.

He rubbed his stubbled chin to wipe away some of the daytime debris of sweat, salt, sand, and frustration. Then his mind snapped back to the task at hand.

"Okay, sergeant, let's keep it that way."

Bachtin was a good noncom—none better. But no matter how hard Douglass tried, he couldn't get the guy to learn what Castle repeatedly had drilled into his own head: Know your territory, know the people in it, and always be aware of what shouldn't be there. Kind of like Sherlock Holmes's dog that didn't bark.

He walked to the edge of the post perimeter and stared into the darkness: only a few house lights on and the usual sounds of activities after sundown. The odors of mealtime blended with crackling noises, as the ground slowly released the stored heat of the day.

Then he heard a piano, just a smidgen out of tune. He had played trumpet in high school and could still remember the dissonance of the untalented and uninspired. But this ... this came from the soul. Yes, Chopin himself would have been proud to play this way.

He stood still, not wanting the music to stop, when he felt the vibrations through his boots. Something heavy, coming up slowly. It definitely did not belong here!

"Bachtin, get the men on point. I think we're getting a visitor to the 'hood."

"Yes, sir. Just picked it up. Standard stop and search?"

"No, I don't want it getting near the post. Take the spot, shine it directly at them. See what they do."

The million-candle spotlight lit the darkness, outlining the old truck moving slowly toward them.

"Truck bomb!" Douglass heard himself yell out as the magnesium-white explosion detonated. He felt himself blown backward by the moving front of superheated air. He couldn't hear the sound, but his eyes witnessed in slow motion the collapse of the building that had stood in front of the truck. In an instant the music and the bakery were gone.

"Sir, are you all right?"

His ears were ringing, but he could make out Bachtin's voice. He felt the hands of the men, as they picked him up slowly and carefully carried him back to the post perimeter. He felt the hands of the squad medic going over him inch by inch and then sighed in relief when he saw the young man give a thumbs up. The rest of his men also showed relief, as their jaw muscles unclenched. From a distance he heard himself say, "Check for civilian casualties."

Then he passed out.

"How many, Corporal?"

"Sixteen, Sergeant."

Bachtin walked around the cloth-covered bodies of the neighborhood dead. He pulled back the sheet on the smallest one, saw the mutilated face of what had once been a young boy, and began to cry. He bent down to adjust the boy's arms and jumped backward when one of them moved.

"Corporal, get the medic!"

"Captain Douglass, I appreciate how you feel, but it wasn't your fault the boy's family was killed."

The colonel considered Douglass the best man in his unit. He understood the young man's feelings, but he also had to follow the rules.

"Look, we'll do what we can for the boy, but we can't take him back with us."

The skin grafts had left his body a grotesque, Harlequin patchwork. He still could hear and feel, and his sense of taste and smell were slowly returning. But the darkness permeated him—mind and body. He raised his hands to his face, felt the contortion of burn scars, and then circled the former homes of what had once been penetrating brown eyes. Scarred lips opened in silent scream.

Dearest Di,

I don't know what to do about the boy. You above all know my soul. I must help him,

yet I am powerless against the rules and regulations. I can't get this out of my mind.
You are always with me.
Lachlan

Diana printed out a copy of the text message and went to the phone.
She waited until a deep voice finally answered the call.

"Sergeant Castle."

Ben drove the patrol car alone now, while his partner served a reserve
stint in Iraq. He traveled the winding mountain roads always watching
for the out of place. But when he saw the familiar driveway entrance,
he slowed down and stopped just in front of it.

What am I doing here? Why should I bother these three with this?

Clenching his jaw, he turned into the long lane and followed it to
the house on the summit. He noticed something that hadn't been there
the last time. It was a wooden sign of large, carved letters standing not
far from the house: SAFEHAVEN.

Maybe it is a sign, he thought.

"Bob, Sergeant Castle is here. He wants to talk to the three of us. Is
Galen around?"

Startled, Edison jumped up from his recliner.

"Has anything happened to the kids?"

They were in school this time of day.

"No, but he said it was important," she replied.

"Okay, I'll see if Old Grumpy is in his room."

He was halfway down the hall, when he nearly collided with Galen
emerging from his room. Edison could tell he was in one of his moods.

"I was just coming to get you."

"I'm not deaf and blind. I saw the car pull up. What the hell's going
on?"

The two men joined Nancy and Castle, who were now standing in the living room.

"Sit down, please, Sergeant," Nancy said, nervously. "Do you like tea? I've just made some butterscotch walnut cookies."

They waited for Castle's cue. When the sergeant nodded that he understood, the trio breathed a collective sigh of relief. The three men sat down, and Nancy went to the kitchen and soon returned with a tray and tea caddy.

Castle didn't know where to begin.

"Do you remember Lachlan Douglass, the young officer who was with me when you had that trouble with Caddler?"

They all nodded, remembering the drunken old farmer who had threatened the children and the wolf pack.

"Well, Lachlan's reserve unit got called up to serve in the Middle East. Sonofagun if that boy isn't a captain in his own right. Anyway, a truck bomb killed a bunch of people in the neighborhood he was monitoring. Somehow a little boy survived the blast, but he was severely mutilated. He's blind now, and his face is distorted. Lachlan wants to bring him to the States for treatment, but you know how it is— regulations, rules..."

Nancy and Edison immediately looked at Galen, who turned to Castle.

"Do you know the unit numbers for Officer Douglass?"

Castle pulled a piece of paper out of his jacket pocket and handed it to the bear-like man. Galen stood up.

"Excuse me."

As he headed to his room, the officer shot a puzzled look at the Edisons.

"Don't mind him. He's in one of his grumpy moods. But if anything can be done, he'll do it."

Nancy smiled and offered the man more tea and cookies. He relaxed a little and savored the midday treat.

Galen dialed a number from memory.

"Plastic surgery. This is Dr. Connors."

Galen grinned to himself.

"Connors, have you finally learned how to treat hyperosmolar coma?"

Silence on the other end, then the man laughed.

"Dr. Galen, what a surprise! Are you still torturing poor medical students with that question?"

Jim Connors was one of the best students Galen had ever seen, and now he was tops in his field of plastic reconstructive surgery of the face.

"I got one for you, Jim."

The old doctor relayed the basics of the case, and the young surgeon asked a few questions and promised to do whatever he could to help.

Galen dialed another number, one that stirred mixed feelings. But this person owed him, so he was calling in the marker.

He impatiently endured the Pentagon's computerized menu voice.

What was so wrong with switchboards?

The others watched silently, as he re-entered the living room and stood in front of the picture window for a few seconds before turning to face them.

"Sergeant, tell Officer Douglass's wife that the Air Force will fly the boy to Andrews and transport him from there to the military hospital at Bethesda…"

He paused briefly.

"And let her know her husband will be accompanying the boy."

Castle sat silent, stunned by what he had just heard. Nancy exhaled and smiled. Edison just shook his head at his friend.

"What skeletons did you drag out for that?"

Galen stared at him with haunted eyes and replied, "Some of my own."

The tall young man in captain's uniform ran to his wife and surrounded her tightly with his arms on the tarmac at Andrews Air Force Base, southeast of Washington, D.C. He was elated, but he was no longer the happy soul who had left her. She could see the look of pain relived in his eyes, and she held him tightly as well.

"Galen, it's Jim Connors. We've done what we can. He'll look human again."

The surgeon's voice cracked, as he asked his old teacher the unanswerable question: "Why does a just and merciful God allow men to do this to children?"

Galen hesitated a second before replying. He remembered another time, another war, when children suffered for men's hatred.

"It wasn't God, Jim, it was Shaitan."

The doctor removed the boy's bandages, and he brought his hands once more to his face: long, delicate fingers touched lips, nose, and ears. Then he felt the prosthetic eye globes now housed in the empty sockets, a pretense of the reality of sight. He began to cry, but there were no tears. There never would be again.

The table held three guests that evening, as the children sat down for their dinner and discussion of the day's events. Galen, Edison, and Nancy had told them that Sergeant Castle, Officer Douglass, and his wife Diana would be there to talk about something that would affect them all. The adults had agreed that this decision should involve the youngsters.

Carmelita was fifteen now, Freddie nearly fourteen, and Tonio almost thirteen—old enough to contribute their unique outlook as adolescents.

Galen stood, after they all had filled themselves with Nancy's gourmet meal. He surveyed the eight around the table then addressed the children.

"I've already told you about Officer Douglass and his tour of duty in Iraq. And I've told you about the young boy who was severely injured by the bomb blast. Here's what we know about him. He's about twelve. His name is Faisal Fedr, and he's lost everything: his mother, his father, his dog, his home—and his eyesight. He has no living relatives, so Mr. and Mrs. Douglass are planning to adopt him.

"He's just gone through major reconstructive surgery. The doctors have fixed him up on the outside. But on the inside, his soul and mind need help.

"Your tio and tia and I have talked it over, and we'd like to have him stay at Safehaven to recuperate.

"You are nearest in age to him, so he would spend the most time with you. That's why we want to know what you think."

The children looked at one another. They were smart enough to understand what their tio hadn't said: They, too, had been lost and then found.

Nine years ago Galen, Edison, and Nancy had rescued them on Bald Head Island then adopted them and brought them here to live at Safehaven. Memories of their parents, Sandoval and Felicita, of their birthplace in Cuba, and of their harrowing journey across the water, had been steadily fading. This was now their home, and they loved their guardians.

Carmelita was first to reply.

"Tio Galen, does he speak or understand English?"

Galen turned to Douglass, who answered for him.

"Yes, the town where he lived was multilingual, and many residents spoke English fluently. But he hasn't said anything since the blast."

Then Freddie piped up.

"What does he like, I mean..."

He hesitated at the awkwardness of his question.

"What did he like to do before this happened?"

Douglass again answered.

"He was just a normal, bright kid, according to the neighbors. He excelled in one area. Even the local imam, the holy man, said Faisal had been blessed with a talent for music."

He paused, remembering the last notes of the polonaise, just as the blast erupted.

Galen waited for one more voice to be heard.

Tonio looked at his favorite tio.

"He can stay with me."

The children cleared the table before heading to their rooms to finish their homework. The adults returned to the living room, where Nancy served brownies and some of Edison's favorite Jasmine tea. Its aroma put everyone in a more relaxed mood. This time the old sergeant broke the silence.

"Pretty amazing group here, folks. Those kids picked up right away on what was needed."

Douglass held his wife's hand. He tried to speak, but the emotion overwhelmed him.

"What Lach wants to say ... what the three of us feel ... can't be expressed."

Diana smiled at her husband, so tough on the outside but tender in the heart. She had known they were meant for each other from the moment the tall-but-awkward, high-school basketball player asked her for a date. She had never doubted he was the right man for her.

Edison savored his tea.

"Think we can handle it, guys?"

Nancy looked at the younger woman seated across from her, and in that telepathy shared by women she conveyed that she, too, had found a keeper.

The boy sat silently in the car, feeling the vibration of the ride through his feet. The American soldier and his wife had picked him up from the hospital. He said nothing, when they talked about his coming to live with them. He said nothing, when they said he first would be staying with friends who had children his own age. And he said nothing, when he felt the car make a hard turn and begin a long climb up a road, its tires crunching the gravel, stopping at a place where the air felt cooler and fresher.

"Tio Galen, Tio Galen, he's here!"

Tonio rushed into the living room, as the big patrol car pulled up out front. It was early in the day, but Nancy was already outside fixing up a new planter box. She heard the approaching car and moved toward it. Edison was working on a storage cabinet for the garage, and he, too, hurried to meet the new guest. But it was Galen, moving at steam-engine speed out the door, who reached the vehicle first.

Lachlan stretched his long frame, as he got out of the driver's seat. Diana, Dresden-petite, sat in the front seat for a second before getting out.

Galen opened the right-rear door and looked inside. The boy sat impassive, unmoving. Galen stared at him, as flashbacks of an Asian village and napalm-covered, burning, screaming children tore at his psyche. He reached in and touched the boy's right arm.

"Faisal Fedr, assalamu alaika, bi rahmati wa qudrati Allahu Taala wasalta ila huna."

Faisal Fedr, Salaam Alaichem. Allah's Grace and Will has brought you here.

The boy turned toward the voice and reached out both arms.

Galen picked him up and carried him from the car. As they approached the sign, he stopped, set the boy down, and took his hands in his own. Slowly, he guided the long, slender fingers over the nine letters: SAFEHAVEN.

"Inna daruna mahallun amin ya Faisal, wa huna beytune. Wa talama tahibbu al baqua maana wa huwwa baituka aithan."

This is Safehaven, Faisal. It is our home. For as long as you need to stay, it will be your home.

The children lined up on the stairway, as Galen, guiding the boy by his left elbow, moved him forward. He whispered what was in the path ahead as they moved forward to the steps.

"This is Carmelita, Faisal."

The boy extended his hands, and Galen placed them on the girl's face. His fingers moved and felt the wetness of her eyes and the softness of her hair. He was startled to hear her, as Galen did, greet him in his native tongue.

"Ahlan wa sahlan wa marhaba ila baitina ya Faisal."

Welcome to our home, Faisal.

Freddie was next, but he stood awkwardly, unsure what to say. Then he blurted out, as the boy's hands touched his face, "I'm going to teach you how to play baseball! And maybe you, me, and Tio Eddie can work the radios together, too."

They moved up a few steps, and Galen placed Faisal's hands on Tonio's face.

"You're going to stay with me, Faisal."

And then, to everyone's surprise, Tonio blurted out, "And someday, I'm going to make you see again!"

Nancy looked at Faisal, smaller than Tonio. A ragdoll, patchwork child, she thought.

How can such things happen?

She stepped forward, as Galen approached the top of the stairs. Edison stood right beside her. Already, his mind was in motion, realizing that this boy's life was now sound and touch.

Shouldn't be too difficult to put sound emitters of different frequencies around the house to guide him.

He thought of Freddie's comment about baseball.

Easy enough to put a sounder in one of those, too.

Nancy knelt down, and once again Galen guided the boy's hands to her face. Edison also squatted and stared at those artificial eyes— stuffed-toy fabrications no matter how cosmetically real they looked. He made another mental note to ask Galen about nerve implants and electronic eye feasibility.

"Faisal, this is Tia Nancy."

"Hello, Faisal," she said, her voice quivering. "We are pleased to have you in our home."

She was glad that the boy lowered his hands just as her tears began to flow.

"And this is Tio Edison."

"I'm glad to meet you, Faisal," he said, taking the boy's right hand in his and shaking it.

"Faisal, you can call me Tio Galen if you like. It will be time for lunch soon. Your guardians will stay with us for lunch, then we'll get you settled down. We hope you will like living on the mountain."

"Come sit next to me, Faisal," Tonio said, as he followed Galen's lead in guiding the young boy by his left elbow into the dining room. He placed the boy's hand on the back of the chair he was to sit on and helped him pull it away from the table. He waited until his new room-mate had seated himself before sitting next to him.

"In front of you are your knife, fork, and spoon, Fai. Feel their location."

Galen noted Tonio's immediately familiar manner with the boy and felt pleased.

As the meal progressed, Faisal began to relax. It was difficult not to. He smelled the rich scents of simple food, the smooth, cool taste of fresh milk, and finally the rich sweetness of Nancy's brownies. What had become the habitual tightness in his neck eased, and his jaw muscles gave up their near-constant, clenching tension. Hesitantly, in the direction he had last heard Nancy's voice, he turned and stammered, "Thank you."

Edison raised his hands and started to clap slowly, then faster as the others joined in.

"Faisal, we're going to come here every day, until you feel ready to come with us to your new home. We'll be back tomorrow."

Diana and Lachlan each hugged the boy, who ran his fingers over their faces then raised his hand in a tentative effort at goodbye. Lachlan helped his wife, whose eyes had filled with tears, into the car. The adults and children gathered in front of the house and waved, as the cruiser rolled slowly down the driveway.

He felt Freddie take his left elbow and heard him as they started to move.

"Come on, Fai. I'm going to give you a guided tour of the house and the neat stuff we have here. Carm and Tonio are coming, too."

The three former orphans took their new charge on a word-and-touch tour of the house. They reached Tonio's room last, where an extra bed and dresser had been placed.

Tonio led Faisal to the bed. Sitting on the smooth, cotton sheets and soft quilt suddenly made him very tired.

"May I rest now?"

Carmelita and Freddie left him with Tonio.

He was running, running with his little dog, Fez, back through the dusty streets of his hometown. It was early morning, and the sun had not yet begun to heat the sandy dirt of the roads and raise the shimmering light waves that cooked the earth like his father's big ovens.

He smelled the yeasty scents of the flat breads and the sweet honey cakes his father and mother would make daily for the townspeople, and he ran. He ran in circles of play, Fez dancing a four-legged jig around him. He ran, and his mind conjured up the music he would play for his parents. He ran, and the notes danced in his head. And then the sky exploded in unbearable brightness, and he screamed and screamed and screamed.

Nancy sat on the bed and held him in her arms, rocking him back and forth.

"We're here, little one. We're here."

The early, Sunday morning sky was cloudless blue. Galen knocked gently on the door to the boys' room. Tonio, pajama clad, opened the door quietly, and Galen stepped in. He saw the boy everyone now called Fai curled up on the bed but not asleep.

"I hear you, Tio Galen."

"Fai, today is a special day of the week for us. There is a place here on the mountain that your new friends and I call our Garden of Remembrance. Every Sunday we visit that place. Would you like to come with us?"

He put on the new clothes they had bought him: the blue jeans and polo shirt and comfortable shoes Tonio called "sneakers." He followed Tonio on his own now, the sounds of the house and the feel of the wall giving him direction to the breakfast table. Then Tonio took his left elbow, as Carmelita and Freddie met the three adults at the top of the steps. They all walked down together.

Faisal smelled the morning dew and the aroma of trees, grass, and flowers—so different from the scented oils of his hometown. The air felt cool on his face, and he seemed to float with the little band, as they walked down the mountain. The trees parted, and a grassy clearing filled with scents of seasonal flora overwhelmed the boy. Tonio took his hand and helped him move it over the various flowers and shrubs, while the peeps of sparrows and the rawkish calls of bluejays filled his ears. Galen spoke in quiet tones.

"Fai, this is our Garden of Remembrance. It is a garden of flowers, birds, and memories—memories of those whom we all have loved and who are no longer with us. Tio Edison, Tia Nancy, Carmelita, Freddie, and Tonio ... and myself ... each hold precious thoughts here. We celebrate the goodness of those we remember, and we mourn their passing. Now, we would like you to bring your memories here."

Nancy and Edison held hands, thinking of the baby daughter they never had the chance to raise. They looked at the children and blessed the Fates for bringing them three to care for so late in life.

Carmelita, Federico, and Antonio thought of the storm-tossed raft, each straining to recall the faces of their parents, who had sacrificed themselves so their children could live in freedom.

Galen stared ahead, seeing in the flowers the faces of Leni, Cathy, and June, and those of his friends now gone.

Faisal heard music in the light breezes and the caressing touches of warmth from a sun he could no longer see. He cleared his throat and began to speak.

"Al dumuu tamlau al ayun wal qualbu maqbuthin bil alam wal ahzan."

Galen translated for the group.

"The eyes shed tears and the heart is grieved..."

Faisal hesitated, his voice quavering with emotion.

Then he heard Galen's voice, and he joined in the prayer the prophet Mohammed spoke upon the death of his own son:

"Walaakin soafa la neshtaki aw naqula illa ma yurthi Allahu Taala."

But we will not say anything except which pleases our Lord.

"Inna Lillah wa inna Ilaihi rajaun."

We came from Allah and we will go to Him.

Two voices, one boy, one man, echoed across the mountain.

A few months passed. Faisal had grown an inch since arriving at Safehaven. Nancy had lengthened his jeans and trousers to match his new height. He now knew the house well and could walk unguided to each of the rooms and workshops, running his fingers over the radio equipment and shop tools, in which Edison took such delight.

He sometimes sat in the kitchen, listening to Nancy and Carmelita talking what Freddie called "girltalk," as they mixed ingredients for Nancy's baked delights. Once he had knocked on the door of Galen's room on a dare from the other children, who giggled when the bear of a man appeared.

Galen saw the boy standing expectantly and noticed the other three watching from a safe distance in the hallway. He remembered the days during his internship and residency, when the nurses and hospital staff would play tricks on him. But now, with age and circumstance changed, he growled only to delight the pranksters.

"Fai, I understand that you are a musician. Would you like to try my electric piano?"

He left the door open, allowing Faisal to follow the sound of his voice and footsteps. He removed the dust cover from the full-keyboard, Yamaha electric, pressed the on switch, and touched a note.

The boy moved toward the sound but then hesitated, his sightless eyes pleading.

"May I try it?"

Galen pulled out the piano bench, guided Faisal's hands to it, and then stepped back, as the boy sat and touched the keys.

"Is there a forte pedal, Tio Galen?"

Galen placed the boy's foot on the pedal control for loudness.

The three children stood in the doorway, watching as Faisal tested the keys. Then, quickly, the room filled with the sounds of Bach's

"Toccata and Fugue" in D Minor. Soon Nancy and Edison joined the audience, marveling at the boy's fingers moving like centipedes across the keyboard, his body swaying in time, his voice humming along. As he finished, there was a second of silence, then six pairs of hands clapped loudly, and his mind flashed back to that yeast-scented night, and he sobbed, tearless and in silence.

"Tia Nancy, remember how you used to read to us when we were kids?"

Nancy smiled at the beautiful, fifteen-year-old girl who was no longer a child.

"Yes, Carm, it was one of the things your tios and I loved to do— reading, playing the parts in the story, and watching the three of you jump and laugh, as you joined in. Why do you ask?"

"Well, Freddie, Tonio, and I were thinking maybe Fai might like that—hearing stories, I mean. Could you ask the tios?"

The children sat through dinner with unusual anticipation. They knew normally this would be the time for suggestions, thoughts, complaints, or whatever, but tonight would be different. They ate silently, commenting only on Nancy's custard dessert.

When the table had been cleared, Galen rose as if to leave but then retrieved a book from the top of the bookcase and sat back down.

"It's been a long time since we had a story hour. I came across one of my favorites while straightening up the bookcase today. Does anyone remember 'The Jungle Book' by Rudyard Kipling?"

"Faisal, have you heard of this story?"

The boy shook his head. His story books had consisted of tales about the great Caliphs and the beautiful girls they rescued from evil doers.

"No, Tio Galen. Can you tell me what it is about?"

"We'll do better than that, Fai," Edison joined in. "We'll let you meet the characters. We'll all play parts in the story. Afterwards, you can tell us who did the best job."

At first, he didn't know how to react. He had been told that Americans did strange things for fun, and this sounded strange. But there was a man in his village—an "old one," a teller of legends. Maybe it would be like that.

They moved from the table to the big, woven rug in the center of the living room and formed a circle around Nancy, now seated in her favorite rocking chair. She took the book from Galen and said, "We'll start with one of the stories. It's about a little boy—a boy named Mowgli—who was raised by wolves and who grew to manhood as the protector of the jungle creatures. I'll read the narrator's part, and as the passages describe each of the characters, I'll pass the book around, so that each of you..."

She stopped, suddenly realizing that Faisal could not participate.

"Fai, " Galen said, "we'll read you the story tonight, but soon, if you wish, I will get some books that you can use to read stories to us."

Nancy silently sighed in relief then began the first chapter:

It was seven o'clock of a very warm evening in the Seeonee hills when Father Wolf woke up from his day's rest, scratched himself, yawned, and spread out his paws one after the other to get rid of the sleepy feeling in their tips.

As they took turns reading the parts, Faisal created mental images of Mowgli and the Seeonee, the wolves who fed him and cared for him; of Father Wolf and Raksha, the Mother Wolf; as well as Bagheera, the black panther who vouched for him, and Baloo, the wise old bear. He marveled at Kaa, the great python, and cheered as Mowgli defeated Shere Khan, the tiger. He remembered his little dog, Fez, as Mowgli adventured with Akela and Grey Brother, the great wolves of the pack.

Then, the written words ended and the voices stilled, he heard the wise old bear call out to him.

"You are Mowgli."

Another weekend and the children released their energies as would any prisoners released from captivity. They jumped off the bus and ran up the mountain driveway, cutting across the field to the old blind and the den where their friends lived.

"Athena! Zeus! Mercury!" Freddie called out then waited, as the pack leaders followed by the young ones slowly moved toward them.

Tonio, busily petting the young ones, called to his brother and sister.

"Why don't we bring Fai down here?"

Carmelita sternly reminded her brother that they had no way of knowing how the pack would respond to a stranger, no matter how friendly the animals had become to them.

"I'll ask Tio Galen tonight and see what he thinks," he replied, and then the siblings headed home, as luminous-green, lupine eyes followed the uphill journey of the two-legged ones.

He heard his roommate coming down the hall. Tio Edison and Tio Nancy had told him he would be attending the same school as his friends, as soon as he fully recuperated. The older folks kept him busy during the school week, but he missed the company of the other children, his new friends.

He heard Tonio open the door, and then he smelled something. It was a dog! No, not quite, something doglike but outside, wild. He remembered the feral dogs outside his village and the warnings his elders would give him and all the other young ones.

"Tonio, have you been with dogs at school today?"

The boy laughed but said nothing.

He heard Tonio's quiet breathing punctuated by an occasional snore. He rose from his bed—he needed no light. His pajama-clad feet cast no sound, as he carefully opened the bedroom door and, led by his ears, slipped down the hallway to the living room. He felt his way to the large picture window overlooking the mountain vista. He pressed his right ear against the glass and listened. Faintly, from a distance, he heard the triple-toned cry of the Moonsingers.

"Tio Galen, your piano, it is electric?"

"Yes, Fai, and it can make many sounds, not just piano. Would you like to try it again?"

"Oh, yes, Tio!"

He sat at the console, as the old man guided his fingers over the buttons that would switch the digitally created sounds into different instruments. Faisal's fingers pressed each key as he sampled the sounds of oboe, flute, horn, organ, bass, and more, and as the notal tones swirled in his brain, his fingers carried them forward to the keyboard.

Galen listened in amazement, as the swirling sounds conjured up the boy's native land: blowing sands, the five calls to prayer from the muezzin in the minarets, the movement of people in the bazaars, and the ever-shimmering heat.

Nancy and Edison once again stood in the doorway. As the adults listened, the music shifted effortlessly to cool breezes, birds, mountain forests, water, and air, reaching a crescendo in the startling, elemental, harmonic howl of the wolves.

Sightless glass eyes pierced them, as the boy turned and asked quietly, "Where are they?"

The band of seven moved slowly down the mountain path, Tonio guiding Faisal. The forest sounds played counterpoint to their footsteps, the crunching leaves serving as tympani to the birds and crickets.

They reached the observation blind, and the boy's nose twitched, its alar wings expanding to take in the multitude of forest smells: decaying leaves, and tree and plant scents blending with the feral.

"Zeus! Mercury! Athena! Come out," Freddie called. Faisal's sensitized ears picked up the quiet padding of the four-legged ones.

They came in threes, moving slowly toward the pack that was of them and not of them. Now their moist, black nostrils took in the scent of a new, two-legged one. They stopped. The three oldest sat, as their three successors moved forward, green eyes watching, ears on point.

Faisal took three steps and dropped to his knees. He extended his arms slowly, performing the ancient prayers he had been taught. He had no prayer rug, but Allah would grant the forest floor that honor. He bowed his upper body the ritual four times, then placed his hands on his thighs and waited.

The young alpha male walked forward first, inhaled deeply of the boy's scent, then touched its muzzle to Faisal's right hand. The two others followed in turn, then they returned to sit by the three seniors. From the remainder of the pack, a young, medium-sized, dark-gray male approached slowly, tail at half-mast. It went down on all fours and slowly inched forward. Its muzzle touched both hands, then it stared upward into the sightless eyes and whimpered.

Faisal reached out gently, placed his hands behind the beast's head, and whispered, "Akela."

CHAPTER 4

Heartbeats

The drumbeat of life begins in the womb and continues until the Three Sisters select, measure, and cut the strings that bind us to this mortal coil. It is a steady yeoman's beat, regular with few skips. It speeds up in love or fear and slows down at rest. But there are times, maybe a warning of the approaching scythe, when it performs a Tango of Death.

He felt the sudden fluttering. There was no pain, just the sensation of wings beating inside trying to escape from within a cage of muscle and bone. He rubbed his chest, hoping it was just fatigue, and it seemed to abate. He was a man, after all, so he ignored it.

Ben Castle, sergeant, Pennsylvania State Highway Patrol, got dressed. It was good to have his partner back on duty again. Lachlan Douglass was quite a guy—a good cop, loyal soldier, loving husband, and now adoptive father to young Faisal. The boy who went to the Iraq war had come back a man, one whom Ben would have been proud to call son.

The former high-school basketball champ was turning into one damned fine cop. He soaked up Ben's advice like a sponge.

The old trooper stood in front of the mirror. Everything looked straight and spit-polish bright. He adjusted the badge over his left chest and felt the flutter again.

That'll teach you to eat pork chops before bedtime!

He looked in the mirror once more and saw his father's face staring back: stocky, almost bald, with rounded lopsided grin, and azure-blue eyes that still caught the ladies' attention when he pulled them over for speeding.

Not bad for an old guy in his fifties. Must be those good Polish genes!

He adjusted the crown of his trooper's hat and strode out to the patrol car.

Time to pick up Lachlan and the kid.

Faisal, guided by his wolf-dog, Akela, waited outside the Douglass house, ready to be dropped off at the bus stop, where he would meet the Hidalgo children. Another year at the private academy then off to The Juilliard School of Music in New York City.

The Douglasses still couldn't believe it. The three old-timers up on the mountain had said they would pay Fai's tuition and cover his expenses at Juilliard.

Lachlan heard the honk of Ben's patrol car. He kissed Diana and headed to the driveway to join Faisal.

Then the horn became one steady, ominous tone.

At usual, Diana watched her husband depart from the front window. Each time he left for work, she would recite the universal prayer of wives and husbands of all police and service officers:

Dear God, let my loved one return safely.

She knew as they all did that every phone call or unexpected visitor could be the one bearing the message of loss.

Then she saw Lachlan dash toward the police cruiser and fling open the driver's side door. She raced outside.

"Tio Benny, Tio Benny!"

He heard Faisal's voice from the bottom of a mental well. He sensed vaguely that his face was pressed against the steering wheel, but he couldn't move. He tried to speak, but nothing came out. A loud noise was roaring inside his head, reminding him of a childhood visit to the beach and the pounding surf that used to frighten him. Then he drifted away from what was happening around him.

Lachlan gently grasped Ben's shoulders and pulled him back against the seat, stopping the horn. The right side of his face was drooping, and his right arm hung loosely. His breathing was labored. Saliva dripped from the flaccid right side of his mouth.

"Tio Benny, Tio Benny!" Faisal repeated.

Douglass grabbed the car microphone and called in.

"Central! Central! Sixteen-oh-eight. Officer down! Need Medevac now!"

"Roger, sixteen-oh-eight. Who is your ten-five-three, and what is your ten-four-five?"

"Central, it's Sergeant Castle. He appears to have had a stroke. Please notify Medevac EMTs. We're in front of my house."

Momentary silence from the radio voice.

"Uh ... Roger, sixteen-oh-eight. Dispatching Medevac. ETA your position ten minutes."

"Copy that, Central—tell 'em to hurry!"

"Will do, Lach."

"Sixteen-oh-eight, out."

He turned back to his partner, as Diana cradled the older man's head and kept repeating, "It's going to be all right, Ben."

Faisal and Akela sat next to her.

The outside speaker for the phone was ringing—ringing insistently, it seemed.

"Now what?" Nancy asked aloud, putting down her garden trowel and heading for the house. She had just finished changing the annuals in her bathtub plant holder. The resident chipmunk raced back and forth from under the tub, where it found safety from the hawks and other creatures that preyed on its kind. She had carefully begun placing small piles of peanuts and seeds near the tub, so that the frenetic little rodent could stuff its cheeks and safely bring the food home to its burrow.

Edison and Galen were working about a hundred yards away. He had dragooned Galen into helping erect one of his antennas, and the two men were soaked with sweat, as they attempted to raise yet another part of the mountain communications array.

"I'm too old for these shenanigans, you old goat. Why can't you just listen to local radio stations?"

Galen took off his workman's gloves and massaged his hands, while Edison grinned back at him.

"Do you good, you fat old couch potato. About time you got some real exercise like the rest of us."

Edison was younger by a year and a half, and he never let his friend forget it. But they both knew they weren't spring chickens anymore, especially when their joints started acting up. The two limped back toward the doorway of the house, where Nancy was frantically waving them inside.

"It's Lachlan. Something's happened to Ben!"

She handed the phone to Galen, who listened for a few seconds.

"Yes, it does sound like he's had a stroke, Lach. If we're lucky, and it's the right type, it might be reversible. But it's a race against time. How did they take him? By Medevac? Good. I'll call the hospital, and we'll meet you at the ER."

The three friends quickly changed, Edison fired up the van, and they rolled down the mountain in silence, each one thinking about the officer they had first met while trying to protect the wolves.

They found the children still waiting for the school bus. Edison pulled over and Galen called out, "Get in. Sergeant Castle has been taken to the hospital. Faisal and his parents will need us."

He felt them lift him onto the stretcher, but only on his left side. He was vaguely aware of the instruments they were applying to his body: the stethoscope on his chest, the needle entering his left forearm. But where was his right arm? He felt them wiping the left side of his face and gently opening his mouth to be sure that nothing was blocking his breathing. He felt his left eyelid being lifted and a bright light being shined in his eyes. He saw the faces staring down at him and heard them asking if he understood what was going on. He felt the left side of his chest go bare, as they opened his uniform shirt, the one he had worn so proudly just a short lifetime ago. He felt the stickers being placed on his left chest. And he heard someone call out something that sounded like, "He's in A-fib! Bet a clot did this to him."

He wanted to escape, but his right side wouldn't follow orders. So his subconscious mind took over and led him into the past...

·   ·   ·

"Papa, tell me again about the old country."

Ben looked up from where he was playing with his toy soldiers made of lead on the floor of their small apartment's living room—the soldiers his father had cast for him and his brothers.

Jerzy Zamek watched his youngest son. The coal dust would never leave the heavyset man's lungs, even when the wracking spasms of coughing could not expel it. His mine-pale skin would turn pink only when he smoked, and that habit was increasing day by day.

Big, hairy arms reached down, picked up the boy, and set him carefully on thick knees. Ben was his and Sophie's last child. His Warsaw wife had given him three healthy boys, and he grinned as he saw her plump shape peering through the open kitchen door.

Jerzy loved Sophie in so many ways, not the least of which was her skill with sweet cabbage, sour cream, and sauerkraut. His bright-blue eyes sparkled, as he told his son how his own father had organized a resistance group against the Nazi invaders, and how the family had escaped, when Joseph Stalin decided to pluck the golden pear that was Poland.

Jerzy laughed while telling young Ben about how he and Sophie had met after arriving separately in the United States as war refugees, finding friends in the local Polish American community, and eventually settling in the coal country of eastern Pennsylvania.

He laughed even harder, barely avoiding a coughing spasm, as he told his son how red-faced his older twin brothers, Stanley and George, were when they were born.

"But Ben, my little Ben, you came out thoughtful and quiet. You seemed to be watching everything."

And both would laugh, as his father bounced his knees up and down, shouting "Hi-yo, Silver, away! The Lone Ranger!" until he began to cough again.

Sometimes the boy would reach up and touch the soot-stained sputum that darkened his father's lips, his blue eyes peering into his father's, his mind filled with questions.

.   .   .

"Papa, where does our name come from?"

He was twelve now. Girls noticed him—and he returned the favor. His growing self-awareness now extended to his origins. He knew the songs and tales of the old country. But his name, the magical talisman of family ties, remained a mystery.

He knew what it meant in Polish: Castle. Many famous and royal ancient buildings began with the word *Zamek*.

His father, skin sallow and loose, the color of his eyes now fading, told him that his ancestors were soldiers, guardians of royalty, like the rooks of the ancient game of chess.

Ben grew proud.

.   .   .

At last he was eighteen—draft age. His two older brothers had gone before him to the killing fields of Southeast Asia. Papa was gone, too, the big, happy-faced man shrunken to a death's head by the lethal crab devouring him from within.

He enlisted, not waiting for the lottery to call his number. College wasn't for him. The stories of his ancestors defending the kings of Poland moved him, as only a young man with no life experience can be moved. He relished the military life of discipline and structure, and he believed in the cause that his superiors offered him.

And so it was that his unit moved to Saigon, and then Da Nang and the Mekong Delta. The coal miner's son saw his friends die, singly, in pairs, and in some cases groups. Yet his beliefs remained fixed, until the day he and his best friend—the big, black kid from Chicago everyone called "Bandana"—went to help the old lady with the baby carriage. The machine-pistol fire cut Bandana in half and wounded Ben in both legs, before he pulled his sidearm and shot a bullet into the woman's brain.

After that he was shipped home, a hero with medals and lifelong guilt for not having been more observant. He would never make that mistake again. But he knew it wouldn't bring Bandana back.

.   .   .

At twenty-three, honorably discharged, and seeking meaning to his life, he faced the world with wounds that had healed and no residual weakness in his slightly bowed legs.

The G.I. Bill would pay for his education. His natural inclination was law enforcement, so he took some courses at the local community college before applying to the Pennsylvania State Police Academy in Hershey. Then he took one final step.

Ben was never quite sure why he did it. Maybe it conferred on him an added sense of protection, or perhaps he needed to hide from the ghost of Bandana. He changed his name to its English translation: He became Ben Castle.

·   ·   ·

College still wasn't for him, but it did bring him Irene—beautiful Irene Strzewski. Shortly after completing his training at the academy, they dodged the rice tossed at them and headed with his wedding party to the reception hall. His mother greeted the couple at the entrance, holding out the traditional offering of bread and salt to the newlyweds. His two older brothers, sharing their younger sibling's haunted look, slapped him on the back and told him he would always be a Zamek.

They danced, the stocky blue-eyed state policeman and his auburn-haired, hazel-eyed Irene. She seemed doll-size next to him, her petite body complementing his intrinsic strength. But she fed him the doughy, triangular piroghis and the bowtie-shaped, sugar-coated cruller cakes— the *krusziki*. She also decided the order of those with whom she danced the *Pani Mloda*. And she held him tightly, her tiara of mock orange blossoms scenting the air below his nose. As they danced to the final verse of the Polish Money Dance, the rest of the party sang, "Take the bride away with you and love her 'til your death."

·   ·   ·

He heard voices hovering above him.

Is that Dr. Galen?

"Get the interventional radiologist to TPA him now. His atrial fibrillation is controlled, and the scan shows definite embolic blockage in the middle cerebral artery where it branches. Ken Drake's a good man. Had him as a student."

More gibberish, Ben's brain decided, and retreated back in time once again...

.   .   .

He felt on top of the world, as he joined his sergeant in the patrol car. Even the veteran of the force who had mentored him mellowed his usually gruff voice, as he spotted the unmistakable symptoms.

"So, what's it going to be, Ben, boy or girl?"

The words startled him, but he grinned and nodded up and down.

"I don't care, as long as it has Irene's good looks."

The sergeant laughed and added, "Hopefully her brains, too!"

They headed along the road just outside Scranton, Ben reading the dispatch reports he had picked up on the way over.

"She's going to see the doctor again today. It's getting pretty close."

Just then the squawk box blared, "Car one-twenty-one, car one-twenty-one, robbery in progress. Go to..."

The sergeant hit the siren and flashers, made a quick U-turn, and headed to the outskirts of town. They approached the business district, just as a dark-green sedan pulled away from the State Bank & Trust building, wheels squealing.

Local police joined them in pursuit down the highway bordering the town. At one point, just on the verge of boxing in the fleeing sedan, the green car suddenly crossed the median and moved into the opposing traffic stream.

Neither the fleeing driver nor the driver of the small, tan-brown coupe saw each other, as their cars fused together.

The sergeant pulled the patrol car onto the median strip. Both officers jumped out and rushed to the tangled mass of what had been two vehicles. Ben stared at the small brown coupe for the shortest moment before screaming, "No, No! Irene, Irene!"

He tried to lunge forward to the wreckage, but the sergeant's powerful arms restrained him.

"I'm sorry, Officer Castle, there was just too much damage to your wife's head. If it means anything, she didn't feel any pain. Your daughter is in our neonatal-intensive-care unit. With the premature birth, she'll need to be watched for quite a while. The accident may have disrupted her blood and oxygen supply. We don't know if there will be any lasting effects."

.   .   .

"Dr. Drake, he's ready."

He felt something moving inside him, and then a sudden rush of liquid heat moved up the left side of his neck. It created a sensation inside his head like crawling ants.

He heard Galen's voice again, this time strangely exuberant.

"That's it, you've got it Ken! The damned clot's lysing!"

Then, nothingness.

Nine anxious people crowded into the patient's room of the county hospital's special neurology-intensive-care unit. One was a young blind boy led by what looked like a large dog. Not exactly by the book, but this case was different.

The nurses said nothing, as they stared at the harnessed guide animal, although one, older and from the Midwest, kept muttering, "That ain't no dog, that's a wolf!"

"Tio Galen, will Sergeant Castle be okay now?"

Tonio stood next to Faisal, while Carmelita and Freddie flanked the other side of Castle's hospital bed.

"It's going to be a while before we can tell how much function will return," Galen said. "His face isn't sagging like it was, and that's a good sign.

"Whatever happens, Ben is going to need therapy for both his body and his mind. It's not unusual for someone who has had a stroke to become very depressed afterwards. The physical part is easy to handle—it's his emotional outlook that can become tricky."

They heard sounds coming from the semiconscious man. Edison and Carmelita seemed the most aware of what was going on.

"It's Polish! He's trying to talk, but in Polish."

Edison turned to the others.

"My grandmother on my mother's side was Polish."

Carmelita bent her head toward Ben's face and listened intently then stood up when the sounds stopped. She began crying, as she told them what she had learned.

"He had a wife and a daughter. His wife died in an auto accident. He saw it happen. His daughter's name is Miriam."

Galen turned and walked out of the room.

Diana looked at Nancy, who said quietly, "The same thing happened to him."

Silence reigned for a few moments, and then Freddie spoke.

"Carm, where's his daughter? Did he say anything about her?"

Carmelita shook her head, as Lachlan, now holding his wife and standing next to their adopted son, interjected, "I never knew. Ben never talked about his personal life. But I can find out."

Freddie grinned. "I bet I can find out quicker than you can."

Nancy shot a scolding glance at Edison, who looked at Lachlan then at Freddie.

"Searching—no hacking!"

Faisal guided himself to the head of the bed. He bent over and whispered into Ben's left ear.

"I will come and play for you, Tio Benny. My music will make you better."

What the hell you doin' in bed, Honky? Thought you were tougher than that!
Sheeit, the way you took that ol' mamasan's head off, you should be joggin' by now.
He tried to focus on the voice in the darkened room. The shadows seemed even darker as they took shape.
Bandana? Bandana! But I thought you were. . .
Dead? Yeah, man, I am. But you ain't, least not yet. You gonna let a lotta folks down, you keep lying on yo' ass like that. The lady here, too bad I never got to meet her befo'. She's gonna be pissed off, too.
Suddenly the darkness brightened, and the air filled with the scent of mock orange blossoms.
My dearest Ben. I loved you in our brief life, and I will love you after death. But you have much to do.
The music of the *Pani Mloda* filled his ears and his soul.

The old floor nurse made her rounds of the cubicles in the stroke intensive-care unit then stopped by the secretary's desk.
"Millie, I thought flowers weren't allowed in here."
The secretary looked up at her.
"They aren't, Ms. Pratt. Why?"
The battle-hardened nurse took the young girl by the arm and led her to cubicle three. The scent of orange blossoms wafted toward them.

The night air was still on the mountain, and even the wolves seemed subdued. The six residents of Safehaven sat around the dinner table as usual, but the normal, give-and-take conversation didn't seem appropriate. Finally Freddie broke the silence by asking Galen the question everyone wanted to ask.
"Tio, what happened to Ben? What made him so sick?"

"His heart betrayed him. No, not love, but turbulence. Ben's heart started to beat funny. The heart is a four-cylinder engine and, just like a car motor, its cylinders have to contract in sequence to squeeze blood through our bodies in just the right way. The two smaller chambers of Ben's heart, the atria, started to act independently from their big brothers, the ventricles. That created a disturbance in the flow of blood, which allowed some of it to harden into clots.

"Those clots are like bullets, and when they form, they can break off and travel up into the brain, disrupting the blood flow to critical areas. That's why Ben became paralyzed."

"Will he have permanent damage?"

Tonio wore his worried look well, Galen thought.

"We don't know yet, Tonio. Sometimes, when the food and oxygen supply is cut off too long, chemical changes happen that cause the death of brain tissue. We're trying an experimental drug on Ben. It's called a Lazaroid, to try to block that chemical destruction. Now we have to wait and see."

Carmelita looked puzzled.

"Tio, why is it called a Lazaroid?"

Galen smiled.

Of course, she wants to know the meaning behind the word.

"Do you remember Lazarus in the Bible?"

Her face lit up in understanding.

Edison looked at the others.

"Nancy and I were talking this over earlier. We'd like to have Ben stay here when he's discharged from the hospital. He has no one at home. Lachlan and Diana have offered to help out, but we think it would be too much of a strain on her. We have the room, and the mountain air will do him good."

He waited. One by one, the children nodded agreement. Then he looked at Galen, who shut his eyes and nodded as well.

He lay in the bed, feeling his right hand opening and closing. Feeling the pillow on the right side of his face. Feeling his tongue move, but with lingering numbness, like a visit to a dentist would produce. But his mind dredged up thoughts he had not harbored in years.

Ben, you're just like your old man. You couldn't stand school. You couldn't apply yourself. You couldn't discipline your mind. Just like old Jerzy, you always craved action. And it cost you your daughter.

Tears welled up as he remembered...

.   .   .

"She's a beautiful little girl, Officer Castle, but ... well ... you see..."

The doctor had no good way of telling Miriam's father.

"We think she may be autistic."

Sophie Zamek had become mother to her granddaughter the way she had been mother to her son. It was she who noticed the detached manner of the child, when Miriam was almost two.

"Ben, I took her to the doctor. He wants to talk with you."

He accompanied his mother and his daughter, the woman still wearing widow's black, the young girl in a red-and-blue-colored jumpsuit, trailing the uniformed Ben, as he entered the doctor's office. He listened, but most of what the white-coated man had to say made no sense. What was wrong with his daughter? Nothing!

He couldn't see anything wrong with her.

Miriam sat in the play area of the waiting room. Lights reflecting off the ceiling fan cast a kaleidoscope of colored shapes on the light tan rug. Seemingly fixated on the moving shadows, the girl sat and watched the multihued variations, and she began to rock back and forth.

Ben sat down next to her on the carpeted floor.

"Miriam, show Daddy how you can play. Show Nana and the nice doctor how you play, please, Miriam."

His voice was rising, desperate to hear his daughter call him Daddy. The doll-size reminder of Irene appeared to ignore him, as he picked her up and held her in his arms.

"Miriam, my little Miri, Daddy loves you, Daddy loves you!"

The little doll's eyes remained fixed, but not on him.

.　　　.　　　.

He watched Miri grow up and his mother grow old. The strong Warsaw lady eventually could no longer handle the energies of a girl with the pervasive, developmental disorder of autism entering adolescence.

He used up his savings and insurance benefits for special therapies, none of which helped her to interact with other people. She seemed intractable within a world of her own. She was one of the soulless ones.

Then, on a starlight night in late August, in Miri's sixteenth year, Jerzy Zamek came to reclaim his Sophie. Ben was alone once more, now facing the terrible decision of whether to try to raise his daughter on his own or place her in a facility for those with her condition.

What haunted him most was that Miri suddenly looked directly at him as he left her with the attendant of the home. Those hazel eyes pierced him to his very core, as he kissed her and whispered, "Daddy loves you."

He thrashed in his bed, and his voice howled in agony.

"Daddy didn't mean to leave you!"

.　　　.　　　.

"The hospital is discharging Ben."

Galen had just sat down in the living room with Edison and Nancy, who were sipping tea in the quiet of the evening. The children, their homework completed, were preparing for bed. The next day was a Saturday, but rules were rules: Homework assigned must be finished.

Nancy nodded.

"The back guest bedroom is set up and aired out. Are we picking him up in the morning?"

Edison joined in.

"I've set up the van to take a wheelchair in the back. Does he need any other adaptive devices?"

Galen shook his head.

"He's moving very well now. His speech seems to be just about normal. It looks like the clot-busting and Lazaroids did the trick. But he's definitely showing signs of depression. Has Lachlan had any luck tracing the whereabouts of his daughter?"

They said no.

Just then Carmelita and Tonio, both in pajamas, literally dragged a similarly clothed Freddie into the living room.

"Tell him, Freddie," Carmelita growled at her younger brother, who was starting to tower over her.

"Tio Galen, I ... uh ... I did some research and came up with this."

The boy offered him a piece of paper then backed off sheepishly.

Galen examined the paper and handed it to Edison.

"St. Ignatius Home," Edison noted. "Isn't that a custodial home for children and adults with developmental and mental disorders?"

Galen nodded.

"I'll call them in the morning, before we head over to the hospital."

Saturday morning entered with the cool crispness of late fall. Galen was on the phone, as the five others filed into the dining room for breakfast.

"This is Dr. Galen. Do you have an inpatient by the name of Miriam Castle? Yes? Good. I'll be coming by later today. Her father has been ill, and we needed to contact her. She's what? I see. I'll come by this afternoon."

He replaced the phone and walked slowly to the table. The others saw the frowning concern on his face.

"Stranger and stranger," he muttered, as he took his seat. "Ben's daughter, Miriam—she's autistic."

It was quiet in the van, as they drove down the mountain road toward the Douglass home. They would form a caravan—patrol car and mini-van—to the hospital, an honor guard to bring the old trooper to his new living quarters.

Galen turned back toward the children.

"You heard me say that Ben's daughter is autistic. I'll explain more to you later, after I see her at St. Ignatius. For now, though, I don't want you to say anything to Ben or the Douglasses—and that includes Faisal. I want to see for myself what's going on. With everything that's happened, I don't want to stir up an emotional hornet's nest for Ben. Promise?"

Edison added, "That includes you, Freddie."

Ben was dressed in the civilian clothes that Lachlan had picked up for him. He wasn't used to the loose-fitting, pale-blue shirt or the khaki trousers and the flat, rubber-soled shoes. Where were his boots and uniform?

Diana picked out that shirt, he thought. *Shows what a good woman notices!*

He wanted to walk out of the hospital, but the nurse in charge must have taken classes in bullying from his old sergeant. It was her way—the wheelchair—or no way.

The unit secretary gave him the envelope with his discharge instructions, and the attendant wheeled him to the pickup site the hospital staff had nicknamed "The Loading Doc."

"Tio Benny, Tio Benny!"

Four children and one wolf-dog crowded around Ben, as five adults endeavored to help him into the police cruiser.

"Ben, think you can ride in the back seat?"

Lachlan looked at the man who was more father than senior partner to him.

"Hell, yes, boy! I see you drove Old Betsy. Are we going on patrol now?"

Lachlan gave a worried look to Galen. An unspoken question crossed the divide between the doctor and the police officer: Was Ben in his right mind? Ben spotted it and laughed.

"Think I'm nuts, eh? Okay, where are we headed to, my apartment?"

Nancy spoke first.

"Ben, we'd like you to be our guest at Safehaven, until you get your sea legs back. How does that sound?"

She hoped his pride wouldn't be insulted at the implication that he needed recuperation.

Edison added, "You'll certainly be more active than the old goat who lives there now."

Galen frowned at him and turned to Ben.

"I don't know why Edison just insulted himself, but we all would like you as our guest."

Some of Ben's old bravado energized his next words.

"Hell, if it's for free, how can I turn you down?"

For the first time he sat in the back of his police cruiser.

How appropriate, I'm a prisoner—a prisoner of my own body!

"Hello, I'm Dr. Galen. I called earlier about Miriam Castle."

He shook hands with the home administrator and offered his credentials. The younger man nodded.

"We know who you are, Dr. Galen. No need for that. What can we do for you? You mentioned Miriam's father being ill. We wondered why he didn't show up for his weekly visit."

"He's had a stroke. Fortunately it was the kind that we could do something about. But none of us knew he had a daughter. What's the story?"

Jesse Orth was a native Pennsylvanian who had worked at St. Ignatius since high school. He had risen to the rank of administrator and now knew each of his charges personally.

"Miriam has one of the more severe forms of autism," he explained. "She has almost no verbal skills despite attempts at repetition training. But there is something interesting about her. Please, come with me to her room. Right now she's with the group in the sunroom area, so I can show you something without upsetting her."

Galen followed the tall, heavyset man down a hallway marked EAST WING. The area was clean but sparsely decorated and devoid of any meaningful wall hangings. They arrived at an open door marked 3E and stepped inside a dormitory-sized room containing standard, institutional, blond-oak furniture with a desk and chair on one side and a very low-to-the-floor, single bed on the other. Galen was struck by what adorned the walls. They were covered with drawings, done with a mix of charcoal and watercolor and pastel, all of Ben and photographic in quality: his face, full length in uniform, from the side, from the front, and at different ages. And one was of a woman dressed in white wearing a tiara of mock orange blossoms.

Orth pointed to the picture of the lady.

"She did that one just this week. I don't know where that face came from. No one like that has ever visited her. Fact is, only her father has ever come to see her."

They walked to the sunroom. Galen saw them standing or sitting—mostly men and boys, alone in a crowd, but that was the nature of the illness. Each resided in his own world. Some stared at the rainbows cast by sunlight coming through the skylight glass in the ceiling. Others sat pushing and pulling at toy blocks on the floor.

Among the few girls and women, one sat on the floor, a lump of modeling clay before her. Her hands moved seemingly independent of her eyes—kneading, twisting, shaping.

Galen watched, mesmerized at the movement of the delicate-featured girl, her hands nearly a blur of activity. Then he saw her creation and was startled. She had brought out of the clay a lifelike image: a full-bodied, seated wolf.

"Mr. Orth, her father is recuperating with us at our place on the mountain. He needs to heal in many ways. After he settles in, would it be possible to have Miriam join him?"

Orth eyed the old doctor. He had heard about what this man and his friends had done for the young Middle Eastern boy. Such news circulated fast through the endless mountains of Central Pennsylvania.

Maybe they could pull another rabbit/hat trick.

"Yes, Dr. Galen, I think we could arrange that. Just let us know when you're ready for her."

He hesitated a second, and then, almost embarrassed, he asked Galen a question.

"I understand that you and your friends call your home Safehaven. Why?"

Galen smiled.

"It's a long story, Mr. Orth. Let's just say we call it that because that's what it is."

As he drove home, Galen mulled over what he had seen that afternoon. No question Miriam was autistic, but she was one of those rare forms— what the French would call an idiot savant—an artist of high quality. Yet how could her brain produce such works, when it was so genetically or chemically or traumatically different from so-called normal people?

He remembered Manu Kumar, a young boy from India, one of his last patients before retiring, with his doe eyes and vacant smile. Manu was the son of a diplomat. He, too, was what his countrymen called a soulless one. The boy was a perpetual-motion machine, arms waving like the Avenging Kali, pushing away any stethoscope or hands that attempted to examine him. And yet, when left alone, his movements adopted a panther-like grace. Galen had thought he moved like a dancer, and he wondered now if that might be Manu's talent.

Galen realized his mind was wandering, as he swerved to reenter the right-hand lane of the highway.

Better keep your mind on the road.

He made one stop on the way back home. His beloved red Jeep was loaded by the time he drove up the curving mountain road and pulled into the house driveway.

"One more thing, and then we shall see what we shall see," he said to himself, as he lumbered into the house.

Ben's presence made seven at the dinner table that evening, with him enjoying the place of honor at its head. The other adults and children sat on either side of the maple table Edison had made after the kids had moved in.

"Ben, we have a little ritual here," Edison said.

"Yes, and any guest has to join in—unless he doesn't want to," Nancy quipped.

"What they're saying, Ben, is that you'll have to sing for your supper—figuratively, that is," Galen concluded.

The old trooper looked confused, until Tonio explained, "We eat, and then we gripe, boast, complain, whatever, about what happened during the day."

Nancy served a citrus-and-almond salad, followed by chilled potato soup, and then to applause she brought out thick slices of roast beef sautéed in garlic butter with mushrooms and stuffed tomatoes. She wowed them again with fresh-baked *focaccia*—Italian tomato bread—and then a treat she made only for special occasions: *crème brûlée*.

"Don't worry, Ben," Edison joked. "The way Nancy cooks, there's no fat. Even the garlic butter doesn't have butter."

The children cleared the dishes then returned to the table.

Ben looked at them and wondered, *Why? Why do this for me?* He laughed nervously.

"I don't sing too good, folks. All I know is some Polish folk songs, but I doubt you'd be interested in those. What can I say? Thank you, really."

"I'd like to hear those songs, Tio Benny," Carmelita said. "But I guess what we're all interested in is you. We'd like to know how you feel—are you having any problems? Is there anything we can do to help you?"

He blushed. He hadn't expected a question like that from the girl. Then he remembered: He had missed his visit to Miri. The lopsided grin he had worn as protection against the world started to fall in sadness. He caught himself quickly, hoping they hadn't noticed.

"That's very nice," he said, regaining himself. "I can't believe how fast things have gotten better. I thought I was never going to talk or move right again. Whatever you did..." and he looked at Galen, "whatever was done, sure seems to have turned the corner for me."

He turned to Freddie and laughed, as he challenged the boy to an arm-wrestling contest. But the looks from his siblings and guardians stopped the teenager from accepting.

They moved to the living room. The curtains were open to the final remnants of the evening light, as it filtered through the deep, multicolored foliage of the fall trees. Nancy looked at Ben. He seemed tired but also restless.

"It's probably best if you get some early nap time, Ben. It's been a busy day, and tomorrow we'd like to show you around the place.

Bob and Galen will help you to your room."

Galen and Edison guided their guest down the hall and helped him settle in.

"There's an intercom button by your bed, Ben. Just press it if you need anything."

Edison looked at Galen and grinned.

"It's hooked directly to Doc Grumpy's room."

"I'll help you with your exercise program in the morning," Galen said, ignoring Edison's jab. "We need to be sure your muscle tone remains intact."

He felt that total exhaustion of mind and body that had overwhelmed him only twice in his life: in Vietnam after Bandana had been killed and when Irene had died. He lay back, resting his head on the home-made pillow and pulling up the patchwork quilt to ward off the slight chill. Nancy had made it from pieces of the children's long-outgrown and worn clothes. She cherished it especially for the scraps she had salvaged from their first sets of clothes. To her it represented the beginning of a new life for herself, Edison, and Galen.

Ben didn't know that. He only knew it comforted him.

The sky was dark now, but he could see just a glimmer of quarter moon peering through the top of his bedroom window. He heard the sounds of the house, the creaking and snapping, as its joints, like his, settled down for the night. The wind cast up some of the fallen leaves, and he heard, faintly, a tripartite howl.

What the hell was that?

Then he remembered Faisal and Akela.

Ah, maybe the wolves are welcoming me, too!

He smiled, as he drifted off, and soon he was with his wife and daughter in the little house he had planned to buy after Miri was born.

They were laughing and dancing around him. He tried to reach out and hug them, but they always stayed just beyond his grasp.

Why do they run away from me? Irene, it's me, Ben. Miri, come to Daddy, come to Daddy!

They danced in circles around him, tantalizing him like forbidden fruit. The room turned, as his Miri looked at him—looked into his soul with those piercing eyes.

He cried out, "Daddy didn't mean to leave you, Miri! Daddy didn't mean to leave you!"

Galen heard him talking in his sleep and quietly stood outside Ben's bedroom door. As the sounds subsided, he thought about his own losses.

That won't happen to you, Ben. I promise.

He returned to his room and dreamed his own troubled dreams.

Sunday entered windy, cool, and overcast. There were six at the table for breakfast.

"Where's Dr. Galen?" Ben asked, as Nancy brought out a platter of her special, multigrain pancakes.

Edison laughed.

"Hard to believe, him missing a meal, but he said he had to do something in town, and that he'd meet us a bit later. By the way, Ben, we have another little ritual around here. I'll tell you about it after we eat."

Edison's eyes had become as large as the pancakes, and he couldn't wait to dive into them.

Soon the six sat satisfied at the table.

"Freddie, why don't you tell Ben what we're going to do next."

And Freddie, usually seeking the center of attention, suddenly became tongue-tied. So Nancy took over.

"Ben, every Sunday that we can, we visit a special place on the mountain. We call it our Garden of Remembrance. It gives us a chance to recall and thank those who are no longer with us for who they were and what they meant to us. We always ask our guests, our friends, to accompany us. Will you?"

Edison looked at Nancy.

"Ben, do you think you might want to use the wheelchair? It's a bit of a walk on the side of the mountain."

"Nah, just one day here and I got my sea legs back already."

He looked at Carmelita.

"Little lady, want me to sing some of those Polish songs I know?"

She smiled a yes.

They walked quite a bit more slowly than usual. The chilly wind gusted now. Ben took a deep breath. It felt so good to do that. Then his lopsided grin grew broader, as he started to sing.

"Hej, górale, nie bijcie si . Ma góralka dwa warkocze podzielicie si !"

Edison and Carmelita both laughed. Nancy and the boys looked at them.

"What's he saying?" Tonio asked.

Carmelita blushed, and Edison's eyes took on a glint that Nancy knew all too well.

"Give us the clean translation, Bob."

"Let's just say it's about two mountain boys fighting over one girl ... and leave it at that," he replied.

They reached the special spot. The flowers were now frost-bitten and faded, but the surroundings still subdued everyone. Ben stood with the others, each gazing into wherever in the universe his or her loved ones resided. He thought of his Chicago friend and then his beloved Irene, and then the what-ifs: What if he had been more observant that day in Saigon? What if he had stayed home that day and driven Irene to the doctor? What if Miri had been born normally?

Footsteps, several different pairs, approached, disrupting the meditation.

Ben turned and saw a tall figure in uniform and two women, one leading the other. Galen, Faisal, and Akela were close behind. He wiped the tears away and stared at the latecomers: Lachlan and Diane and...
Miri! Miri is here!

Diana led the child-woman toward her father. She stepped awkwardly, hesitantly. She emitted guttural sounds, low at first then rising. Akela's ears went on point, and he started to do the same. The girl turned toward the wolf, staring. By then Ben had reached her and put his arms around her. He felt the resistance in her body and let go.

Galen intervened quickly.

"Everything's strange and different for her, Ben. Let's all go back to the house. It's getting colder."

The fireplace crackled, its flames a semaphore of warmth and comfort. Eleven humans and one wolf-dog crowded the living room. Miriam sat on the floor, staring at the flickering flames, humming to herself and moving her torso forward and backward. Faisal drifted toward her, guided by the sounds she made. He gently ran his hands over her face before she could react.

Miriam did not respond the way she normally did, when other people touched her. Instead of pulling away or pushing away the offending hand, she placed her own hand on Akela's head, and the great canine sat down between the blind boy and the mute girl.

Galen watched the interplay carefully but said nothing.

"So that's why you left so early," Edison spoke up. "I knew it had to be something like the End of the World or the Second Coming to keep you away from Nancy's breakfast. What other sneaky things have you been up to, big brother?"

The laughter from the group quieted down as Ben interrupted.

"How did this happen? How did you know about Miriam?"

"Are you angry with us?" Galen asked.

"No!" he replied. "I couldn't have asked for a better surprise..." and he hesitated before adding, "or a better gift."

He lowered his head to hide the welling tears.

"Ben, you did so much for Lachlan, Faisal, and me," Diana said. "How could we not do this?"

Ben looked at his daughter, who stared intently at the flames.

"How can I get her to forgive me?"

There, he had said it out loud. What would the others think of him now?

Galen stood and walked toward the big picture window, hands clasped behind his back.

Strange, how many times had Papa done this when he talked to me? Now I'm my father's image.

He turned to the group.

"Ben, nothing that you did or didn't do made Miriam the way she is. Yes, she's autistic. But we don't know what happens to cause the condition. So many possible causes—from vaccinations to trauma to food contamination—have been debunked. And if you think that being in the car with Irene that day..."

He paused at the astonished look on Ben's face then spoke even more emphatically.

"If you had been in that car at that point in time, Miriam would have had no parents left to love her. Yes, she cannot communicate the way we do, but I want to show you all something remarkable."

He left the room momentarily and returned with a large box. He set it down on the floor, opened it, and spread out the contents. Lifelike pictures of Ben in different poses and uniforms stared back at the crowd. And one special picture, a young woman wearing a tiara of mock orange blossoms, smiled radiantly at them.

Ben broke down.

"It can't be!" he sobbed.

"This is your daughter's voice, your daughter's soul."

Galen left again and brought back another box. It contained a large, amorphous gray lump. He walked over to the girl and placed the clay mass in front of her. She appeared to glance at it briefly then picked it up and began kneading and working it. Her hands moved faster and faster, no longer awkward and uncoordinated. They moved purposefully, fingers rivaling Faisal at his keyboard best, and suddenly the spirit of the clay emerged. Her hands stopped, lifted the piece, and placed it in front of Akela.

The clay had morphed into the life image of a boy and wolf lying side by side.

It was a three-day weekend for the kids. Founders Day at the academy fell on a Monday, and by tradition it was a school holiday. Faisal pleaded with Lachlan and Diana to stay overnight with his friends, and after a brief conversation and apologies for the perceived intrusion, he claimed his old bed in Tonio's room.

Nancy and Carmelita agreed that Miriam would stay in her room. Carmelita set the drawing and modeling-clay supplies near Miriam's bed. The staff at St. Ignatius had packed clothes for the girl, and they placed these few nondescript items—drab tans and faded greens—in a small side cabinet.

Carmelita placed a pair of her flannel pajamas on Miriam's bed. Then she and Nancy helped to prepare the girl for sleep.

Four adults sat in the living room enjoying a late evening cup of bi lo chun tea. Ben was restless. He couldn't seem to stay seated. Edison watched the younger man, prematurely aged by grief and sickness.

"What's wrong, Ben?"

"That picture, it was Irene."

He kept moving his hands back and forth over his forearms then stood up again.

"How could she draw a picture of Irene? She never saw her mother, and I never showed her any pictures, especially of Irene dressed like that. That was our wedding day. That was the only time Irene would have appeared like that."

Nancy had just come in from getting Miri settled down.

"Are you sure that Miriam never saw any wedding pictures, Ben?"

He shook his head.

Galen wondered about the statue of the wolf Miri had made at the home but said nothing.

The night closed in with its mid-fall, Pennsylvania mountain chill. The moon was outlined in full clarity, unobscured by clouds or fog, and even the remaining crickets had quieted down. Ever so faintly, the sounds of howling echoed through the darkness. And ever so quietly, four paws and two feet padded through the house and out the back porch door.

As dawn began its slow rise in the east, two shouts rose simultaneously throughout the mountain house.

"Akela!"

"Miri!"

Four adults came running to find Carmelita and Faisal standing in the hallway, almost hysterical.

"She's gone, Tia Nancy, I didn't hear anything but she's gone!"

Carmelita hid her head in Nancy's chest, sobbing as she tried to tell the others what had happened.

Faisal stood bewildered beside Tonio and Freddie.

"He's never done this! He's always been by my side, even at night. Akela would never leave me."

Galen turned to Edison.

"Go turn on the outside sensors. If they're still on the mountain, we'll pick up their sounds."

The seven quickly converged on Edison's communications lab, as he and Freddie sat at the consoles of the remote-sensor units, changing the inputs from location to location.

"There," Edison said, "something's going on down by the pond. The wolves seem overly active. Freddie, bring up video. Let's see if we can pick up what's happening."

Two large overhead monitors lit up, one showing an optical image, the other infrared.

"There she is!" Nancy called out, and the sighted ones saw the shadow image of the girl sitting near the pond edge. Surrounding her in apparent council style sat seven of the wolves.

Galen threw a coat over his pajamas and headed for the door, followed by the others.

"Hold on to me, Fai."

Tonio reached out for the other boy's arm, but Faisal shrugged it off.

"My ears can guide me better than your eyes, my friend."

The group headed down the path to the migratory bird pond at a rapid pace, but they slowed when Galen raised his hand and signaled for quiet.

Seven sets of green eyes watched the approach. They remained seated before the strange one. By scent they knew it was a female and two-legged like the others, but it was different. It spoke to them as one of the pack, and they responded in kind.

"Listen," Faisal whispered. "She's talking to the wolves!"

In the morning stillness, lit by the first salmon-pink rays of sunlight, they heard the guttural exchanges between wolf and human.

Akela rose from his position at the edge of the pack and padded slowly to Faisal. The gray wolf seemed apologetic in its behavior, as it resumed its place at his side.

A small, brown-gray wolf, female, rose and moved to the girl. It looked at her then placed its head and muzzle on the girl's lap.

The air was suddenly perfumed by the scent of orange blossoms.

CHAPTER 5

Genesis Two

"C'mon, Carmie, get out of the bathroom!" Freddie yelled.

"Yeah, you've been in there for hours!" Tonio wailed.

The two stood there, still in pajamas, towels in hand, waiting and waiting. Their voices resonated with the timbre of young adult males, as they complained loudly about a certain sister.

Freddie was now seventeen, with a full head of jet-black hair and what a past generation would have called bedroom eyes, which flashed dark brown when he smiled. Once frail and small, now he towered over his brother and sister and had developed a muscular physique from working out with weights. At six feet, two inches, and one-hundred-fifty-five pounds, he possessed enough olive-skinned good looks and tight butt to drive his female academy classmates wild.

Unfortunately, he knew it, and he flaunted it confidently. Freddie moved from one conquest to the next. If Lilly didn't want to go out, that was fine with him. There was always Patti, or Mary, or Beth.

But Tonio took rejection hard, perceiving it as an assault on his very existence. Younger by one year, he was still growing. Standing almost six feet, at one-hundred-seventy pounds and wearing glasses, he didn't have quite the sex appeal of his brother, but his piercing dark eyes conveyed thoughtfulness, and his dark hair and eyelashes were the envy of the girls who dated him. And despite not lifting weights regularly like his brother, Tonio's body was supple, with enough speed and balance that he could beat Freddie at wrestling.

And both boys were smart—too smart in some ways.

Dealing with two active teenagers tried the souls of their aging uncles, particularly because Nancy wisely stayed clear. When it came to laying down the law about curfews or escapades, she would walk away, laughing inside and leaving Edison and Galen to deal with the Lothario or the brooding Werner.

"Isn't there some sort of manual we can buy ... you know, 'Raising Teenagers for Dummies?'" Edison would gripe. "If I had known parenthood would be like this, I would have entered a monastery!"

Galen understood all the physiology that motivated Freddie's behavior. He also understood all too well the emotional trauma that underpinned Tonio's melancholy nature. A lot of good it did. Much of the time, their actions left him clueless.

Edison had no formal training in such matters, but he thought he knew the best way to deal with young males.

"I'll reason with them," he had told Nancy before the teen years began. "I'll just calmly explain my point of view to the boys, and they'll recognize the logic of it and follow it."

She immediately shot him a "What planet are you from?" look.

Of course, she was right. They were good boys, but they were still boys. The only saving grace was that their antics often forced Galen and Edison to reflect on their own youthful indiscretions. And doing so made the old men shake their heads in wonderment at how they had managed to survive.

As Nancy watched the men grapple with the problems of the boys, she conceded she had not been spared entirely the angst, or *Sturm und Drang*, as her own mother would have put it, of raising her adopted niece.

Carmelita was eighteen, legally an adult, but still with the cherubic, olive-skinned face of her childhood, and highlighted by iridescent black hair and penetrating dark eyes. Her five-foot-nine-inch height and one-hundred-twenty-five-pound body made the other girls hiss in jealousy. But no one ever said a misplaced word against her character. Carmelita was growing up to be the proverbial oil on water, seeing both sides of any problem and calming tensions before they erupted on the surface. Maybe that's how she survived the two boys, who called her "sister" but treated her like another brother. She was the grandee of the house.

Early on, Nancy had sworn to herself she would never let Carmelita go through what had happened to her. Working at her parents' nursing home had sucked away much of the time a teenage girl needed for socializing. Young women deserve lives of their own and the time to enjoy them.

Carmie, as her brothers called her, had no end of boyfriends. She was beautiful, smart, and wise enough not to scare them off with her intellect. She would be starting college soon, living on her own with all of the incumbent risks and benefits.

Nancy prayed she had prepared her sufficiently for the challenges that lay ahead.

On her birthday—an approximation based on Carmelita's memory, her guardians had pooled their resources and bought her a car. She needed it to get to the local hospital each day, where she worked as a translator. The burgeoning Spanish-speaking population in the area needed a voice to help them.

Galen had checked out the situation before allowing Carmelita to become involved in hospital work, and Edison had given her a cell phone to carry in case of emergency on the road. He even installed his own, custom-designed tracking system, in case she was unable to contact them for help.

Despite all the precautions, the care and concern, the elders worried more and more as the children grew older. They understood that the world the youngsters were about to enter was much less forgiving of mistakes than the world of their own youth.

God help them.

"I wish we could have found some photos of their parents," Edison mused.

"The boys are most likely their mirrors," Galen added. "Maybe someday, if Cuba ever becomes an open society again, the kids can obtain the official files on Sandoval and Felicita Hidalgo."

"Okay, I'm done," she said, emerging finally from the bathroom. "You'd think I was living in there for all your complaining."

Both boys shoved past her, as she walked out with her hair rolled up in a towel. Neither could think of a reply that wouldn't have earned a reprimand from their tios and tia.

"Tia Nancy, I'm going over to the hospital tonight. The supervisor wants me to help out with the trainee translators. Is that all right with you?"

"What time do you expect to be back?" Nancy asked.

"Probably by eleven-thirty. It's Friday, so I can sleep late tomorrow."

"Carmelita."

"Yes, Tio Galen?"

"Is he nice?"

She blushed.

How does he always know?

Michael Dimitriades was a second-year engineering student working in the hospital tech lab part-time to earn tuition money. His dream was to become an aerospace engineer. He had met Carmelita in the cafeteria two weeks before, when crowding forced them to share a single table. He had spent so much time staring at her he couldn't finish his food. She laughed when he lifted his soda can and missed his mouth, because he was so distracted by her.

She brought paper napkins to help dry his wet trousers and ego, and the gates of introduction opened.

Michael's parents were from Greece, and he had grown up in a bilingual household. Soon Carmelita started using him to practice her Greek language skills. He was amazed at the ease with which she picked up the words and grammatical constructions of his parents' mother tongue.

He began thinking of inviting her to meet his parents, but he hesitated. He had a career to pursue, and she hadn't even started college yet—though from what his co-workers had told him, she'd probably finish before he did.

"Yes, Tio Galen, he is nice. His name is Michael Dimitriades. He's studying engineering and working part time in the tech lab."

"Well, just be sure you're home before midnight, Cinderella," Nancy called out.

The brothers climbed into their sister's car. The guardians watched them through the living room picture window, each wistfully remembering the energies of youth.

"Carmie, Tonio and I want to go with you to the hospital this afternoon. We found out there might be some part-time work for us there. Okay?"

Great, just what I don't need, two brothers getting in the way of me and Michael.

"Do the folks know you guys are doing this?"

"Uh ... not yet," Freddie replied. "We were going to call them from school later today."

"You'd better get permission, or you're not going anywhere but back home."

"Sure! Can we borrow your cell phone later?"

School couldn't pass quickly enough. Freddie kept thinking about the opening he had heard about in the tech lab, while Tonio entertained thoughts of becoming a pharmacy technician. And Carmelita ... well ... Carmelita just dreamed of Michael.

"Hello?"

"Tia Nancy, Tonio and I have found out about some jobs over at the hospital. They sound really neat. There's an opening for a pharmacy tech and another for electronics lab tech and ...uh ... we ...uh ... thought we could go with Carmelita after school to check it out— okay? "

"Why didn't you tell us about this at breakfast, Freddie?"

"Well ... uh ... we ... we ... just heard about it today."

Tonio stood near as his older brother continued to stammer.

"What's she saying?" he whispered.

"Shh! She's thinking."

"What's the work schedule?" Nancy asked.

"Friday and Saturday evenings from seven to eleven," Freddie replied. "We could ride home with Carmie tonight."

Nancy considered the prospect. The boys were doing well academically, and they wouldn't be working on schooldays.

"All right, go look it over. But we'll want to talk about this when you get home this evening."

"Great ... I mean ... thanks, Tia Nancy. Bye!"

Her gut told her something was not quite kosher. She called the men into the living room and related what she had just heard. They also expressed some concern about the way the boys had sprung this news, but they agreed to wait before making any decisions.

Nancy brought the teapot and cups from the kitchen. She opened the curtains, and Edison put on their favorite classical-music radio station. They sat there, staring at the rolling hills and thinking about the kids taking their first steps toward independence.

Carmelita led her brothers to the side entrance of the hospital. There the boys split off and headed toward their potential employment sites, while she walked down the main corridor to the interpreters' office.

She liked her job immensely. Imagine, actually getting paid to meet so many different people admitted to or visiting the hospital! As soon as she reached her desk she made a quick call to the tech lab.

Better warn Michael about Freddie!

She had barely finished her call, when the supervisor came through the door.

"Ms. Hidalgo, there's a strange situation down in the ER. The floor nurse says the police have brought in someone who appears confused, and he doesn't speak English."

"Do they know the language he's using?"

"No one's quite sure. Would you see what you can find out?"

It's going to be one of those nights—first the boys and now this.

"Yes, ma'am."

She took the side stairs down to the emergency-room level and entered the circular nursing station. Things looked quiet. She went up to the unit secretary.

"Ginny, what's the story?"

"Hi, Carm. We've got a weird one tonight. Glad you're here to cover it. The cops brought in this big guy. He must weigh three-hundred pounds and looks like a sumo wrestler, but he's not Asian. They found him wandering around the town park chasing pigeons and throwing small stones at people. They were able to restrain him, but no one can get near enough to determine what's wrong. And he's jabbering away something awful."

"Why can't they get near him?"

"He keeps lowering his head and charging like a bull. Good thing his hands are cuffed."

"And who might you be?" the lab supervisor sniffed.

"Sir, I'm Federico Hidalgo. I called about the part-time opening in the tech lab. My sister works in the translators' office, and my uncles are Dr. Galen and Dr. Edison."

He stared at the electronics array, the heart of the ongoing maintenance and upkeep of all the expensive medical equipment and computers for the hospital: row after row of testing devices he already had become familiar with from Tio Eddie's workshop.

The supervisor led Freddie to another young man as tall and darkly handsome as he was.

"This is Mr. Dimitriades. Mr. Dimitriades, this is Mr. . . . what did you say your name was?"

"Hidalgo."

"Show him the ropes, Mr. Dimitriades."

He turned and left.

"Hidalgo?"

"Yep, and I'll bet you're the Michael my sister is crazy about."

She's crazy about me? Wow!

"Well, if you're the Freddie your sister talks about, you're an electronics wizard. Let's see what you can do."

Carmie thinks I'm hot stuff with electronics? Wow!

Michael showed Freddie a bench holding the guts of a defibrillator.

"It's not holding a charge, and when it does it's erratic at best."

Freddie immediately began mentally deconstructing the chassis.

Hmm. Simple circuit, regulated voltage going to a storage capacitor, which would discharge a measured amount of joules when the firing button's closed. The amount stored and discharged would depend on the condition of the capacitor. If there's leakage, the charge level would drop. And if it's erratic, the regulator in the charging system would also be defective.

"Where are the spare parts, Michael?"

"Call me Mike."

He pointed to two cabinets and filing drawers.

Freddie rummaged through the parts and picked out a replacement for the capacitor and a new triac regulator. He sat at the bench, disconnected the bad parts, wired in the new, and stood back.

"Give it a try, Mike."

He turned on the power, held the discharge plates a few inches apart, and pressed the firing button. A satisfying electrical snap between the plates made both of them smile.

"Fast work, Fred."

"Call me Freddie."

"Okay, now let's see if it holds and is putting out the right juice. If so, we're home free. By the way, I'd like to ask you something about your sister..."

"Antonio Hidalgo, please come in."

He was the last of the applicants for the pharmacy-tech position. He had waited nervously, while the other seven in turn entered the director of pharmacy's office, and he watched as each departed, disappointed faces saying it all.

Wonder what happened?

"Tell me, Mr. Hidalgo, why should I hire you?"

What could he say? That he wanted to earn money? No, that didn't sound right. That he knew chemistry backwards and forwards and, thanks to Tio Galen, he knew more about pharmacology than most of the students in the pharmacology program?

Uh-uh. Too much like bragging—even if it's true, which it is. Okay, let's try something simple.

"I know chemistry, Dr. Turnisky. I am precise in what I do, and I know how to follow orders."

Turnisky stared at him and smiled.

"That last comment saved your neck, Mr. Hidalgo. What we do here requires knowledge, that's true, and we need utmost precision. But we don't want hotdogs. If you are told to process a drug order, you must do it correctly and precisely, and follow the orders given you."

Tonio held his breath.

"All right, let's try you out tonight. Sam here will show you you duties."

Carmelita arrived at the holding cell used for prisoners and ER patients who appeared violent. The two town police officers guarding him watched her admiringly.

"I'm Carmelita Hidalgo. I work with the translator's office here. What's the story?"

The officers took turns repeating what Ginny had already told her. She approached the locked door and opened the viewing window, which was heavily barred and glass-enclosed. Inside she saw the large, handcuffed man. He was dirty and bruised from the nightstick blows necessary to subdue him. He sat on the metal bench, rocking back and forth. She couldn't hear his words through the protective glass, so she started to unlock the door to go in.

"Whoa, Miss! You don't want to go in there!"

"Yes, I do, and I'll need the help of you two strong officers to protect me."

She opened the door and stepped in. Now she could hear the man's words. *Strange, Spanish and yet not Spanish. Sounds almost like Romany. No ... wait ... it's Basque!*

For fun about a month earlier she had read about the strange and mysterious Basque people and their language, and now here was a person who actually spoke it.

She moved farther into the room and tried a greeting phrase. The man looked at her through bruised eyelids and facial swelling. She kept her voice low and spoke slowly. It seemed to work. He stopped rocking and focused on her words. His facial expression softened, as he heard simple words in his native tongue spoken by this pretty young woman.

He immediately felt the need to be polite, so he stood up to offer her his seat. That's when the mistake happened. The two policemen, thinking he was threatening the young woman, rushed into the cell holding out their sticks. He saw his former attackers coming at him and began his head charge, butting one officer right out of the room. The other one backed out and closed the heavy door behind him, leaving Carmelita still inside.

Merde! Now what?

The big man started pacing back and forth becoming more and more agitated. He slammed his cuffed fists against the seat frame, until the chain connecting the two cuffs snapped. Then he turned and looked at her. He shook his head like a confused bull and pointed to the bench. She came forward hesitantly and sat down beside him, watching his every move.

He's just a big, scared kid in a man's body.

She began to sing a children's song from a book she had read about Basques.

His agitation melted away. He smiled through his swollen face and accompanied her in a heavy rough bass. Then he started to cry. She put her hand on his shoulder and attempted to ask him what had happened.

"My wife leave me," he answered, in English. "She take kids. I no know where they went. No one tell me."

He had come to the United States to make a better life for his family. Now he had lost his family, and no one would help him. He had reached the end of his rope.

Carmelita tried her best to acquire more information: his name and address, where he worked, all of the necessary bureaucratic bits of information without which we are non-entities. Then she stood up, still keeping an arm on his shoulder.

"I have to leave you for a few minutes. I am going to speak with the authorities about your situation. Maybe we can help you."

She removed her arm slowly, walked even more slowly toward the door, turned, and smiled at him. He remained seated, while the two astonished police officers opened the door and let her out.

"Tonio?"

"Yeah, Sam?"

"We need to get this filled, stat, for room three twelve. Let's see you do your stuff."

Tonio examined the order sent by the unit secretary. Dr. Grimaldi had ordered high dosages of IV third-generation cephalosporin for one of his elderly patients with atypical pneumonia. The appropriate cultures were pending.

Tonio pulled up the patient's medication profile on the computer monitor.

Uh-oh!

The patient also was taking high-dose Coumadin, a blood thinner, to prevent clots forming on his artificial heart valve. This particular antibiotic was correct and good, except when the patient was on blood thinners. Then the thinning effect went wild and the patient could easily bleed to death.

He looked up at Sam, who was watching him in a deceptively casual manner.

"Sam, I can't fill this. It'll kill the patient. Can we get the ordering physician on the phone?"

The older man checked the order again, then the computer screen, and saw the patient's drug profile. He picked up the phone, dialed the paging office, and asked the operator to page Dr. Grimaldi. Fifteen seconds later, he heard the gruff voice.

"Grimaldi here, what's the screw-up?"

Sam held out the phone to Tonio. He grinned as the boy took the phone and tried to get his voice lower than a squeak.

"Dr. Grimaldi, this is pharmacy tech Hidalgo. I'm sorry to disturb you, but we have an order written by you for your patient in…"

Grimaldi cut him off.

"So fill it, damn it, and quit bugging me!"

"Sir, your patient is also on high-dose Coumadin. The drug you ordered will send his INR through the ceiling, and he could bleed to death."

No immediate response through the telephone receiver, but Tonio could hear Grimaldi mutter, "Oh shit!"

The doctor cleared his throat.

"Uh … thanks, kid, you're right. You saved my ass tonight. What's your name?"

"Antonio Hidalgo."

"Aren't you old Galen's nephew?"

"Yes sir."

"I studied under him. He would have had my head if I'd made that error in residency. Give him my best and tell him I'll give you my highest recommendation if you need it for med school."

"Freddie, come on, we need to get over to OR five. Leave your stuff here. We'll need to suit up and get gloved to go in there."

"What's the problem, Mike?"

"They've got an old guy in there for pacemaker replacement. He has one of the models that can be programmed and recharged externally, and it has a built-in defibrillator. The pacer won't take the reprogramming, so they want to replace it. The problem is the patient is very frail, and the replacement procedure could kill him."

They ran down the hallway and took the staircase to the operating suite section, where Mike led Freddie to the changing room. They stripped, put on scrub suits and shoe and head covers, and did the mandatory five minute scrubbing before being assisted into gowns and gloves. The automatic door opener hissed, as Freddie made his first entrance into an OR.

Mike approached the vascular surgeon, who filled him in on the pacer/defibrillator model and specs. Then Mike and Freddie assessed the reprogramming unit.

Was the embedded unit or the external one at fault? There was no substitute to try empirically, so Freddie looked the machine over, flipped back the cover, and studied the microprocessor circuits. His mind was racing.

Tio Eddie says a lot of times with complex equipment the simplest explanation is a loose or ill-fitted chip.

Carefully he manipulated each primary chip then looked at the loop antenna that would carry the changing signals to the unit inside the patient. He spotted a loose connection. He tightened it and closed the cover.

"Dr. Bakerson," Freddie said, "please try reprogramming one more time."

The surgeon looked questioningly at Mike, who nodded agreement. Then he set the external antenna over the patient's left chest wall, where the unit was embedded in a pocket of skin. He activated the external programmer, and the surgeon keyed in the activating codes, while the anesthesiologist watched the heart monitor. Within seconds, the telltale spike of the internal pacer appeared on the screen, a metronome of life for the old man lying there.

"Geez, it's midnight! The folks are going to be royally pissed when we get back," Tonio muttered.

"Well, if *La Belle Dame Sans Merci* hadn't spent so much time smooching with my tech partner after we got done, we would have been home in time," Freddie groused.

"I did not smooch, mush head, and we are home! Keep quiet, and maybe we won't get grilled for hours."

The trio opened the door quietly, hoping that the oldsters had gone to bed. The light in the foyer switched on suddenly, and three obviously tired and stern-looking guardians stood there in pajamas and robes.

"We got a phone call," Nancy said flatly.

"Actually we got four phone calls," Edison added.

"Each of your department supervisors called, and then we received a conference call from the hospital administrator with Dr. Grimaldi on the line," Galen said softly, looking intently at the kids.

"Each of you in some roundabout way saved a life this evening. And when all is said and done, that's what counts. But in some way, each of you also broke rules that were established for a purpose. We will have to deal with that, but tonight you brought honor to the family. Now, go to bed, and we'll talk more in the morning."

The teens, their ears red, started up the stairs when Galen called out, "Carmie, you have our permission to date Michael. He seems to have a good head on his shoulders."

Now awake and well experienced with disruptions in their sleep routine, the adults sat in the living room. They needed to relax before heading back up to their rooms.

"Did we ever do stuff like that when we were young?" Edison asked.

Galen remembered the night the two of them had encountered the victim of an automobile accident, and the unorthodox—and unauthorized—treatment they had administered to restart his heart.

"Car battery," he whispered.

Nancy saw Edison's face turn beet red.

"Want to tell me about it?"

He shook his head.

"Tomorrow."

CHAPTER 6

Suffer the Little Children

PART ONE

The flames climbed higher and higher, matched only by the crescendo of screams from his dying family. He felt the heat sear his face and arms, as he sought to rescue his loved ones. He knew it was too late.

Cracking walls and support beams drove him from the inferno that was once his home. He stood there watching the death throes of his life. He turned away and saw the boy, backlit in orange-red. The boy was smiling...

The old man awoke with a start and a cry of anguish. He lay sweat-soaked on the long-unwashed bed sheets, feeling the familiar onset of the tremors that would soon become uncontrollable shaking. He grabbed the half-empty bottle of grain whiskey lying on the unfinished wooden floor and began drinking from its open top. The dirty-brown liquid overflowed his trembling lips, adding its own unique hue to his sweat-yellow undershirt.

He fell back, the bottle slipping from his fire-scarred right hand. The alcohol-induced amnesia caught hold once more, and he did not dream this time.

She sat at the reception desk watching the minutes slowly tick by. It was almost noon. Her father had promised she would only have to work the morning shift to fill in for the girl who was sick.

Come on, Dad! I need to leave here soon.

Tony said he would try to come and get her, and he would take her to his home up on the mountain.

The phone rang. She sighed and picked up the handset.

"Still want to go, Betty?"

He hadn't forgotten!

"Yes, Tony, I'm just waiting for Dad to get through interviewing the family of one of our new residents. I'll meet you outside. 'Bye."

Come on, Dad!

"Tío Galen?"

"Yes, Tonio?"

He looked at the young man, now taller than he was, and thought how lonely he must be with his sister and brother away at college. Even his friend, Faisal, had left early to start at Juilliard. Hard to believe Tonio would be leaving for college soon, too.

"Tío Galen, could I invite my friend Betty over this afternoon? We thought we could … you know … walk around the mountain, and I could show her the wolves, and…"

Well, well! The boy has indeed grown up! He has a girlfriend now. Never thought I would be serving in loco parentis at this age.

"What's Betty's last name? Is she a classmate of yours?"

"Oh, yes, Tío! She's the smartest girl I've ever met. We've worked together on projects in chemistry and biology, and she wants to be a doctor, too."

Galen caught the word "too" at the end of the boy's sentence, and his heart jumped.

He does want to follow in my footsteps!

His mind recalled the little boy following him, walking side by side in the woods, learning to read his journals and notes. Maybe, just maybe, he would have the son he always wanted.

"And what's her last name?"

"Oops, sorry, Tio, it's Betty Orth. Uh ... can I borrow your Jeep?"

The old man sat in the back of the courtroom, dressed in dirty-blue bib overalls. His hands clenched and unclenched, as the trial proceeded all the way to summation. He watched his boy, now a hard-faced man, backlit by the mixed, yellow-and-blue light of the worn-out, fluorescent tubes in the courtroom ceiling. He saw the jury reenter the room and the foreman hand the small paper to the court clerk, who then handed it to the presiding judge. He held his breath, as the judge nodded and handed the paper back to the clerk, who read the verdict.

"By unanimous vote of the jury, you have been convicted of the crimes of kidnapping, homicide, and interstate flight to avoid prosecution. You are hereby sentenced to mandatory life imprisonment in the United States Federal Penitentiary at Allenwood, Pennsylvania."

Jesse Orth walked down the north corridor of St. Ignatius Home, as he escorted the family of its latest resident to the lounge. It had been a difficult session. Family expectations often exceeded the staff's ability to treat and help the type of patients residing there.

He spotted his daughter sitting at the receptionist's desk impatiently drumming her fingers on the counter. How like her mother! Betty was the spitting image of Hisayo—beauty, brains—and an iron will. He had been truly blessed with the women in his life.

"Okay, Betty, everything's quiet. Now, tell me again, what are you doing this afternoon?"

His daughter's delicate Amerasian features took on the universal exasperated look of teenagers, as her eyebrows rose in disbelief. She had told him twice already!

"Tony and I are going for a drive up the mountain to his house. He has some great stuff to show me, all of the tame wild animals and plants."

"Tony who?"

"Tony Hidalgo, Daddy, and you know it already. He's on his way down to pick me up now."

He looked at her, remembering the little girl riding horsey on his back and asking him to read to her at bedtime.

"Tony is one of Dr. Galen's wards, isn't he?"

She nodded.

He deliberately paused, holding back the laughter as he saw the anxious frustration in her face.

"Have a good time, honey."

In one motion, the beautiful young woman stood up from the desk, smoothed her light-yellow blouse and tan skirt, kissed him, and ran out the door.

The old man sat in the stick-frame rocker staring out the front window of the ramshackle farmhouse. He had only partly rebuilt it after the conflagration that had robbed his life of meaning. A half-empty bottle of rotgut lay on the floor beside the chair.

The tremors weren't too bad now. He could hold his hands outstretched to hug the ghosts of his wife and oldest boy, as his mind conjured up the image of that last day...

.   .   .

"Hey, Pop, let's ping some, while Ma and Meemaw get the turkey ready."

His boy was tall, like him, but with his wife's delicate, Tennessee nose and eyes. He wanted to be a soldier like his dad, and he had always looked for an excuse to target practice on the tin cans they had hung up in the woods.

"C'mon Pop. Bet Granpaw'll wanna come with us."

"Ain't yer brother comin'?"

"Nah, he's readin' his books again."

In his memory the old man watched, as the back door opened, and his wife and mother stood framed in the doorway. He heard each of them call that Thanksgiving dinner would be ready soon. He saw his father squeeze past them and waddle out to where he and his son stood waiting. He grinned at hearing his father's guffaw about escaping "the wimmin."

.   .   .

The old man slumped in his rocker, haunted by ghosts. He began to cry.

Ben Castle's lopsided grin grew broader, as he watched his daughter sketching and throwing clay, bringing to life the images her mind had captured in whatever universe it inhabited. The she-wolf sat beside her, a study in calmness contrasting with the restless energy the autistic girl could not control.

Ben was retired now. His stroke had made him ineligible for anything but permanent disability from the State Police. He could have taught at the academy, but he was not attracted to that classroom stuff. He felt perfectly fine in all ways, but the bureaucracy considered him damaged goods, at risk in the daily struggle of law enforcement.

The generosity of the Edisons and Dr. Galen still amazed him. They had provided a guest cottage and studio for Miriam and him at the base of the mountain property. Not only had they helped with the costs of the small, four-room residence, but they also had helped to build it, and they had even granted him and his daughter rights in perpetuity to live there.

Truth be told, Ben didn't want to go back to work. He was with his daughter now, giving her the care and love he never had time for in the daily grind of police work.

The guilt was finally abating.

"Where's Tonio going?"

Edison and Nancy had just walked out on the back deck, as Galen's ancient red Jeep took off at warp speed down the mountain driveway. At first Edison thought it was Galen driving badly as usual, until he saw him standing in the shadow of the deck railing. Galen was quietly staring at the vehicle receding in the distance.

Nancy also saw Galen and recognized that distant look. She made a hushing sound to her husband and walked over to the old doctor.

"They do grow up before we know it," she said softly.

Galen turned toward Nancy and Edison.

"You would think I'd be used to this, now that Carmelita, Freddie, and Faisal are away at school. But each time it's just as bad. I wonder if it's easier for younger parents, when their children want to leave the nest and fly on their own."

The three stood together and watched the Jeep make its descent to the highway, suspecting that its driver was feeling like a bird in flight.

"Lach, come in here! Look what Faisal sent us!"

Diana Douglass had opened the cardboard mailing envelope and removed a DVD carefully wrapped inside. She slid it into the player, and the two sat in front of the TV to watch and listen, as the image of the young man and the wolf that served as his seeing-eye dog appeared on the screen.

"Hello, everybody! One of my friends here at school is making this recording. Say hello, Jacob."

The camera did a one-eighty and found another young man, dressed in Chasidic garb, black hat, and beard. He waved and pivoted the camera back to Faisal.

"He's not supposed to show himself in pictures, but he wants to be a movie producer someday. Strange, isn't it?"

Faisal knelt down and stroked the head of the wolf-dog at his side.

"Akela and I are doing well. They keep us pretty busy with music theory and actual composition classes. When we come home for Thanksgiving break, I'll play some of my stuff for you. I hope maybe this year we can all get together on the mountain for the holiday dinner. I miss you."

The brief scene did a slow fade, as piano music rose in the background.

Diana and Lachlan stayed silent for a while afterward, hands intertwined.

"Betty, I have something for you."

The two youngsters sat at a side table in the little sandwich shop. Both had finished a lunch of veggie hoagies and root-beer floats and felt halfway between sugar-buzzed and contented.

She took the small, square box from his outstretched right hand and carefully opened it. Inside was a smaller, silver box with a songbird incused on the cover. She lifted the lid and the box began to play "Somewhere My Love." Inside was a silver friendship ring.

They gazed at each other, as Tonio took the ring from the little music box and placed it on the third finger of her right hand.

The Pennsylvania mountain weather chilled rapidly soon after Halloween. The last flutter of fall foliage had fallen. The local stores already displayed Christmas decorations.

The old man sat nursing his bottle. Once there was a time when he would have been out hunting wild turkey, just like that Thanksgiving week when his life died. He could still hear his wife's voice, as he and his oldest son had headed out that frosty morning, the scent of fireplace smoke lending its aroma to the chill November air...

Come on, Pop, them turkeys ain't gonna wait fer us.

Ain't Tommy coming?

Nah, you know how he is, Pop.

When he had turned toward the house, he saw the younger boy staring at them from the front-bedroom window. The boy's jaw was clenched, his eyes fixed unmoving on his older brother.

"This place is beautiful in the fall, Tony."

They walked hand-in-hand along the wooded path leading to the migratory bird pond and the wolf den. The leaves formed a scarlet-and-yellow carpet that crunched under their feet.

She wore his ring and told him that she would never take it off. He wanted to tell her that she looked beautiful, but he didn't. That would sound too corny, he thought, and he didn't want to seem stupid in front of her.

They stepped into the clearing and, one by one, the wolves appeared, led by the alpha male. They formed a half-circle around the two youngsters, taking in Tonio's familiar scent and sniffing the new two-legged one to see if she was safe or not.

"Tony, these can't be wolves. They're so tame!"

She reached out to touch the head of the nearest one, a medium-size, gray-and-brown animal that sat on its haunches looking at her. But he backed away, ears down and whimpering.

Then all of the wolves followed suit keeping their distance and whimpering.

"Betty, I've never seen them do this. Did you handle any chemicals at the nursing home?"

"No, nothing, Tony," she said nervously. "Let ... let's go up to your house. I'd like to meet your aunt and uncles."

He stood there a moment, puzzled.

"Sure, let's go—and if you're real good, I'll introduce you to Miriam and her father."

He laughed, and she punched him on the shoulder and kissed him.

Ben was cleaning up the room where Miri did her drawing and sculpting. She seemed tired, more so than usual, and lay down on the floor mat that she used during the day to rest. He tried to move quietly around the sleeping girl and her wolf companion, as he picked up the sketch papers and clay figures she had generated during the day.

Normally he would look at the sketches and try to sort them by subject matter and file them away. But one charcoal drawing caught his eye. It was a picture of Tonio and a young girl, Asian by the looks of her, standing in the forest. The light filtering through the trees cast an ethereal illumination on the girl's face.

"You know, Lach, Faisal's idea is a good one. Why don't we all get together at Safehaven for Thanksgiving dinner? Ben and Miri are up there now, and I'll bet Nancy could use some help getting things in order for the kids when they come home. How about showing her the DVD and seeing what she says?"

Lachlan nodded—he had just been thinking the same thing. He also had been thinking about stopping by Ben's place to see how his old partner was doing.

The tall state trooper, still in uniform, got up, stretched lazily, and then kissed his wife. As he headed for the door, the phone rang. Diana was nearest, so she answered, heard the voice on the other end, and then handed the phone to Lach.

"Douglass, the fit's hit the shan," he heard the gruff voice of his new sergeant say. "There's been a breakout at Allenwood—three maximum-security prisoners."

He listened to the details and turned pale, as he heard his sergeant's final comments:

"We think they're coming after Ben. He was the one who put them away, and the worst one swore he would take him down. Better get over there and warn him. He doesn't answer his phone. We'll send backup as well."

The old man had dozed off in his chair and awoke to the sounds of harsh laughter. His eyes took several seconds to lose their sleep blur and focus on the three figures standing in front of him.

"Hello, Pa. Didn't think I was coming home for the holidays, did you?"

He saw them clearly now: three men in ill-fitting clothes, probably stolen, including the one he recognized.

"Yeah, it's me, Pa, your little Tommy. Remember, you drunken sot?"

The seated man just stared not saying a word. He knew if he did he would feel the blows on his face, just like that last time when the police took Tommy away.

"Got some unfinished business, old man, and you're part of it. Don't know how you escaped the first fire, but it's your turn again to be the roast turkey."

The other men guffawed, as they watched their cellmate take a five-gallon container of gasoline and start pouring it around the perimeter of the man's room. Their friend wasn't called "Tommy the Torch" for nothing.

His father watched motionless and without expression.

Maybe it'll be better this way.

He stayed still, as the last drop gasoline fell from the can's spout. Then he heard his son's parting words:

"Say hello to the others when you get to hell, you..."

His ears shut out the obscenities, as his eyes saw the cigarette lighter being clicked. He began to cry as the flames licked at his chair.

"Tonio, why don't you introduce us to your friend?"

Nancy watched the young girl sitting uncomfortably on the sofa in the living room. She could see that he was ill at ease, too. This was the first time he had mentioned having a girlfriend, much less invited one to the house.

"Tia Nancy, Tio Edison, Tio Galen, this is my friend, Betty Orth."

Galen looked at the young woman.

"Your father is Jesse, right?"

Betty nodded.

"Yes, I help out over at St. Ignatius Home on the weekends. I remember seeing you there, when you came to get Miriam."

Nancy looked at the girl again, harboring a private joke she couldn't share with the others—at least not now.

Oh, Betty, I know exactly how you feel. Someday, we'll talk ... just you and me.

"Would you like to stay for dinner, Betty?" Edison asked. "You haven't eaten until you've had one of Nancy's gourmet meals."

Tonio exchanged glances with Betty.

"That would be great, Tio. First, Betty and I would like to visit Tio Ben and Miri. We'll walk down to their place and be back in time for dinner. Okay?"

Lachlan had tried several times to reach Ben by phone. Nothing.

Maybe he's sleeping.

Then he dialed another number.

"Hello, Safehaven, who's calling?"

He watched the flames rising, the heated air curling the remaining hair on his arms. He didn't try to escape—he didn't want to. As the smoke spiraled up, it conjured a memory.

Come on, Pa, we gotta go huntin'. Can't just sit there, can ya?

He rose from the chair to follow his boy and stumbled outside.

Get your hunting rifle, Pa. We need to bag some varmints.

Yes, son, we do need to nail some varmints.

The alcohol haze began to lift, as he reached his old pickup truck and removed the rifle from its gun rack. He checked the load then got in and drove off.

Firefly sparks, rising up from what was left of his home, lit up the darkness.

"It's right down this path, Betty. It's a neat place, just right for Ben and Miri. Tio Edison and Tia Nancy even helped build it. I didn't know they could do things like that, but Tio Galen told me they did a lot of work for Habitat for Humanity and actually worked side by side with a former president way back when they were younger. Look, there it is."

The little cottage sat in a sheltered clearing, a true-to-life, Hansel and Gretel, gingerbread-style house.

"I hope the big bad wolf isn't in there," Betty joked.

"Funny you should say that," Tonio replied.

Ben had finished cleaning up and felt like lying down himself. He hadn't really done any heavy work today. Maybe it was the cool air and the wind rustling through the mountain forest that relaxed him. He sat down in the stuffed recliner that had been a gift from Nancy and tilted it back to take a quick nap.

He looked over and saw Miri still asleep. Her dog—he couldn't get used to the fact that it was part wolf—lay beside her.

Then he heard the click-whoosh, as the front door opened, and he saw three grim men entering the room.

"Well, look, guys, it wasn't Goldilocks in here after all. Lee, Quint, meet my favorite copper, Sergeant Ben Castle, a genuine Pennsylvania State Trooper.

"Sergeant, meet my pen buddies."

He recognized the one talking, and his mind shifted to an earlier time. The face was younger then but just as mean.

Tommy—Tommy the Torch! How many people has this one killed, including his own family?

"Whatsa matter, fuzz, cat got yer tongue?"

That was Quint—barrel chest, broken nose, unfocused eyes, stupid with animal cunning. Ben had met that type before.

"Lee, go out and check the perimeter. We wouldn't want to be interrupted, would we, Ben?"

The third man, short, wiry, gray eyes fixing on everything and nothing, nodded silently and walked out.

The she-wolf had opened her eyes and was watching the strangers. She emitted a low, gutteral growl, and the girl awoke at the sound. She let out what sounded like half-groaning, half-grunting noises and rose to her feet.

"This your kid, Ben? Looks real pretty, don't she, Quint?"

Both men laughed.

Ben sat up in the chair and faced the trio's leader.

"She's my daughter, Tommy. She's not right in the head. Leave her be. This is between you and me."

"Sure, Ben, sure. We're old friends, after all. You got me free food and housing for the last ten years. Who could have a better friend than that, right Quint?"

Miri started to move around the room, holding out her arms and touching the clothes of the two strange men. She moved her head from side to side, her mouth emitting "unnh, unnh."

"She really is a retard, isn't she Ben? What a kick in the teeth that must have been for you. Better get her away from Quint. He doesn't like being touched."

Ben rose very slowly from the chair keeping his hands in front of him, palms up. He move to Miri and guided her over to her drawing papers.

"She's autistic, Tommy. You know what that means?"

"Don't you remember, Ben? I was the smart one in the family."

Ben watched the younger man holding the tight-lipped, cold smile on his face.

"She likes to draw, Tommy. Just leave her alone."

The three turned toward the door at the sound of Lee's monotone voice.

"Get in there, you two."

A frightened Tonio and Betty appeared in the doorway, followed by Lee holding a handgun at their backs.

"What did you find, Lee?"

"Couple o' kids. Too bad for them," he laughed.

Ben stared. It was Tonio ... and the girl in the picture!

Nancy had immediately recognized Lachlan's voice. She listened to the young trooper and began to tremble. Edison and Galen spotted her reaction and immediately sprang from their chairs. Edison reached the phone first and took it from his wife's hand.

"This is Bob Edison. What's going on?"

"Bob, this is Lachlan Douglass. Listen..."

Now Galen saw his friend blanche, and he put his ear to the receiver just as Lachlan added, "They're after Ben. I'm on my way, but you've got to warn him. He's not answering his phone."

A shaken Edison put down the phone and stood there holding Nancy.

"Do you have any firearms here?" Galen asked.

Edison thought for a moment.

"There's an old hunting rifle I got the first year we were here. I thought I would try shooting at tin cans, but Nancy doesn't like guns. And when the kids came, I locked it up in one of my workboxes downstairs. It hasn't been touched in decades."

"Get it. I just hope the ammunition is still good."

He had a good idea where he could find Tommy. He knew his second son was smart enough to have tracked down the state trooper's address even before the prison break. He just had to get there in time.

"Quint, go outside and keep an eye on the grounds. We don't want anyone else paying a visit."

Tommy's crooked grin never changed, as he eyed the two youngsters. The girl was a looker. After he took care of the copper and the boy, he'd have fun with her, and maybe even the daughter. He'd spent an awfully long time in stir.

Miri seemed oblivious to the commotion. She sat on the floor, cross-legged, her hands holding charcoal drawing markers and moving like windshield wipers, tossing out drawing after drawing. The she-wolf sat strangely quiet beside her.

The heavyset con moved slowly in a large half-circle around the house. It was past sunset, and the air was still. The summer insects had died off in the early frosts, and all he could hear was his own heavy breathing.

He turned toward the side of the house and suddenly saw several pairs of luminescent green eyes outlined by the cloudless moonlit sky.

Must be animals. Too low to the ground for people.

Then he heard the growl, and just as he looked back, the alpha male leaped forward. Quint's dying screams were confined to a bloody gurgle in his torn-out windpipe.

"It's time, Ben."

He turned to Tonio.

"You, kid, go stand by the copper."

Tonio moved toward Ben, and Betty took a step to follow him.

"No, not you, little lady, just your boyfriend. You and Ben's daughter are going to be my special guests. We're going to celebrate the holiday."

Tonio stood at Ben's side. He couldn't think of anything to do. Ben's mind was racing, playing and replaying all the possible attack and escape scenarios he could imagine. At the moment there seemed no way out. It was fairly obvious what was going to happen to him and Tonio. And then the girl and his daughter would be...

They heard someone approaching the open doorway.

"You find someone else, Quint?"

No reply.

"Come on in, Quint. Join the party."

"There's no party, son, just me."

Tommy saw the tall shadow of a man walk in, rifle at the ready. He quickly grabbed Betty and held a knife to her throat, while Lee pointed his gun at the intruder.

Tommy was genuinely stunned.

"I killed you! I saw the house burn! Why didn't you die?"

The she-wolf smelled the heavy scent of fear emanating from Tommy and Lee. She began a low growl again.

Miriam's hands flew faster and faster over the paper, pages falling like snowflakes to the floor, as she finished one and started another.

Tommy screamed, "I'll kill her! I'll kill you! I'll kill you all, just like I did before."

He held the point of the knife on the right side of Betty's neck and a drop of blood welled up underneath the tip.

Just then a set of heavy footsteps approached the doorway.

"Quint," Tommy screamed, "Where the hell. . .?"

It was a bear-sized man carrying another rifle.

Twin blasts rocked the air in the small room.

The first blew Lee backward, his forehead shattered by the round from Galen's rifle. The second shot caught Tommy square in the chest, knocking him against the wall. His eyes glazed over as he slid down to the floor.

Lem Caddler ran to his dead son. He knelt down and held him in his arms, sobbing.

As Galen lowered the smoking weapon, one word entered his mind: *Absalom.*

CHAPTER 7

Suffer the Little Children

PART TWO

Lachlan Douglass entered the front door of the cottage, followed by a phalanx of state troopers, all with guns drawn. When they surveyed the carnage, they holstered their weapons. Lachlan walked up to Ben and hugged him.

"Did you find the other one, Lach?"

The younger man swallowed.

"The wolves did."

Galen stood over Tonio, who was sitting on the floor, shaking uncontrollably, and holding Betty in his arms. He knelt down and put his hand on the young man's shoulder and used a word he had only dreamed of.

"Son, are you all right?"

"Something's wrong with Betty, Tio Galen. She's still bleeding!"

"I'm okay, Tony. It's just a scratch."

The old doctor saw the paleness in her skin and the dilation of her pupils. He felt her neck then turned to Lachlan.

"Call the Medevac. We need to get her to the hospital."

When the meat wagon arrived to pick up the three dead convicts, Ben gently pulled Lem away from his son's body, so the attendants could bag it and carry it out to the waiting coroner's vehicle. Lachlan had called in the medical-evacuation helicopter and stood by as it picked up Betty, accompanied by Galen and Tonio.

After the 'copter took off, he returned to the blood-stained studio. Lem had collapsed into Ben's chair. Ben was standing over Miri, who had lain down on her mat again, the she-wolf by her side. The tall trooper walked over to his friend and former partner, bent over, and began picking up the pile of sketches, hoping to save Ben the trouble. As he did so, he examined them. The subject matter startled the young man, even though he had seen death many times in the Middle East: Multiple views of the three prisoners graphically displayed the moments of their deaths—even the moonlit destruction of Quint.

There was one more. It depicted a young, Amerasian girl lying in a hospital bed.

Lachlan stared at Miri

"What are you, girl?"

Empty eyes stared out into space.

They had followed the stretcher carrying Betty into the ER, Galen consulting with the attending physician about her condition. He convinced Tonio to sit in the waiting area, where Nancy and Edison soon arrived to join him.

The young man sat, head in hands, torn between the desire to run to the cubicle where Betty was being examined, and the understanding that he would probably be in the way. Edison and Nancy sat beside him in silence.

All three looked up, as Jesse Orth walked out with Galen. The big man's face was ashen.

"Mr. Orth, can I see Betty?"

Jesse shook his head.

"Betty's mother is with her now, and the doctors aren't quite finished yet. Tony, tell me what happened."

Galen stood outside the cubicle with Frank Farber, the ER doctor on call.

"You called it, Galen. She's got ALL. Her white-cell count is over a hundred thousand, and the smear is loaded with blasts. Who do you want to call in for consult?"

Both men knew what lay ahead for the young girl with acute lymphoblastic leukemia, the most common blood cancer striking children. It demanded a regimen of drugs, radiation, and even bone-marrow stem-cell transplantation. The toll on the patient's well-being would be magnified by the emotional turmoil normally occurring in the teen years, as the young person attempted to stake out his or her identity and independence.

Whatever happened, it was bound to be a rough ride.

"I'll call in Jay Greenberg. He and his team are the best pediatric and adolescent specialists I know."

Galen walked out to the waiting area and approached his friends.

"Betty needs to be admitted for her bleeding," he told them.

He pulled up a chair and straddled it. He looked first at Jesse then Tonio, Nancy, and Edison.

"Betty has a problem with her blood. It's making too many white cells of a type called lymphocytes. Because of this, her body—her bone marrow—isn't able to make other blood cells like platelets, which help control bleeding when she gets cut."

He looked again at his ward.

"You were very observant, Tonio. Most likely you saved Betty's life. The problem she has often goes unnoticed until something very serious happens."

Jesse had been a nursing-home administrator too long not to realize what Galen was saying. His words were both question and statement.

"Betty has leukemia?"

He braced himself for Galen's reply.

"Yes."

Just then Lachlan walked in leading a very shaky Lem Caddler.

"Lem wanted to know how the girl was doing. I think maybe he needs to be admitted, Doc."

Galen saw the combined effects of grief and incipient DTs—delirium tremens, the withdrawal effects of heavy alcohol use. He got up and found Farber, who was writing his final notes on Betty's chart.

"I think we have another admission here, Frank. Lem Caddler just lost his son, and the alcohol is wearing off."

"All right, we'll get him admitted to CATS unit."

Galen returned to Lachlan and Lem.

"Lem, what you did tonight took more courage than any battlefield you fought on. You saved multiple lives. Do you have the strength to find yourself again?"

The man was shaking even more now. He looked past the trooper and the doctor. In the shadows near the entryway he visualized his oldest son, Lemuel Jr., and his wife, Tara. Was it the DTs again, or did he actually hear his boy say, *Go for it, Pa,* and did he hear his wife say, *I love you, Lem?*

Lem nodded, and the attendant escorted him to the beginning of his new life.

"Tio Galen, can I see Betty now?"

Galen looked at Jesse, who nodded.

"Go ahead, Tonio, but remember she's exhausted from all the excitement."

The young man dashed across the waiting room to the cubicle. He opened the door carefully and saw an older version of Betty sitting by the bed. He suddenly felt awkward, but he moved near.

"You're Tony, Tony Hidalgo. Betty has told me so much about you—how smart you are and nice and..."

The petite Japanese woman smiled at Betty.

"She also said you were cute."

"Mama! Don't believe her, Tony!"

Betty blushed, whether in anger or at hearing the truth, Tonio couldn't tell. He was blushing, too.

"Thank you, Mrs. Orth. May I visit with Betty?"

"Yes, by all means. Maybe you can persuade my stubborn daughter that she needs to stay here for treatment."

Hisayo Orth smiled again at the two young people then made a graceful exit. They sat there in awkward silence for a moment, before they both started to talk at the same time.

"Betty, I ... uh ... I just wanted to tell you that I'll be here for you."

He put his hand over hers and felt the little silver ring on her finger.

"I don't want you to see me like this, Tony. Besides, it's not fair. What did I do to deserve this ... this blood thing?"

"You didn't do anything."

He bent over and kissed her forehead. She started to cry, so he sat there holding her, growing silent again.

"Nancy, I'd like to invite Lem Caddler to stay here when he gets out of the detox unit. He has no place to go. His son burned down the farmhouse, and he can't live out of his truck."

She looked proudly at her husband. He never ceased to amaze her with his willingness to help one more person, even someone who had caused him trouble in the past.

"Of course, dear."

Galen had just entered the room, but he caught the gist of the conversation.

"I see we're still taking in strays," he muttered.

Edison placed his tongue in his cheek.

"We did so well with you, we figured to make it a habit."

Galen plopped down in the wing-backed easy chair he had claimed as his own in the living room, his own tongue in cheek as well.

"Glad to have been of service. And, for the record, I do agree with you both. Lem certainly does need a home. He mentioned that a developer wants to buy his farmland. Then he said something else. He wants to live here, like Ben and Miri. Even said he could help with the animals and do other chores. He offered to give the money from the sale of his farm to the trust fund we've set up for the Agape Mountain Wildlife Preserve.

"Think we have room for another small cottage?"

Edison and Nancy smiled and nodded.

"Tomorrow's Thanksgiving," Nancy said. "The kids will be coming in tonight. Should we still have the big dinner tomorrow with the Douglasses and Ben and Miri? I've got everything ready. I just didn't know, with all that went on yesterday ... if we felt up to it."

"Of course we'll have Thanksgiving here," Edison replied. "Having that gunfight at the OK Corral, with our own Doc Holiday shooting up the place, stirs up a man's appetite. Besides, all the kids will be home."

Nancy turned to Galen.

"How's Tonio doing? I haven't seen much of him lately. He's always out."

"He's spending as much time as possible at the hospital. Betty's started the first phase of her chemotherapy, and it's making her pretty miserable."

Nancy and Edison exchanged glances, and Edison asked the unanswerable question.

"Is she going to make it?"

Galen threw up his hands.

"It's hard to tell. Based on all the testing and the special, chemical markers that we look for as favorable-outcome signs, we still don't know. But I do know that what Tonio is doing by being there for her is just as crucial as any treatment we can give her. It's hard enough being old and creaky and ugly like you, Edison, but can you even imagine what a young adult would be going through with what might be a fatal condition? She's supposed to have her whole life ahead of her—career, love, marriage maybe—but she's got to deal with this instead.

"No older person can truly empathize with what she's experiencing. But a member of her peer group, and one I suspect she loves? Now that's therapy!"

Edison aimed a set of beady eyes at Galen.

"I resent being called 'creaky.'"

All three laughed.

"Which reminds me," Galen added, "how are the kids coming in?"

"Freddie's driving down from MIT with Lilly and picking up Carmelita at Yale. Then they'll drive through New York and pick up Fai at Juilliard. I expect we'll be treated to a typical Freddie arrival."

Edison grinned.

"Freddie is turning into a real chip off the old block. He's got his pick of every girl at school, but he seems to be sticking with Lilly."

"I guess he never got over that kiss at the riverside," Nancy said, grinning back at him. "Oldest trick in the book: Bat your eyes at the right man and he never forgets."

"Yeah, that young man thinks he's got the best girl in the world. Too bad she's only second-best."

They clasped hands like school kids.

"What about Carm and Mike? Is he coming in from California?"

"Sure, unless we ring the place with wild horses," Nancy laughed.

The day passed uneventfully. The frost from the previous evening had remained on the ground, and the weather report predicted light snow for Thanksgiving.

Tonio was the first to arrive home from school. After a brief greeting he headed to his room. The elders saw the worried look on his face, and Galen headed down the corridor. He stood in front of the closed door then gently knocked.

"Can I come in, Tonio?"

No reply.

He slowly opened the door. The boy was lying facedown on his bed, crying. Galen sat on the edge of the bed.

"The medicine is making her so sick, Tio. And I heard the nurse tell her that she would have to get a wig, because her hair might fall out. I don't know what to do or what to say to her."

Galen's mind flooded with memories of holding Leni and Cathy and of being powerless to help them.

Dear God, if you exist, are you going to make this boy relive my life?

He remained quiet, while Tonio continued to sob.

The late-afternoon stillness was shattered by the sounds of an automobile approaching the house and sliding to a stop on the gravel in front, accompanied by Wagner's "Entry of the Gods into Valhalla."

The kids were home!

"Come on, Tonio, put on a good face. Your brother and sister are here."

The troubled boy had found restless sleep, but Galen had kept a vigil by his side, overwhelmed by his own dark memories of loss. But now, now was a time to show a more positive face to the world. It was something he hoped the boy would, by necessity, learn to do if he really did want to follow in his tio's footsteps. Part of the art of medicine is playing *Pagliacci*, bringing relief to others while appearing rock-like in the presence of personal adversity—empathize, advise, be available despite your own troubles.

Tonio sat up, his face creased from lying on the blanket.

"Go wash up and change into something comfortable and bright. I'll let them know you're coming out. Hurry up now."

Galen's joints ached, as he shuffled down the corridor and heard the rising cacophony of young adults coming back to the nest. He paused, removed his glasses, and rubbed his eyes then took a deep breath and entered the living room. He wore a smile.

Carmelita rushed up and hugged him.

"Tio," she scolded, "did you forget to shave?"

She rubbed her hand over the old man's face and laughed.

He smiled back.

"You've gotten used to the smooth faces of the young men at school, Carm."

Her blush matched the color of her sweater.

How she had grown and matured, he thought. Only her second year as a linguistics major, and already she was taking graduate-level courses, to the amazement of her professors.

"Tio Galen, you and Tio Eddie and Tia Nancy don't appear any older," Freddie joked.

He hung back a bit. Leaning against the living room wall, he presented a casual air, but Galen could see he was taking in everything going on. Gone only a few months his face already had lost some of its youthful innocence.

The world isn't kind, is it, Freddie? It doesn't laugh at your jokes and pranks like we did. It bites back at anyone who too aggressively seeks his position in the hierarchy of authority and power.

He looked at the lanky, Latino-handsome young man and smiled once more.

"You've matured into quite a man now, haven't you Freddie. Are you treating Lilly well? How are your grades?"

His face turned pink at the mention of Lilly's name.

"We're both acing the grades, Tio."

He turned toward Nancy.

"Could Lilly come for dinner tomorrow? Her father is away on mission, and her mother and sister are visiting relatives."

"Certainly, Freddie," Nancy replied.

Edison agreed. He liked Lilly. Too few young women understood electronics.

Tonio entered the room dressed in jeans and a red-flannel shirt. With sleeves rolled up and his shirt untucked, it gave him a carefree look, Galen thought.

That's good. He's learning.

After hugs and handshakes, the three youngsters sat down together.

"We dropped off Fai and Akela on the way up. He said they'd all be over for dinner tomorrow. Can we handle the guests, Tia?" Carmelita asked.

"Of course we can, dear. Why do you think we wanted you all home? Everyone's going to help."

She laughed at the look on their faces.

How soon they forget.

"Anything exciting happen here?" Freddie asked.

Tonio started to speak, but then he stopped himself, got up, and left the room.

"What's eating him?"

The story came out, bit by agonizing bit. The two college kids sat shocked. Carmelita looked at Galen sitting there quietly. She had flinched when Edison told of how Galen had unhesitatingly killed one of the convicts. Then she remembered his unwavering determination that long-ago day on the island. He always did what was necessary, no matter what it took.

Brother and sister rose and asked to be excused. They headed to Tonio's room and knocked on the door. Carmelita opened it. He was sitting at his desk staring at the wall.

"Little brother, Carm and I would like to go visit your friend with you tonight. Would that be all right?"

Freddie and his sister waited for a reply. They saw their brother's head nod.

"Then it's settled. We'll head over there after dinner. I'm starved," Freddie added.

Dinner was quiet. Maybe the group was saving up the excitement for the next day's holiday festivities. Or maybe it was just the comfort of having everyone home again. Long-learned training took hold, as the young people stood up after dinner and helped clear the table. It was like old times, but the elders understood that soon all three would be living their own lives.

Growing independence or not, the three did not forget to pay their respects.

"Tios and Tia, we're heading over to the hospital with Tonio to visit Betty," Carmelita said. "Is that all right?"

"Go ahead," Edison replied. "Give her our love. Just don't blast that radio down the driveway tonight. Ben and Miri might be sleeping."

The youngsters used Galen's physician's pass to park Freddie's car near the hospital entrance. They took the elevator to the ninth-floor wing, where the special-pediatric and young-adult cancer patients stayed.

As they walked along the corridor, they saw the children in their multicolored hospital gowns, IV tubes hooked to either arm. Some were able to walk alone, pushing the poles carrying the fluids that were attempting to ward off the spread of disease. Others sat in miniature wheelchair/feeding-chair units, while the nursing staff tried to interest them in games or conversation.

And there were some, their doors open, lying there unmoving, their parents sitting vigil by their beds.

They passed two nurses, eyes wet, pushing a domed cart out of one room while the cleaning crew removed the debris of a failed code. They walked by the guest lounge, door closed, where they saw through the window a haggard man and woman sitting across from a clergyman.

"This is her room."

Tonio pointed to a door numbered 903. Carmelita stepped forward and held her brothers back.

"You guys wait here. I want to go in first."

She had brought along a small carrying case. She knocked on the door before opening it. The girl, her face drawn from the effects of the chemotherapy, tried to smile.

"Are you a new doctor?" she asked.

Carmelita approached the bed. She carefully put her hand on the girl's arm and spoke gently.

"No, I'm Carmelita Hidalgo, Tony's sister. He and our brother Freddie and I have come to visit you. I thought you might like to freshen up a bit before the guys come in. I brought some makeup with me."

Betty looked at the beautiful young woman, and female understanding brought a smile to her face. Carmelita opened her case, examined the shades and scents she had packed, and showed Betty what she thought would match her complexion.

Twenty minutes later two very impatient males were admitted to the room, where Carmelita and Betty were talking like two sorority sisters. Tonio looked at Betty and flushed—she was gorgeous!

Freddie nudged his brother.

"I thought I was the only one with an eye for the good-looking ones, little brother. Lucky for you I have Lilly!"

"Come on, Freddie," Carmelita said. "Let's leave these two alone for awhile."

"Call me if you need help, Tonio," Freddie laughed, as his sister yanked him from the room by his elbow.

"She's quite amazing, Tony. How did she know what to do?"

"She's always known, ever since we were kids stranded on that island."

"She told me about that. You guys really lucked out with the Edisons and Dr. Galen."

"Yes, we did," he sighed.

He looked at the bedside table and saw the small music box sitting on it.

"I asked Daddy to bring it in. And, see..." she held up her right hand, "I still have it on."

He saw the silver friendship ring glowing from the reflected rays of the bedside light. He reached over, took her hand, and touched it to his face. She turned and kissed him.

The door opened and their brother walked out. He went to Carmelita and hugged her.

"Thanks, Carm," he said, his eyes glistening.

The three rode home in silence.

Just as predicted, light snow spotted the ground on Thanksgiving morning. Galen got up early hoping for a quiet, predawn walk on the mountain. He had tried to maintain his lifetime habit even after closing his office in Northern Virginia and moving to Pennsylvania. The mountain weather here was harsher than the relatively mild climate of the Piedmont Plateau, but he had managed to adapt to it and continue his one concession to exercise.

He put on boots and took his walking stick—no telling if there were ice patches under the snow. Quietly he made his way out the back door and slowly trudged down one of the side trails that wound past the now-frozen, migratory-bird pond.

Wonder if the wolves are up and about.

No, they were smarter than humans. They had enough sense to stay in their den when it was dark and cold. He continued walking, his boots making sharp, crystalline crunches in the shallow snow. The sky was brightening a bit, and the early dawn cast an amber glow over the leafless trees.

There was a strange scent in the air, not just the aromatic smoke from the many wood-burning stoves and fireplaces across the valley below. No, this was something else—something musky and wild!

With that thought he came to a full stop. He looked ahead and saw the large tracks in the fresh snow. These were big—bigger than the wolf paw prints he was used to seeing on the trails. He arrived at the lightly frozen pond and saw the cracks where something had attempted to drink at the edge.

Then he heard the snuffling noise behind him and turned slowly. *Urso americanis*, a black bear! He stood still, walking stick held tightly at his side.

Weren't they supposed to be hibernating by now? Maybe not. Even with the snow, it had been a relatively mild autumn.

Suddenly Galen experienced a strangely giddy moment, his thoughts seeming ridiculous and sensible at the same time. He almost wanted to laugh out loud, as he thought about it. Ever since childhood, his nickname had been Berto, and as he grew older others had called him the Bear. Maybe, if the Indians were right, the bear was his totem—his spirit symbol—and it had decided to pay him a visit.

"So, what's your name, Bear?"

Before he realized it, he had spoken out loud. His voice shook as he said, "Did you know that my nickname is Bear?"

The critter, undisturbed by the ruckus, sat on its backside and watched Galen. It was a full-grown male, about three hundred pounds of muscle. It brought its left front paw up and scratched its muzzle. Then it yawned and made a noise halfway between a groan and a belch.

"By all the gods that sure sounded like Balloo," Galen laughed.

Then both turned toward the sound of crunching ice crystals and saw the wolves approaching, the alpha male on point, deciding whether to attack the ursine stranger. The bear rose up on its hind legs, standing at least five feet tall, a deep, rolling growl emanating from its throat.

Another giddy moment hit the old doctor. He raised his arms like Moses spreading the Red Sea and spoke to *Lupus* and *Urso*.

"Stop it, both of you! You will both live here in harmony. There's plenty of room and food for you all."

He caught himself.

What the hell am I doing? I'm talking to wolves and bears like that? I must be going senile!

Both bear and wolf were watching him now, so he stared back. The wolves calmed down and sat. So did the bear.

"That's better. I'm going up to my own den now and get back into bed. I'm sure this is all an old man's dream and none of you exist. Now…" and he laughed again, remembering the priest's blessing at the end of mass when he was a boy, "*pax vobiscum.*"

He turned away from the animals and began trudging back up the path.

Better not say anything to the others. They'd probably have me committed for mental testing and blame it on the stress of the last few days.

After all, he had killed a man, even though the police said it was justified. But in his soul he wondered.

Green lupine and brown ursine eyes followed his passage up the mountain.

The State Police car pulled into the driveway in front of the mountain home. A light dusting of snow sat on the wooden sign at the entrance, little mounds highlighting the letters.

All the occupants, save one, looked at it before opening the doors and stepping out into the crisp, wood-scented air. Lachlan and Diana got out first then helped Ben and Miriam. The two wolf-dogs jumped from the car and started to roll in the snow, before Faisal called out "Akela, come here." The large male rose quickly and went to his master's side, waiting until the young man stepped from the car and grasped his harness lead. The smaller, gray-brown female, nameless except in Ben's mind, also rose and stood by her charge.

Ben had wanted to call the dog Irene but thought it might be regarded as a sign of disrespect for his late wife. And, besides, the wolf seemed to need no name or command. It was Miri's shadow at all times, and the two seemed to understand each other on some level that other humans could not.

Faisal hadn't seemed to need eyes to guide him for some time now. He ran up the steps to the door faster than the sighted could move and was met there with a hug from his friend Tonio.

"Wait till you hear what I've written for you, for all of you. It's still in my mind, that is, I actually haven't written it on paper yet."

Faisal was so excited he would have rolled in the snow if he were a dog.

Ben led Miri up the steps. He carried a shopping bag with him and presented it to Nancy in the kitchen.

"Ben, you didn't need to bring anything. There's plenty here," Nancy told him.

"This is special stuff, Nancy. Don't tell Fai. It's a honey-nut cake from a Middle Eastern bakery. A friend of mine from the force brought it back from Philadelphia."

After exchanging greetings and hanging up coats in the hall closet, they all crowded into the living room. Edison had stoked the massive fireplace well. Nancy and Carmelita brought out trays of cups and a large pot of tea. Miri sat on the floor in front of the glass fire screen and stared at the flames hungrily consuming the wood logs inside. Her wolf companion lay next to her.

The youngsters listened, as Ben described the cleanup that had been done in Miri's studio. Faisal stretched out his hand and placed it on Tonio's shoulder, when he heard about Betty and their close call with the escaped convicts. And they were astounded to learn who the heroes of the escapade had been.

"Lem's getting out of detox next week," Galen said. "Ben, I'd like you and Edison to come with me when he does. I'll talk with you about it later."

"Dinner!" Nancy announced. "Everyone take your seats."

They filed into the dining room and found places at the now-larger table that Edison had expanded to hold even more than the eleven who were present.

"Ben, why don't you do the honors and say grace," Nancy offered.

"I don't know stuff like that, folks," the old trooper stammered.

"You start it off, Tio Benny, and we'll each add something. How's that?"

Faisal grinned and waited for Ben to reply. Ben took a breath and began.

"Thank you, Lord, for reuniting me with my daughter. And for bringing friendships that exceed anything I've known since I lost Irene and Bandana."

Each in turn added a comment until only Miri was left. As usual she didn't appear to understand what was happening. Then she looked down at the wolf lying next to her. Nothing needed to be said.

When the dinner dishes had been cleared away, Tonio quietly walked into the kitchen, where Nancy was arranging the dessert.

"Tia, could I take some dinner to Betty?"

She saw in him the same love and devotion that she beheld in her Bob's eyes, when he looked at her.

"Certainly, Tonio, I'm sure she'd like that. Are the others going with you?"

"No, just Fai. He hasn't met Betty yet."

She paused.

"I'll let the others know where you're going. I guess you'll want to borrow Galen's car. Does he know about it yet?"

Tonio made a dash back to the dining room to find his tio.

"Come on, Fai, we can't stop to let every kid pet Akela. Besides, that's not what you're supposed to do with a seeing-eye dog."

"He's a seeing-eye wolf, Tonio. That makes it different."

The two friends walked down the corridor of the ninth floor on-cology wing. Families were visiting in droves for the holiday, and many stared at the two friends and the wolf-dog. When they reached Betty's room Tonio asked Faisal to wait, while he checked to see how she was.

"Are you decent, Betty?" he called, as he cracked open the door.

She wasn't there. The blankets were on the floor, the clothes closet was open, and her street clothes were gone. Tonio raced out the room toward the nursing station and almost shouted at the unit secretary, "Where's Betty Orth?"

The young man at the desk looked at him blankly.

"Is she a patient here?"

Tonio didn't bother to reply. He looked around for the nearest nurse and spotted one coming out of another patient's room. He ran to her and tried to stay calm, as he repeated the question. The nurse shook her head then added, "Is she a young woman, about eighteen?"

"Yes."

She checked the log for any tests that might have been scheduled and found none. Then she hurried to the nursing station and called the security desk to report the girl missing.

"Hey, Tonio, we can find her."

It was Faisal. He led Akela into the girl's room and asked his friend to let the wolf sniff an article of Betty's clothing.

Tonio looked puzzled at his friend and then realized what Fai meant.

Faisal sensed the confusion.

"Akela can find things. I would have lost half my homework if I didn't have him. Let's try it."

Tonio waved the discarded hospital gown in front of Akela's long nose, then Faisal called out, "Akela, find!"

The beast turned, almost pulling his charge off his feet. They headed down the corridor and found themselves in front of the stairway door. Tonio took his friend's arm and guided him through to the stairwell.

"She must have wanted to avoid the elevators. We've got nine flights down. Can you do it?"

"Wait 'til you're on a college campus running between buildings, kiddo," Faisal said, as he headed downward, Akela leading the way. They reached the lobby level, and the dog headed toward the exit door. They continued across the large waiting room to a side door and soon found themselves on the street, as Akela moved away from the hospital.

The wolf began a faster pace now, both humans having to jog just to keep up. They were nearing one of the enclosed, Plexiglas bus shelters. Tonio saw her standing there, no coat, both arms encircling her chest. He ran to her, took off his own coat, and wrapped it around her then took her in his arms.

"Why, Betty?"

"It's not fair. This can't be happening to me. I won't stay there."

She began to cry and he held her closer.

"Come on, we need to get back inside. In case you didn't notice, it's cold out here."

He led her away from the bus shelter and over to Faisal.

"This is my friend Faisal and his seeing-eye wolf. Say hello, Fai."

"Hey, Betty, good thing this isn't New York City. Your shoes would be gone by now. Come with us. This big lug brought you some Thanksgiving dinner, and it's going to be colder than the three of us if we don't get back to your room."

They began walking toward the hospital, when a security van pulled up and directed a searchlight at them.

"You folks all right?" the guard asked.

"Yes, sir, we're fine," Tonio replied. "She just wanted some fresh air. We're headed back to her room now."

They walked to the hospital entrance, as the van followed them. This time they took the elevator back up, the other passengers staring at Akela. Tonio stopped at the nursing desk and informed the staff that his friend had just gotten lost in the complex, and they were headed back to her room.

Betty sat on the edge of her bed, head down. He saw the swelling now on her neck and the bruises that hadn't been there before. He didn't know what to say.

"Why is it always left to the blind guy to break the ice?" Faisal quipped.

Betty snuffled then started to laugh.

"All right, you turkeys, I'm ready for some of that food you brought."

"Turkey you want? Turkey we got," Faisal quipped.

Both young men felt the tension easing.

Later that night the two friends sat in Tonio's room back at Safehaven. Faisal had asked Lachlan and Diana if he could stay over.

"You really fell for her, didn't you?"

"She's everything I could ask for, Fai."

Galen stood listening outside the room. He knew the likely outcome and wished he didn't. He made his way quietly back to his own room, took the stuffed toy dog down from its shelf, and held it tightly.

Leni, Cathy, what do I tell him?

The November winds whispered outside his window.

The truth.

CHAPTER 8

Suffer the Little Children

PART THREE

The holiday weekend passed. Carmelita, Freddie, and Faisal reluctantly left to return to college, and despite the tragedy in the cottage, life on the mountaintop returned to normal. Then Christmas brought its own frenetic energies into play.

The three friends sat in the living room listening to Edison's favorite opera, Verdi's *La Forza del Destino*.

"We'll be picking up Lem Caddler tomorrow," Galen said. "Nancy, could I impose on you to stay with Miri, while Ben and Edison come with me? I have an idea I'd like to try. Then we'll bring him back here, until his cottage is ready."

Edison glanced at Nancy.

"Can you handle Miri? She's a pretty strong girl for her size."

"I'll do what Ben does. As long as she has her clay and drawing paper, she'll stay settled. By the way, Galen, Ben left something for you while you were out wandering the mountain today."

She handed him a manila envelope from the end table. Galen opened it and unfolded the sheet of drawing paper inside.

"Look at that!" Edison exclaimed. "I didn't know you had a twin brother!"

Galen held the drawing up and stared at it. The image of a large, upright black bear stared back.

His friends checked their laughter, when they saw he wasn't joining in. Nancy changed the subject.

"How's Betty doing? Tonio's been spending every spare moment at the hospital."

Galen stuffed the drawing back in the envelope. He felt relieved at not having to explain anything.

"She's getting out tomorrow, too. The chemotherapy has her in remission at this point. Now it's up to her body and the drugs to see if it will last. I haven't talked with Tonio about her yet, but I know he's been scouring my books and the Internet about ALL. He probably knows more than I do at this point."

Edison hesitated before asking, "What are her chances?"

"Without getting too technical it's going to depend on the genetic type of ALL that she has. The results of the initial tests on her bone-marrow sample were contradictory. The hematologists say they've never seen one like hers. There are different subtypes, and each one has its own prognosis and possible outcomes. We're still waiting."

They sat quietly, immersed in their own thoughts. "The Force of Destiny" played on.

Lem Caddler waited in a wheelchair at the nursing station for his final discharge instructions. For the first time in years he was totally sober, and it felt strange. All his senses seemed sharper. He felt younger. Everything was so alive and vibrant.

His leaving the hospital stirred up other feelings as well. He was disengaging from the twenty-four-hour support womb that the staff and counselors had provided to all the men and women in the alcohol-detoxification unit. Now he experienced the same emotions as the day before his first real battle in the army: anxiety, fear of failure, and the never-ending death of cowardice while fighting the enemy.

One of his counselors put it succinctly. He had pulled out a copy of the old comic strip, "Pogo." The possum-shaped cartoon character stared at the members of his counseling group, and the word balloon above Pogo's head read: "We have met the enemy and he is us."

Three men walked down the hospital corridor from the other end of the floor, and Caddler's sharp, hunter's eyes recognized them. He felt elation, as he saw Galen, Edison, and Ben Castle, their now-familiar faces smiling as they approached.

"Let's go, Lem. Time to leave this vacation paradise," Ben quipped. "I know I didn't want to leave after my stroke, but look at me—I made it."

Galen picked up Lem's few possessions and discharge sheet, double-checked it, and then put his hand on one of the handles of the man's wheelchair.

"You get the deluxe tour of the hospital, straight to the Loading Doc," Ben joked again, as he grabbed the other handle, and they made their way to the exit.

Edison had gone ahead, opened the passenger door on his van, and waited for the other three to arrive in the parking lot.

"Where we headed?" Lem looked uncertainly at the others, as Galen and Ben helped him into the back seat and climbed in after him.

"We're going back to Safehaven, Lem," Ben said, "but Doc Galen and I wanted to introduce you to some friends of ours, before we take you home. We think you might like to meet them."

Galen and Edison caught Ben's use of the word "home" and smiled at each other. Ben directed Edison to a small building at the outskirts of town that was used as a grange hall and an all-purpose, get-together area. The van pulled into the side parking lot of the old, Pennsylvania-bluestone structure, and the four men got out. They walked down the hallway and turned into a large, auditorium-sized room with rows of tables and chairs set up. On each table were pitchers of water and juice, and thermoses of coffee and tea.

Two middle-aged men walked forward from the crowd that was milling around and approached the newcomers. One was a tall African-American, the other a heavyset white man. Lem recognized the first as the owner of the local hardware store. The other was a prominent town attorney.

"Hello, Ben. Brought us another friend, have you?" the attorney smiled.

"Yep, guys, this is Lem. Lem, this here's Phil, and the potbellied bald guy is Steve."

Caddler was confused. Then he saw the sign on the speaker's platform at the head of the room: AA, Alcoholics Anonymous. He turned to Ben, Galen, and Edison. The three men nodded.

Phil put his hand on Lem's shoulder.

"Pretty confusing and scary, isn't it, Lem? Well, we've all been where you're standing. How about staying for the meeting? There's plenty of the right stuff to drink."

Lem looked at his escorts.

Edison didn't hesitate.

"We'll be right here, sitting in the back."

He turned to Phil and Steve.

"Is that all right with you guys? I know we're not guests, but we'd like to learn."

The two men said yes, and then Phil guided Lem to a table near the front. Steve headed to the stage and rang a little bell sitting on the top of the white lectern. People quieted down and took their seats.

"Ladies and gentlemen, we have a guest here today. This is Lem."

In unison the crowd of men and women called out, "Hi, Lem."

Steve looked out over the group and took a deep breath.

"My name is Steve, and I am an alcoholic..."

An hour later Lem stood next to friends, as Phil and Steve approached them again.

"Lem, Steve and I would like to sponsor you and be available should you need help. I think we've loaded you down with enough reading material. We cannot emphasize how much that little book you have in the envelope means to all of us here. Read it, ask questions, then read it again and again.

"Ben, Dr. Galen, Dr. Edison, thanks for bringing Lem here today."

The men shook hands, and the four headed back to the van.

Lem looked in the envelope. The title of the book inside was simple: "The Twelve Steps."

Betty sat silently in the back of the gray-green station wagon. They had told her she was "in remission," that her blood count and the white cells that had gone berserk were back to acceptable levels. But she didn't feel right. She was weak and tired; and she had no interest in anything.

She looked at her reflection in the rearview mirror.

My God, that can't be me! That isn't my face! I'm not old!

She started to cry.

Hisayo Orth sat in the front passenger seat, while Jesse drove. She sensed the waves of despair pouring from her daughter. She leaned over to whisper in her husband's ear. He nodded. A few moments later the big station wagon turned and made its way up the steep, mountainside road.

Betty paid no attention to her surroundings, until she saw that the car had pulled up and stopped in front of the big, wooden sign. When she saw the letters, her face lit up. She opened the car door and, despite her fatigue, almost ran up the steps to the house.

Tonio had been sitting at his desk pretending to study. He was dressed in what he called his "thinking" clothes: old blue jeans, torn tee shirt, and no shoes. He heard a car coming up the lane and looked out his bedroom window. When he saw the station wagon, he dashed shoe-less out of his room to the foyer and opened the door, just as Betty was about to knock. They gazed at each other.

"Hi."

Oh, God, I must look horrible!

"Hi."

You're the most beautiful girl in the world!

"Uh ... can I come in?"

"Uh ... oh, yeah ... sure, come on in. It's cold out there. Uh ... how did you get here?"

"My parents. We were on the way home from the hospital."

"Oh, geez, Betty, I thought it was this evening. I wanted to be there!"

"No sweat."

Nancy, Edison, and Galen were sitting in the living room, the curtains on the big picture window drawn back. When Nancy heard the car she swung into action quickly.

"We have guests, Bob. Come help me get some tea and biscuits. Galen, use your inimitable charm to entertain them until we're ready."

Galen grunted then headed for the foyer. When he saw the two young people standing there, he walked silently past them, opened the door, and called out to the two adults in the car.

"Come on in, it's too cold to sit out there."

Tonio, seeing Hisayo and Jesse walking toward the door, turned to Betty.

"Give me a minute. I need to get decent."

He ran down the hall, slipped on sneakers and a red flannel shirt, and ran back to the foyer, just as her parents entered the house.

"Sorry to drop in unannounced, Dr. Galen, but Hisayo and I ... well ...we had some questions about our daughter, and we wondered if we could impose on you and the Edisons."

Galen nodded and led them into the living room, just as Nancy entered from the kitchen.

"Would anyone like some tea and biscuits?"

Edison wheeled in the loaded serving cart he had recently made, and the aroma of biscuits and fresh-brewed tea permeated the air.

Hisayo was delighted. She accepted the delicate teacup and saucer that Nancy offered her, then she spoke to the group.

"The specialists and staff at the hospital were wonderful to our daughter. They answered our questions as best they could, but for Jesse and me, the answers only raise more questions."

The two anxious parents looked at Galen. He felt the familiar tightening in his chest that occurred whenever he was called upon to make medical predictions.

They didn't teach us to be fortunetellers in school, but God help us when we don't have an answer to everything.

He steeled himself, took a breath, looked at the man and woman seated across from him, and mentally crossed his fingers.

"Let me start by saying that I don't have all the answers. I can only talk about possibilities. I can't tell you if Betty's remission means a cure or how long it will last. I know the folks at the hospital also covered this.

"The problem with ALL—your daughter's type of leukemia—is that there are different forms of it. Each type carries its own potential for treatment outcome. The sample of bone marrow that was taken from Betty showed an unusual variant form of the disease, which can make it tricky to treat."

"Dr. Galen, my husband and I have one special question."

The petite Asian woman opened and closed her hands then clenched them tightly in her lap.

"I met my husband when he was in the military. He had come to Japan on leave from his base in Korea. We dated and married in my hometown, and Betty was born at the local hospital.

"Dr. Galen, my home was only a few kilometers from Nagasaki."

Both parents looked directly at Galen, as Hisayo continued.

"We have read that radiation is linked to Betty's condition. I was born in 1947, two years after the city was destroyed. I have had no problems, but do you think that residual radiation from the bomb could have disturbed something in me that I have passed on to my daughter?"

Galen's heart sank. He was aware of the higher incidence of the blood disease in descendants of radiation-exposed persons. But this? He shook his head.

"The most honest answer I can give you is, I don't know."

The questions continued. Some he could answer, some he could only guess at based on studies of longevity and remission rates in the different types of the disease. He tried his best to tell the worried parents when his answers were more hunch than fact. He felt relieved when the questions ended.

Tonio and Betty had been standing in the hallway holding hands. They exchanged few words, but much passed between them. Then she noticed the silence in the living room.

"I think my parents are finished interrogating your tio, Tonio."

"Sounds like it."

He didn't want to let go.

Jesse stood up.

"We've taken up enough of your time, and I'm sure Betty wants to get home."

He looked at the two young people now standing in the living room doorway.

His daughter spoke quickly.

"Mom, Dad, Tony has offered to help me catch up on my

schoolwork. Can we get together, alternating between our house and his, to do this?"

The Orths looked at their hosts, and both sides agreed. Jesse headed outside to "warm up the car for Betty," while Hisayo stayed with Nancy, Edison, and Galen.

"You have raised the boy well. I see now where he has learned his manners."

She took Tonio's hands in hers.

"Thank you for giving my daughter a reason for living."

Winter was severe that year. The temperature remained constantly below freezing, and the winds rose in gusty protest against the home on the mountain. Nancy worried about the well-being of the wolves, so she and Edison made the trip to town to stock up on supplies for both animals and humans. She also wanted to do some late Christmas shopping.

While they were gone, Galen invited Lem to the house for lunch. Caddler had been staying with Ben and Miri, helping out and watching over things, until ground could be broken for his cabin in the spring.

"Lem, I've got some ideas for spring plantings along the lower side of the mountain. You know this area like the back of your hand. I'd like your advice and your help in laying the site out."

The old farmer read Galen's list: berry patches, fruit trees, cabbage and tall grass, chinquapin nut bushes, and beehives. He looked at his former adversary and newfound friend and grinned.

"Doc, I've hunted all my life. From the looks of that layout, I'd say you spotted bear spawn around here."

"Spawn? Hell, I saw it. I talked to the damned beast. And it answered me!"

Lem laughed out loud and shook his head.

"You sure it was me that got hit in the head the first time we met, Doc?"

The men laughed, chewed on the ham sandwiches Galen had thrown together, and sipped their tea.

"Promise me, Lem, promise me you won't say anything to the others yet. I don't want them to think I'm crazier than they already do."

They laughed again.

Caddler didn't tell Galen about the drawing he had found on the floor recently after cleaning up Miri's room. He hadn't told Ben, either. He thought it was a good likeness of Galen, but he had wondered about the bear standing beside him and the semicircle of gray wolves. Now it was starting to make sense.

It was late afternoon on that day of the winter solstice. After their lunch Galen walked down the mountain through the woods with Lem. They had surveyed the planned garden plot, and then he escorted Lem back to the little cabin he shared with Ben and Miri. They were approaching the fork in the path—one way leading down to the migratory-bird pond, the other to Ben and Miri's home.

"Think it's possible, Lem?"

"Don't see why not, Doc. Soil's good, and there's a natural break in the trees there, so should be plenty o' light. I'll lay out the area, and then in the spring I'll go rent a tiller at..."

Both men stopped. Three canines stood at the junction. They were older now, but Lem recognized two of them, and they knew him.

"Clyde! I'll be damned ... I thought ye was dead by now!"

The oldest dog, now known as Zeus, pricked up its ears. The younger male did likewise. The female sat on her haunches but remained alert should the need arise.

"He was your dog, Lem?"

Galen was fascinated. How would this play out?

"Yep, Doc, both o' them. Ol' Clyde there damned near took ma leg off, 'fore he and that other critter up and left me."

The old farmer thought a moment then looked at Galen.

"Ya know, Doc, can't say as I blame him, seein' as how I didn't treat 'em none too good."

He looked at the two dogs and shook his head.

"Looks like you picked the right place, you two. Whose girlfriend is she?"

"Zeus ... Clyde is her mate."

He looked at the female wolf who returned his gaze impassively.

Then Zeus stepped toward Lem and let out a whine.

Caddler likewise stepped forward and put out his hand. The old dog stretched his snout forward, sniffed, then sat in front of Lem.

He touched the dog's head and whispered, "I'm sorry."

"*Felice Navidad*, folks!"

The front door burst open and Freddie, with Lilly Daumier by his side, entered the foyer of the mountain home. Carmelita had convinced Mike Dimitriades to fly in from California, and she allowed "her big Greek god" to carry in the mounds of packages she had brought. Faisal likewise had invited a guest who would stay with him and Akela at Diana and Lachlan's house.

"Hey, everyone, meet Jacob, Jacob Geltmacher. He's the guy who stuck his face in the video he made of me. He says his folks are traveling in Europe, and I didn't think he wanted to spend Chanukah alone."

Nancy, Edison and Galen recognized Jacob immediately. Lachlan had shared the video with them when it first arrived. Indeed, the young man, despite his Chasidic outfit and scraggly beard, fit right in with the rest of the young adults.

Almost in unison, the three greeted the boy with "Shalom, Jacob."

The young man's eyes lit up, and he turned to Fai.

"You told me they would understand. I didn't believe it!"

Nancy laughed.

"Jacob, before I was married, my last name was Seligman. My husband Bob and I, and Dr. Galen, grew up in Northern New Jersey outside New York City. It's been a long time, though, so you'll have to let me know how you want your food prepared."

Jacob turned again and whispered in Faisal's ear.

"Tia Nancy, Jacob brought his digital video camera with him. Would it be all right if he recorded footage of us and the grounds at Safehaven? I promised him I would write the musical score for it, and you'll all get copies when it's done."

"Certainly, Jacob, just as long as you make us all look like movie stars," Edison quipped. "And Oliver Hardy can play Galen."

All but one of the young people looked at him, until Freddie finally asked, "Who's Oliver Hardy?"

"Tio is showing how old he is, kids," Galen replied.

They had a simple homecoming dinner, but Nancy brought out special plates she had been given long ago by her parents. These she set in front of Jacob and told him of their origin and usage. He smiled in delight.

"May I also call you Tia Nancy?"

"Certainly, Jacob. So, tell me, where are your parents from? Your name is certainly a meaningful and unusual one."

The boy-man's eyes clouded, and he stared off into space.

"Tia, my great-grandparents came from a little town near Gdyni, Poland. They were captured and butchered by the Nazis, but they managed to smuggle their children—my grandparents—out of the country before they were captured. My grandparents were raised by members of the Chasidim in New York who adopted them and other refugee children."

Nancy stared intently at the young man.

"Jacob, was that town by any chance called..." and she mentioned the name of the Baltic coastal village destroyed by Hitler's killing machine.

He looked in amazement and nodded yes.

"Jacob, that's the same town my father's parents came from!"

Afterward, Faisal and Jacob sat in Tonio's room.

"How's Betty doing?" Faisal asked.

"She's still in remission. She's supposed to have a full-body scan to be sure nothing's acting up. It's scheduled for after New Year's. She's a real trooper, letting them poke her for blood all the time. She looks good.

"Fai, I told you what a remarkable girl she is. She's already caught up on the schoolwork she missed!"

Jacob grinned.

"I take it you don't like the girl ... right, Tony?"

The three laughed, but Faisal, who saw more without eyes, heard the worry in his friend's voice. He was sure Tonio had absorbed every bit of data he could about the complications that Betty might incur.

"Jacob, let's be sure we get lover boy and his squeeze in the video."

"Where did you pick up that language, Fai?"

Jacob looked at Faisal.

"You're right, Tony, he's beginning to sound like a New Yorker."

"Listen, Betty's coming over tomorrow. I hope you'll both be nice and polite to her—and no comments about me. Promise?"

"We promise," the other two replied. Tonio didn't see their crossed fingers.

Freddie drove Faisal and Jacob to the Douglass home, and then he and Lilly left again to take a walk in town. He promised to be back but said it would probably be late, "so don't wait up."

Carmelita took a wrapped gift to Tonio's room.

"What is it, Carm?"

"It's for Betty. It's a special assortment of girl stuff—make-up ... you know. You can give it to her tomorrow, when she comes over."

"Aren't you going to be here? You can give it to her. She likes you."

Carmelita barely hid the blush on her face.

"Uh ... Michael and I are ... uh ... going out tomorrow. We'll be back late in the day, but I'll try to be back when she gets here."

She eyed her younger brother.

He'll do better alone.

She would try to keep her promise. She always did.

"Tio Galen, can I borrow the Jeep? Faisal and I want to show Jacob the mountain, so he can take some video. Lachlan is on patrol duty, and Mrs. Douglass is busy making the stuff she's bringing over for Christmas dinner."

Galen reached for his car keys once again and wondered why the boy never asked to borrow Edison's. He would never admit it, but he actually liked being the one Tonio always approached.

He watched once more, as his beloved red Jeep headed down the mountain with someone else at the wheel. He hadn't told Tonio, but he planned to give him the keys permanently to help him get to and from college. Nancy had given her old car to Carmelita, and Edison's "kid-mobile" van had gone to Freddie. Soon it would be his turn to do the giving.

The telephone rang.

"Galen, it's Jay. We've got the final reports back on the Orth girl. The genetic analysis shows she has a mosaic—bad one. I hope she stays in remission, but you know the odds on that. It's going to be a rough one if she gets a flare-up."

"Have you sent her sample in for bone marrow typing, just in case?"

"Yes, but even that is less likely to work in her case. I'll let you know if anything changes."

The blood specialist paused then added, "Oh, by the way, happy holidays."

Both men knew the irony of that remark.

Galen went to his room and stared at the wall, hoping for an inspiration, something to avert the inevitable. The wall remained silent.

"Come on, Tonio, let's show Jacob the wolves. He's already seen Akela, and I've told him about the pack. He can get some great shots."

Faisal was almost dancing with excitement, as he and Geltmacher piled into the Jeep.

"Uh . . . guys, I'd like to pick up Betty, too. She was coming over anyway."

"I smell love in the air," Jacob laughed.

"Nope, it's the mold in Tio Galen's old car."

Now, all three laughed.

Tonio drove to Betty's house, not far from St. Ignatius. He jumped out and warned the guys not to act like idiots, when she came back with him. Then he ran to the Cape-Cod-style, oyster-white home. He had just begun to knock, when the door opened. She was already waiting for him.

"Hi," he sighed.

"Hi!"

"Faisal and Jacob are with me. We thought you'd like to take a walk in the woods."

He bent over and whispered in her ear, "We can always lose them out there."

She giggled and took his hand, as they walked back to the car. She got in the front seat then turned to the two young men and the wolf-dog in the back.

"Tony, I thought there was only one wolf in the car."

The ride back to the mountain house was filled with easy conversation about life at school in New York and career objectives.

Jacob had his video camera and was recording the ride while asking questions and panning among the occupants of the car.

"What do you want to do next year, Betty?"

"Tony and I are going to take pre-med classes at The University of Pennsylvania then medical school. How's that sound to you?"

For his age Geltmacher already had become a skilled interviewer, and by the time they arrived at Safehaven, all four had talked about their plans for the future. As he slowly zoomed in for a close-up of the sign, he asked Tonio where the name came from.

"It's kind of strange, but it started with an injured female wolf, two stray dogs, and Tio Galen beating the crap out of a drunk hunter who trespassed on the land. After he clobbered the guy he went into a tirade against hunters and said that this mountain was a refuge for animals. When Tio Eddie heard him use the words 'safe haven,' he went back to his workshop and made that sign. The name stuck."

"Really?" Jacob asked from behind the camera.

"Yeah, and what's even stranger, the hunter that Tio Galen hit helped save me and Betty from a bunch of escaped murderers, and now he's going to live here in his own cabin. I think my tia and tios are going to make him a caretaker for the wildlife preserve. He has nowhere else to live. His own son burned down his house and tried to kill him."

Tonio hesitated then added, "He had to kill his own son to save us."

The car stayed silent for a period of time, until Tonio finished his thought.

"You're going to meet him and Ben and Miri. Did Faisal tell you about Miri?"

Jacob kept the camera on Tonio while he replied.

"Isn't she the autistic girl, the one that communicates only with wolves? I thought only Faisal was crazy enough for that."

He reached out to poke Faisal, but Akela saw the outstretched arm and snarled.

"You don't want to upset my seeing-eye wolf, Jacob. He just might eat you," Faisal intoned in a deep and serious voice.

"Tell that lupine friend of yours that I am neither Kosher nor Parve when it comes to wolf meals, and from the beard on the beast he's definitely Chasid."

The laughter rocked the Jeep and echoed across the mountain, as the four youngsters and one large canine arrived at the path and exited.

Tonio led the way to the wolf den, holding tightly onto Betty's hand. Faisal and Akela followed and Jacob, bringing up the rear, kept his camera trained on the other three, frequently throwing out questions and quips to elicit responses from his new friends.

They arrived at the clearing, and Akela let out a loud, groaning bark. Slowly the pack emerged, the alpha male and his two cohorts, one medium-sized male, one female, on either side of him. Akela whined and Faisal let the guide harness slip loose. The wolf-dog loped over to his litter mates and ran in circles of happiness around the pack.

"Amazing, I've never heard or seen of anything like this," Jacob whispered.

The wolves turned at his voice, then formed a phalanx and moved toward the city boy.

"Tony, Faisal, what do I do?" he asked nervously.

Betty moved to him and held her hands out to the wolves. The alpha male came forward and sniffed at her and Jacob. This time there was no whimper, no backing away. He sat down on his haunches and raised a paw, as Betty stroked his head. The rest of the pack followed suit while Jacob kept the camera running.

"Here, Jacob, let me hold the camera. You get in the picture with Betty, then you can let me get in."

Tonio reached for the camera.

Jacob hesitated then said, "What the heck! Next I'll be eating pork."

Tonio recorded his three friends, even Jacob, stroking Akela and the other wolves that came within hand reach, then he handed the camera back. He quickly joined Betty, and they knelt down as the wolves sniffed and licked their fingers.

"Let's go over to see Ben and Miri now, guys," he said. "Then we'll head back to the house for dinner."

Faisal dropped back to walk a bit with Jacob, who continued his recording.

"They look like Hansel and Gretel holding hands and walking, don't they?" Jacob said in a low voice. Then he slapped his forehead at his faux pas.

"They're more like Romeo and Juliet," Faisal replied. "I just hope their story has a better ending."

The door of the small house opened slowly, and the tall and hard-looking man standing in the doorway reminded Jacob of the character, Lurch, in the old "Addams Family" TV series.

"Miss Betty, Tonio, come on in. Ben and Miri are in the studio. It's good to see you doing well, young lady."

"Thanks, Lem, and thank you again for what you did for us."

Lem's eyes instantly glistened, as they followed him into the room, where Ben sat reading a newspaper. Miri was moving slowly back and forth on her sleeping mat, the she-wolf sitting close by her side.

Without seeming to see the quartet that had entered the room, the girl rose and went to her sketch table. Her hands began moving over the paper, weaving in the charcoal markings to form images across the blank page. Faster and faster the fingers flew like knitting needles across page after page. Then she stopped and sat down on the rug once more.

Ben got up to pick up the papers now lying on the floor, but Lem beat him to it. He quickly put them in an empty folder then showed the young people to some chairs. Tonio made the introductions.

"Ben, Lem, you know Faisal and Akela. This is a new friend, a classmate of Fai's from New York, Jacob Geltmacher. Jacob, this is Ben Castle, his daughter Miriam, and Lem Caddler."

Jacob had kept the camera running, but then he handed it to Tonio, while he shook hands with the two older men.

"What's with the camera, Jake?" Ben gave one of his lopsided welcome grins, as he pointed at the small gadget.

"He wants to be a filmmaker when he gets out of school and becomes human," Faisal joked.

Ben laughed, and even Lem cracked what was, for him, a smile.

"We just wanted to be sure that all of you will be at the house for Christmas dinner."

Tonio looked expectantly at the men, and they both nodded.

"Good! I'll tell Tia Nancy. This will be great. Everyone's here, and Betty and her folks will be with us as well. So we'll see you soon. We need to head up to the house. Tia has dinner just about ready."

Lem showed the four young people to the door. Then, when Ben went back to his newspaper, he took the folio holder to his room and laid out the drawings on his bed.

One showed Faisal in formal wear, sitting at a grand piano. Another showed Jacob dressed in casual clothes and standing on a stage. The third showed an older Tonio dressed in white coat. The fourth—and here his heart sank—the fourth showed a misty figure and nothing more.

Christmas arrived as a clarion-lit day of moderate temperature. Refreshing wisps of cool air moved the upper branches of the bare trees. The faint-but-unmistakable scent of multiple holiday dinners being prepared rose from the valley and wafted across the mountaintop, as the sun warmed the ground frozen since before the winter solstice.

Lem had set up a large Christmas tree. It sparkled with twinkle lights, candy canes, and many handmade ornaments, including some of Ben's, which his father and mother had made when he was a child. He even added some little clay figures Miri had fashioned. At the top was Edison's pride and joy: a high-intensity, light-emitting-diode array in the shape of a star, its multicolored, tiny bead lights casting pastel shades of lavender, red, green, blue, and white on the boxes piled beneath.

The guests began to arrive around eleven that morning, and soon the house became a cacophony of young, middle-aged and geriatric voices, each of the latter trying to outdo the others with reminiscences of past Yuletides.

Carmelita, Freddie, and Tonio circulated and refilled glasses of Nancy's special fruit punch, cautioning everyone not to eat too many appetizers before the festival dinner.

Eventually the three youngsters gravitated toward their friends. Carmelita and Mike sat near the tree, gazing more into each other's eyes than the sparkling lights. Freddie and Lilly sat next to them.

Lilly bent forward as if to nibble on her fiancé's ear. What she really did was whisper, "Do you think your brother is up to all this?"

Freddie nodded and sub-vocalized yes, but added, "God help him if she doesn't show up tonight."

Tonio sat with Jacob, who recorded some of the party with his video camera. But he quickly left his friend when the door opened, and Betty and her parents arrived.

Galen brought out a four-and-a-half-by-two-foot-wide box. He smiled at the group and yelled above the crowd noise.

"I'd like to jump ahead just a bit and have one gift opened now. Faisal, would you do the honors?"

Galen carried the package over to him, and Faisal felt it and began to tear at the wrappings, as he realized what it was. Then everyone saw it: a professional-quality, digital-electric piano, complete with stand. He couldn't cry. He just hugged the bear-sized man and said "thank you, Tio Galen," over and over.

Soon the house was filled with Christmas and Chanukah music, as the young man's fingers raced over the keys.

Nancy stuck her head out of the dining room doorway.

"Anyone need to wash their hands? No? Then dinner is served!"

Edison guided the guests to their seats one by one. Seventeen chairs now filled the long, home-crafted table, eight per side with Edison at the head.

"In the spirit of ecumenism, let me make one little prayer," he said quietly, and the room became hushed.

He looked at Nancy, in his eyes still the lovely girl he had married. His gaze moved down the table to Galen, first a savior, now a close friend and colleague, and then to the children, once the wretched castaways on the island, now grown and soon to seek their own lives. Those lives revolved around Mike, Lilly, and, he hoped, Betty.

He looked at Ben and Miriam and Lachlan and Diana.

Strange, how circumstances bring people together.

He looked at Lem Caddler, once unwanted, now invaluable.

His heart twinged, when he looked at Hisayo and Jesse. He prayed that they would not experience what he and Nancy had suffered long ago.

Edison raised his voice in jubilation.

"God bless us, everyone!"

Belts now loosened and small cups of Jasmine tea taken to cleanse the palate, the hosts retired to the living room and called the youngsters.

"Jacob," Nancy said, "As our newest guest, I'd like to give you something. It belonged to my father. He had always hoped to pass it on to a son, but I can't think of anyone better to fulfill his wish."

She handed him two boxes. He opened the smaller one first and pulled out a beautiful, hand-made set of dreidels passed down from father to son for generations. Jacob looked wide-eyed at Nancy, as he opened the second, larger box and found the set of generational phylacteries worn by Nancy's father at temple. He was speechless.

Carmelita came next. Edison and Nancy handed her a small box. She opened it to find two pieces of antique jewelry, a filigree pendant and a simple, gold ring.

"These belonged to our mothers," Nancy said quietly.

Galen handed her another small box. Inside was a small silver cross.

"This belonged to my grandmother. It was the only thing she could give my father when he left the old country to come to America. It is the only thing I have to pass on from my family."

She hugged the old man, her eyes wet with tears.

"Freddie, getting you something posed a problem for the three of us," Edison said. "So we thought maybe you and Lilly could put these to good use."

He handed each of them a package.

"Wow, wireless notebook computers! Thanks so much, Tio, Tia!"

While the quartet exchanged hugs, Tonio handed two boxes to Betty, one large and one small.

"The big one's from Carmelita and Freddie."

She opened it, and her eyes lit up at all the cosmetics. She shot them a big grin. The small one contained a gold, heart-shaped pendant on a chain. Before she could react Tonio reached over and draped it around her neck.

And the all-seeing camera continued to record.

It was New Year's Eve. The bustle of Christmas had subsided, the guests were long gone, the gifts carefully put away, and the debris of the holiday gift exchange neatly packed up and consigned to the recycling bins.

The youngsters, being youngsters, were out with their friends, and the three old timers sat quietly in the living room while Bach's "Violin Concerto in E" played in the background. Light snow dappled the ground outside

"We made it to another one, guys," Edison said between sips of his favorite tea. "I wonder what's in store for us."

Nancy squeezed his hand.

"As long as we're here, that's all that matters."

Galen stared at the fireplace, its hypnotic shades of yellow flame mesmerizing and enticing. All he could do was nod in agreement.

The grandfather clock in the corner started to chime the midnight hour.

Edison kissed Nancy. Nancy hugged Galen, and Galen shook hands with Edison.

"Happy New Year," all said before quietly going to bed.

Winter passed quickly that year. The winds and snows that had persisted into early March soon gave way to days of increasing warmth and gentler breezes. Even the best of students felt the soporific influences of impending spring.

"Did that last equation make any sense to you?"

The advanced calculus class had just finished, and Tonio stretched lazily, as he stood up from his desk. He turned to see what Betty thought. She was sitting there, staring straight ahead, not moving.

Suddenly her arms and legs began to contract and shake, and her head arched backwards. Her eyes rolled upward, and her breath came out in clipped grunts.

Tonio yelled to the teacher, who was just leaving.

"Call the rescue squad. Betty's having a seizure!"

He stood by, as the team started two IVs, one in each arm. He heard the emergency-room doctor instructing the paramedics to administer diazepam. He tried to tell them that she needed Decadron, that the seizure was probably due to the cancer spreading to her brain, but they didn't listen.

He called home and told Galen what had happened. The old doctor directed him to go to the hospital and said he would meet him there.

Galen called the ER and informed the attending about Betty. She was being wheeled in, still convulsing.

The ER doc knew Galen, and he knew the old man could still match any of the younger staff in knowledge and skill. He reached into the crash cart, pulled out the ampoule of Decadron—four milligrams per milliliter—and administered a dose through the IV portal. The girl's body movements quieted down.

"Jay, what's the story?"

Galen stood in the hall outside ICU 3 talking to the cancer specialist.

"It's amazing how fast it spread," the doctor replied. "Her scans and counts were normal just two weeks ago. Now, her MRI looks like the process is disseminated through the entire brain and parts of the upper spinal cord."

"Have you talked with her parents yet?"

"Yes. I don't want to dash their hopes, but I can't lie either. In my experience, this pattern is the worst possible one to see."

"Any use trying a stem-cell transplant?"

"Flip a coin, Galen. We'll either kill her or just buy her a short amount of time. To make matters worse, there are no good donor matches."

"What about intrathecal chemo?"

"Only if the Decadron brings the swelling way down. You know how toxic intrathecal can be."

"So we're talking palliative care."

Jay nodded quietly.

Tonio stood in the corridor waiting for his tio to return from the ICU.

Galen walked out and immediately saw the anguish in his face. He remembered having that same feeling long ago, powerless in the face of nature's whims. But years of experience and countless moments like these had fortified him—he knew no other way.

"Tonio, I know you've read everything you can about Betty's condition. And you were absolutely right about the Decadron. But there's a..."

He was about to say "problem," but seeing the boy's eyes filling with tears stopped the word from coming out. He wrapped his arms around his ward and held him, while he tried to continue, as his own eyes began to water.

"The disease has spread throughout her brain and..."

The boy wailed, "Can't she get a bone marrow transplant?"

"No, son, there are no matches. And even if there were, there's no guarantee it would help because of the severity of the condition."

"Won't the Decadron control the swelling?"

"Only for a limited time."

They stood there in silence.

He was at her bedside. He held her left hand, swollen from the repeated changes in IV needles. Her face was puffy from the effects of the Decadron and fluid input. Her eyes would flutter briefly then stop.

Jesse and Hisayo Orth sat on the other side of their daughter's bed. Both prayed for a miracle. The girl's breathing became more prolonged—quick catches in between episodes of stopping and starting again. Suddenly her eyes opened wide and her upper body moved forward. Then her eyes half-closed and she fell backwards. Her breathing had stopped and the heart monitor went off in the central station of the ICU.

Tonio threw himself across the bed, a loud, shrill "NO!" emanating from his open mouth.

Hisayo and Jesse wept as they gently pulled him away.

It was Easter Sunday. A golden-red sunrise streaked the cloudy sky with tendrils of yellows and light pinks. The air was still as the early plants began their push through the earth in their tropic search for light.

Tonio stood in the Garden of Remembrance, staring ahead, saying nothing. He had gone there every day, but he hadn't cried since that last day. He just stared ahead. He heard footsteps but didn't turn. He heard voices but didn't answer.

"Tonio, I have something. Mr. and Mrs. Orth left this for you."

Galen handed him the little silver song box.

"Jesse said it stopped working after falling off the dresser several weeks before..."

Tonio's eyes were dull, as he held out his hand and took the box. He stared at it, but the emptiness did not go away. He couldn't cry. He turned around to Galen and saw Lem, Ben, and Edison standing there. His voice was flat and barely audible above the faint whispers of mountain breeze.

"Where is she, Tio? What happens after death?"

The four men looked at him, their own hearts and minds seeking the same answer to the same question.

In his hands, the little box began to play.

The young man fell to his knees, and the tears finally came.

CHAPTER 9

Fledgling

She weighed more than he did. That was okay. There was just something about his physique, something about the way he handled himself that really turned her on. Besides, she could tell he was horny.

That was okay, too—so was she.

She got her first glimpse of him high up on the mountain. He seemed a bit disinterested, but she knew how to handle that. She took off, and he soon followed—as she knew he would. The old saying is true: A boy chases a girl, until she catches him.

She stopped, perched comfortably, and called to him, the high, triple-toned question in her voice sending out her best come hither.

"Chk-cher-hoot?"

There! That grabbed his attention. He cocked his ears to pick up the full implication of her siren call.

Yessir, this was one hot chick! But, like all guys, he wasn't sure if commitment was his thing. He preferred laying back a bit—sending her a rather indifferent reply.

"Ch-hoot, hoot, hoot."

Indifferent or not, his deep, triple warble stirred her. She had to respond.

"Chk, ch-hoot?"

He cocked his head—her trap had been set.

He lit out in a masculine display, his almost-five-foot wing spread carrying him high on the mountain air currents. She tried to be coy at first then followed, easily keeping pace all the way back to his lair. No etchings or prints to pretend to study, but she wouldn't have been interested anyway. The prenuptials were over.

"Galen, is that what I think it is?"

"Sure looks like it, Nancy."

"What are you two talking about? I don't see anything."

"Look over there, Edison, up in the pine tree. See it now?"

"Yeah, it just looks like a plain old..."

"No, Bob, it's not a plain old owl. Look at it, isn't it magnificent?"

"Little brother, you are looking at as fine a specimen of *Bubo virginiensis* as I have ever seen."

"Whobo bubo?"

"Don't do a Freddie, Bob. It's a Great Horned Owl, and I'll bet there's a nest up there. You normally don't see them during the daytime."

The three were walking along the mountain trails, a daily ritual now that they were empty-nesters. They had bid their last, off-to-college farewell, as Tonio had headed to the University of Pennsylvania. For the first time in fifteen years, only three lived in the mountaintop home.

The weather was what the locals called "between"—spells of cold and wind, with sudden and unexpected breaks of warmth—which populated the days between New Year's and Valentine's Day. The pattern was just enough to lure the unwary into excessive outdoor activities, which brought about the next day's muscle aches and sneezes. This meteorological restlessness visited before the late-February, heavy snows that would shut down the outside world until spring.

"It's nice out. Why don't we go for a walk?" Nancy's sense of loss over the departure of that last child was greater than she cared to admit.

"Sure it's not too cold?" Galen had grumbled. He despised winter weather.

"Come on, some outdoor walking will do that bear body of yours some good." Edison always sided with Nancy.

His friends had ignored Galen's low rumble about sensible bears hibernating in this weather, and they pushed him out the door.

Spotting the owl family in the pine tree sparked renewed vitality in the three friends.

"Owls usually lay a clutch of no more than three eggs," Galen commented. "Even stranger, they don't lay the eggs at one time, so the owlets are of different ages. I wonder if they've hatched yet. I don't know of any other raptors that produce young in winter."

"I'll put some remote audio-video sensors around here," Edison said. "Maybe we'll be able to observe them when they become active at night."

He was already planning where to disperse his array around the tree site, and Nancy thought about the food needs of her new birds.

"Look at that! There are three of them!"

Edison had turned the video monitors on, and the night-vision cameras clearly showed three, puffball-sized owlets, one larger than the others, wriggling and squirming, as the adults carefully placed shredded pieces of prey in their short, flat beaks.

"They look like Tribbles," Nancy laughed.

"Watch what they do next," Galen added. "There, see that? They're branching."

The biggest one had climbed out of the nest and, like a child with hyperactivity syndrome, was hopping back and forth from one branch to the next. Then, as the three humans watched, a sudden wind gust knocked the owlet off its perch, and it fell into the snow-covered ground below.

Nancy got up instantly, grabbed her coat and boots, and ran to the door.

"Wait, Nancy, don't go out there," Edison yelled, as he ran for his own coat. Galen followed more slowly, muttering to himself and shaking his head in disbelief.

She moved as fast as she could down the snow-covered pathway leading to the big pine tree. She turned on her pocket LED flashlight and cast its faint white beam around the base of the tree, until she saw the small depression in the snow and the silver-gray, down-covered baby bird sitting there not moving. A feather.

Even at its very young age, the bird instinctively knew that movement would attract danger.

"Come on, little one. Let's put you back up there on a branch. I think you'll be able to make your way back up from there."

She scooped up the owlet in her gloved hands and proceeded to place it on as high a branch as she could. Suddenly the air around her became a moving draft across her face. At the same time she felt herself being pushed forward and down into the snow.

"Cover your face!"

She heard the loud screech above her and Edison's yell of "ow," as the mother's taloned claws raked his back. He didn't move. He held his protective cover, shielding his wife's body with his own.

Galen picked up a small tree branch and swung it at the owl. It worked; the mother bird flew back up to her nest and waited, as Edison got up from covering Nancy and helped her to her feet.

"Come on, old girl. Let's get back to the house. What a crazy stunt to pull!"

"Are you hurt, Bob?"

"No, are you?"

"No. I was just trying to put the baby bird back in the tree."

Galen had been patiently quiet long enough.

"Nancy, owls are raptors—predators. That mama bird would have ripped your face off for trying to help her baby. Besides, she would have cared for it on the ground until it was old enough to fly."

Nancy stomped back up to the house without speaking. The two men watched her exit. They looked at each other, shrugged, and followed slowly.

The next day brought more silence. Nancy went about her usual activities, but she remained aloof.

The men sat in the living room, fireplace going full blast.

"I don't know what to do. I've never seen her like this."

"Maybe we were too quick to criticize her yesterday. The more I think about it, the more I understand what she did. She was trying to spare that mother owl the same loss that she experienced."

"The only problem is the bird didn't know it. That mother owl could and would have done serious damage to her."

Silence once more.

Nancy opened the door softly and walked quickly down the path to the pine tree. She saw the snow angel where Bob had pushed her down, and she stared up at the green-needled tree. It was after dawn now, so the owls would be sleeping.

A faint rustling from above caused the snow-covered branches to dust her clothes with a powdery coat, as the baby owlet branched back and forth—in daylight!

She stared up at the downy ball, its small facial disc portending the large creature it one day would become. Its eyes focused on her, taking in her full three-dimensional structure. As she began to speak, its large tympanic membranes picked up every nuance of her voice.

"Tell your mama I was just trying to help you, little one."

"Chk?"

"Yes, you do understand, don't you?"

"Chk."

She felt her eyes watering and dabbed at them before turning and walking back up the trail.

Spring returned to the mountain, and early white Trifolium blooms soon gave way to Jack-in-the Pulpits. Wild raspberry canes began to shoot up and green out. The children had come and gone during Easter holiday, and a certain wistfulness overshadowed the emotional spirit of the friends.

The three elders thought that their adoptees actually preferred leaving to coming home, with maybe Antonio the exception. This was his first year, after all, and the memory of his loss had not yet faded. But soon that too would change, and "home" would become what it had for his brother and sister: an off-campus room serving meals and providing access to friends.

Ben and Miriam and Lem were living nearby, of course, and Lachlan and Diana visited often and shared their news of Faisal. Nancy wondered how Jacob was doing, but according to Diana, not even Fai knew for sure. Jacob seemed to have disappeared this past semester.

"Galen, do you still have any contacts … I mean … anyone who could help find someone?"

She asked in an offhanded manner, trying not to let him or Edison know how concerned she had become.

"Who are we trying to find, dear?" Edison asked cautiously, not wanting to upset her.

Ever since the owl episode, she seemed prickly and more introspective. Time and again she would take off on solitary walks.

"Depends on who it is, Nancy. Anyone we know?"

Galen also watched and waited, as she paused before replying.

"Remember young Jacob, Jacob Geltmacher, the boy who came home with Faisal from Juilliard? Diana says he seems to have disappeared. He didn't show up for classes after spring break. He didn't tell anyone he was leaving, either."

"Maybe he was having academic problems," Edison interjected.

"No, Faisal said he'd always aced his classes, and his creative film projects were prize winners. Something else must have happened. I wish we could contact his family."

"What does the school say?"

Galen's interest was piqued, but he wanted to cover all the public aspects first.

"They can't or won't say anything. Faisal went to the registrar's office and was told in no uncertain terms that the privacy laws forbade them from giving out personal information."

"Can we contact Faisal? I'd like to get as much as I can from him before calling in the proverbial marines."

Nancy seemed buoyed by the interest that the two men were showing.

"I'll call Diana right now and get Faisal's cell number!"

After the call, she surprised them with some of her butterscotch-chip cookies. She didn't say so, but they understood: it was a peace offering.

The phone rang that evening.

"Tia Nancy, what's up?"

"Fai, why didn't you tell us about Jacob? I thought he was your friend."

"Wow, Tia, you sure don't believe in introductory pleasantries."

Listening on speakerphone, the men suppressed laughs. The former little blind Iraqi boy had turned into an American teenager, complete with city manners.

Edison held up his fingers and started to count silently for Galen, as they waited for the explosion.

"Faisal Fedr-Douglass, you watch your manners! Do you understand?"

"Yes, Tia Nancy," he replied sheepishly.

"Now, let's start over again. What happened to Jacob?"

"Tia, you know how Jacob dressed and behaved when he visited Safehaven? Well, this gets complicated. Jacob's grandparents were rescued from the Nazis and raised by Chasidic families here in the United States. His grandparents, out of love and respect for their adoptive parents, took on their dress, beliefs, and mannerisms. They followed all the Chasidic rules and rituals—*shabbos, kasruth, niddah,* and *mikva.* But even though they were fully adopted, they were looked on as *bal shuva,* not part of what Jacob called the FFB—*Frum* from Birth. Apparently you actually have to be born into a family to be one, at least that's what Jacob would say, whenever he started beefing about his family."

"Fai, that's not true. A person's faith has nothing to do with his genetic ancestors. Who told Jacob that hogwash?" Nancy fumed.

Edison looked questioningly at Galen.

"Frum?"

"Think of 'The Chosen,'" Galen whispered, and the old engineer nodded.

Faisal was getting worked up, too.

"Jacob found out about his status just before starting Juilliard. His parents, according to the beliefs they follow, disapprove of his career path. They told him he was a disgrace and ordered him to drop out and join the family business. I think they deal in diamonds and gold. Naturally Jacob refused. He told me the last thing he wanted to do was squint at precious stones and metals through magnifying glasses for the rest of his life. But his parents made good on their threat. They've disowned him and cut off all financial support."

Galen interrupted. "Did Jacob say whether it was both parents, or just his father that started this head-butting contest?"

"I don't know, Tio Galen. All I know is he was able to finish his first year because of some small scholarships he had won in high school, but the money ran out. He applied for financial aid, but that's still pending, so he dropped out of school this semester."

"Did he go back home?"

Almost sixty years later Galen's mind echoed his father's parting words: *"Non ho figlio!"* I have no son.

"No, Tio Galen, they wouldn't take him back. He showed up at my apartment a few days ago. He's staying with me now. He does odd jobs to help out with expenses, but he's miserable."

"Faisal, we're going to wire some money to you for Jacob," Edison interjected. He looked at his wife and friend, who nodded in agreement.

"I want you to tell Jacob to come to Safehaven. Can you do that?"

The boy was ecstatic. He gave Nancy his bank number and address almost faster than she could copy it down.

"I'll tell Jacob as soon as he gets back. I think he's working as a janitor at a nearby soup kitchen. It'll probably be real late. Do you want him to call you?"

Nancy nearly shouted "of course!" but regained her composure and quietly said yes.

"Thanks everybody. Say goodbye, Akela."

The seeing-eye, wolf-dog barked twice, and the call ended.

The three sat in the living room, each staring at the evening darkness outside the wall-sized picture window, each wondering about the happy-go-lucky young man they knew as Jacob Geltmacher.

It was close to one o'clock in the morning, when the phone rang. They were still awake, dressed in pajamas and bathrobes, enjoying the last embers of the dying fire.

"Kinda like us," Edison mused.

"What's that, little brother?"

Galen had lapsed into bygone memories of his childhood and those final, fateful days with his family.

"What he means, Galen," Nancy interjected, "is that we are like those embers. I, for one, would want to go out in a blaze of glory, doing some good in my final days. I don't want to be a never-ending ember, providing nothing in the way of light or heat."

Galen, continuing to stare at the now-dark hearth, said something that surprised even him.

"Do not go gentle into that good night; rage against the dying of the light."

Edison had joined in on the last line with his friend then added, "Dylan Thomas said it all, didn't he?"

Nancy had begun to cry silently, the universal sign of exasperated womanhood.

The men stared at her. Something was gnawing at her, something not even her husband could understand. It had started the day she rescued the owlet, but maybe, like those embers, it had been smoldering a long, long time..

Edison finally bit the bullet. He would say the right thing, or he would trigger off a new cascade of anger. Either way, he couldn't let things stand as they were.

"What's wrong, honey? I've never seen you this way before. Is it anything either of us..." and he looked at Galen for affirmation," is there anything either of us has said or done, or even not done?"

She stared at them, two men older than she was yet still clueless about some things. But she was no youngster, either. And at that moment she didn't know whether she wanted to keep crying or snap at them.

My God, I'm too old for menopause, so why the hell am I acting this way?

She took a deep breath.

"When I was young I said I never wanted to get old. Now I've gotten old. I couldn't stop it. We all had a kind of reprieve for fifteen years when the kids came into our lives, but they're mostly away now, and their adult lives are just beginning. What happens to us?"

"We still have purpose," Galen interjected. "There's always something new happening. Case in point is your owl family. The introduction may have been a bit shaky, but I suspect that little bird knows you're a friend, don't you?"

He stared at her and she knew that he knew.

"I…"

The ringing phone snapped them out of their introspection.

"Tio Eddie, it's me … Jacob."

Edison switched on the speakerphone, and the three heard a flat voice, so different from the ebullient young man they had met a year ago.

"Jacob, we're going to help you," Nancy cut in. "We're wiring money to Faisal's account. You're going to use it to buy a train ticket to Philadelphia. We'll pick you up there."

"Are you sure you want to do this?"

He wasn't used to receiving anything without hidden strings, so he couldn't help feeling uncertain about why these people—friendly but hardly family—were getting involved.

Edison had the final word.

"Jacob, this is not the time to look a gift horse in the mouth. We know things have been rough for you, but now you need to get off your ass, leave the self-pity behind, and develop a plan of action. Listen, young man, the three of us have been where you are. Now we have our own demons.

"I'll wire the funds first thing in the morning. You should be able to access them by noon. You can catch a train from the city to Philly. Let us know what the schedule is. Got that?"

Jacob's voice was a mixture of hope and confusion, as he answered yes.

Edison punched off the speaker button and looked at Nancy and Galen.

"Maybe this is our way of exorcizing our demons."

Nancy looked back at her husband. He really did understand— Galen, too.

They turned out the lights and retired. Tomorrow would be very busy.

As he turned off the bedside table lamp, Edison turned to Nancy.

"Dear, what the hell are *shabbos, kasruth, niddah* and *mikva?*"

She grinned. "I'll tell you in the morning … but only if you're a good boy. Now, go to sleep."

The excitement of anticipation, of being needed, of being alive, brought restful sleep to the three.

They drove to Philadelphia to meet Jacob's train. It was scheduled to arrive at the 30th Street Station at 4:45 p.m. The city's afternoon rush-hour traffic delayed their arrival until 5:20, so Edison began circling the old station on the west bank of the Schuylkill River, while Nancy and Galen kept watching the departing crowds. As they made a third circuit of the 1930s-style, Greco-Roman building, she called out, "There he is!"

A clean-shaven, short-haired young man dressed in blue jeans and spring-green, flannel shirt stood near the taxi bays tightly holding two suitcases. One was standard traveler's fabric. The other appeared to be wood, heavily grained and well polished. Jacob's eyes lit up, as he saw the three in the Subaru four-wheel-drive wagon that had replaced Edison's minivan.

Galen quickly opened the rear door, and Jacob almost jumped into the vehicle, as Edison sped off, before the local police could ticket him for illegal standing.

"We didn't recognize you, boy," Nancy said.

Actually, she was startled by what she saw: fading bruises and facial puffiness that capped more extensive bruising on his arms.

"What happened, Jacob?"

"It's what I am, what I'm going to be, Tia Nancy."

"Tell us what happened. Were you in a fight?"

Galen spotted the telltale marks of fist-bruised skin.

"I ran into some skinheads. They didn't like my long hair and beard. I decided not to fight. You ought to see what their boots did to my back."

"Have you noticed any blood in..." Galen started to ask.

Jacob cut him short.

"The emergency room didn't find any kidney damage, Tio Galen."

Edison put a classical recording in the CD player, and they drove home to the music of Mozart's *Nozzi del Figaro*.

The four grew livelier, as they approached the turnoff to the mountain home. Jacob kept moving his head, looking out both sides of the car, his mind reliving those last, fun-filled days with his friends and the old people he now chose to call Tio and Tia.

A spring storm had darkened the skies by the time the car crunched the gravel in front of the house. Light spatters of rain dotted the windshield, as Jacob climbed out, grabbed his two suitcases, and walked toward the familiar, handmade wooden sign. He ran his fingers over the letters, tracing out each of the nine that made up the word SAFEHAVEN.

He remembered how lovingly Faisal would do the same thing each time he visited here. The wetness on Jacob's cheeks was not from the rain.

"Come on in, boy, don't let yourself get too wet," Galen said.

"We've fixed up Tonio's room. It's yours for the duration," Edison added.

"Everyone go wash up. I'll start dinner."

Nancy seemed more buoyant and interested in life than she had been for days.

Jacob shyly spoke up.

"Tia Nancy, you don't need to use the special kosher dishes for me. I'm normal now."

She shot him a look but said nothing.

The old men loosened their belts and stretched in satisfaction at the conclusion of the meal. Jacob ate well, too, but he seemed listless, almost apathetic. Galen knew that feeling. So did Nancy and Edison. How do you play the game of life when it deals you Jokers?

"Jacob, tell us what you've been doing. We know you haven't been in school. Do you still have the DVDs you made of us the last time you were here?"

Nancy watched him, trying to be both observant yet unobtrusive.

"I ... I had to sell most of what I had, but I kept my recordings, and your gifts, Tia, before the fit hit the shan..." and here he paused to make sure no one took offense, "I had a special wood case made up for your father's phylacteries—and the dredels. There are some things I'll never part with."

He lowered his watering eyes and barely avoided crying.

"Tomorrow we'll go into town and get you some clothes and, if the price is right, some new tools of the trade."

Edison smiled at his own perceived bon mot. The old electronics expert felt rejuvenated by what the friends had begun calling their "Project Jacob."

Galen piped up.

"What the geezer means is, if you're meant to be a cinematographer, you need to have a camera. Drawing on your arm won't work."

He watched the young man and wasn't surprised, when Jacob lowered his head to conceal his face.

"Come on, now, I think you need to rest. The four of us will make our battle plans later."

The friends sat in the living room, the radio set on low as Borodin's "Polovtsian Dances" played in the background. Galen broke the silence.

"What complicates this whole thing is the religious aspect. It was bad enough when I had to deal with the difference between old- and new-world cultures with my parents—but religion? How many people have died in the name of religious beliefs? Once that enters the picture, there's no reasoning."

"It may be the only weapon we have," Nancy interjected. "I still can't believe his parents—most likely his father—told him he didn't belong. I don't doubt the man's sincerity, but nowhere in the Jewish faith does it promote what he's saying or doing to his son. It's just plain pigheaded!"

Simultaneously Edison and Galen burst out laughing at the incongruity of her last remark.

"Cut it out, you two!"

But even she couldn't stop joining in, and the men felt glad to see the old Nancy once more.

"We need to question Jacob about everything that led up to this. I think we may have to visit his parents, so we'd better be well prepared."

Edison said nothing, but he couldn't help what crossed his mind.

She's going to try to set another baby bird back on its perch, and this bird's parents are even more dangerous.

Jacob lay in troubled sleep, twisting and turning, until finally he fell out of bed. The impact on his bruised skin made him yell out in pain. He picked himself off the floor and pulled his shirt over his head. He answered the knock on the door and saw the two old men standing in the doorway.

"Are you okay, boy?"

Edison flinched at the massive purple bruises, outlines of work-boot soles on Jacob's back, a giant monochrome tattoo of violence.

"I'll be right back," Galen said.

Edison sat on the edge of the bed and looked at the victim of bigotry.

"Where's he going, Tio Edison?"

"Probably went to get his magic little black bag. No doubt the old quack will bring back some concoction made of gopher guts and claim that it has healing powers—though I have to admit that what he prescribes usually works."

They both laughed quietly, just as Galen returned with his cherished, worn, black-leather bag.

"I'm sure Edison has told you that my medical skills stop at leeches and blood letting, right? Well, see how this feels."

He pulled out an unlabeled jar, opened it, scooped a gob of off-white cream into his hand, and slopped it on Jacob's back.

"Yeow!"

The young man shivered, as the icy cream hit his skin. Almost immediately, though, the pain disappeared. He grinned at Galen.

"What is that stuff? How come they didn't give that to me at the hospital?"

"Didn't Edison tell you? From the look on your face he probably said it was skunk extract or something just as delectable. Just for that…" and the old doctor turned to Edison, "I'm not going to tell you the secret of this rare and soothing balm devised by the ancients and passed down to their successors."

"Just like I said, kid, he's peddling snake oil again."

Edison got up, opened the dresser drawer, and took out one of Tonio's tee-shirts.

"Here, put this on. It'll keep the quack's goop from getting on Nancy's clean bed sheets.

"You feel well enough to come to the living room and let us give you the third degree about what happened?"

Jacob sighed—he did feel better.

"Yes, sir."

"Then get cleaned up. We'll meet you there."

The three oldsters sat in a semicircle with Jacob in the center. Nancy fixed her attention on his face—she had to know for sure what the real story was.

"Take it from the top, Jacob. I'm sure your parents loved you, didn't beat you or starve you. I'm sure they were proud of your scholastic success. Tell us about them."

"Tia, my father's great-grandparents, Herschel and Deborah, were diamond and gold merchants, as their ancestors had been for centuries. When they adopted the baby boy who would become my grandfather, they named him Abraham and gave him the family name of Geltmacher. Someday I would like to go back and research who my true ancestors were. I'd also like to find out more about the Geltmacher line.

"Anyway, Abraham was raised Chasidim. When he came of age, the elders introduced him to Sarah Glikberg, another adoptee from the war, also Chasidim. Abraham and Sarah had my father, Isaac. He was introduced to my mother, Rebekah Farber, granddaughter of another adoptee. That's how I got here."

He stopped, gazed into some unfathomable distance, and continued.

"All along the way the Chasidim community seemed to steer the adoptees and their children toward other adoptees."

Galen noted the increasing discomfort in Jacob's facial expression and body language. He tried to diffuse the young man's tension with what he thought would be a humorous comment.

"Well, Jacob, if you follow your lineage, you'll have your choice of two potential mates."

"Funny you should say that, Tio. I've already been introduced to two sisters, one named Leah, the other Rachel. And, yes, they come from an adoptee family."

"It sounds like you've grown up in a very supportive, loving community, Jacob."

Edison knew what the answer would be, but he had to see if that was part of the young man's perception of himself.

"On the surface it would seem that way, wouldn't it? So why do they herd us all toward each other—all the adoptee descendants—like sheep on a breeding farm?"

"Maybe there's wisdom in that, Jacob."

Nancy could see an alternative plan here.

"Think about it: Your ancestors—and the others—probably came from the same village in the old country. Marriage and mating were kept within the confines of that social structure. It's possible the old ones, those who opened their hearts and homes to the victims of the Nazi monsters, wanted to preserve that pattern. But that's only a guess on my part."

"You don't suppose it was a deliberate attempt to segregate us—that we were looked upon as outsiders, unfit to marry within the community, Tia?"

"No, Jacob," Galen added, "everything you've told us says otherwise. Your genetic family was Jewish; your adoptive family was also Jewish. I know there are differences in some of the external practices, but you come from a great heritage, and those who took in your grandparents continued that tradition."

"Then why did my papa do what he did? I told him and Mama that I loved art—that I loved to capture life as it is and preserve it. That's what cinematographers do. Someday, I told them, I would trace our family and bring its history to life. But Papa became angry and said I would bring shame on our family by having anything to do with that *yetzer hara* box."

Galen whispered to Edison, "The TV."

"He ordered me to go into the family business, because it was tradition—and a son must obey his father's wishes."

Galen blanched at those last words. He steadied himself, not allowing Jacob to see the tremor in his hands.

"I don't think your problem is with Judaism," Edison interjected.

The young man started to interrupt, but Edison held up his hand.

"Wait, let me finish. It's so easy for older folks—parents, teachers, whatever—to forget that one of the bittersweet joys of youth is to dream. All young men and women dream of conquering the world with great deeds, righting wrongs, becoming heroes and heroines."

Edison was surprised by his emotional response. He remembered his own dream and the power structure that shot it down. Then he almost laughed out loud, realizing for the first time that the Powers That Be had not stopped his idea from happening. He had received no credit, but the Internet—his dream child—had become a reality.

"Your problem is with Isaac the man..." and Edison looked directly into Jacob's eyes, "and with yourself. You are your father and he is you—two identical magnetic poles. It's natural to have conflict. You're both afraid of your futures."

"I don't understand..."

"Yes you do," Nancy countered. "Your father is getting older. He sees his mortality coming closer day by day. He wants to be assured that something of him will carry forward, that what he views as part of himself will respect and remember what he was. You are an extension of him. How can he deal with what he considers self-betrayal?"

"You mean..."

"No, I am not saying that you are betraying him. Remember, he was young once and had his own dreams. Who knows what he would have done, if he hadn't entered the family business."

Jacob nodded.

"Papa is a fine violinist. He and Mama play violin-piano duets together. I even studied it for awhile, but I'm not nearly as good as he is."

"The artistic soul resides well within your family, Jacob," Galen said. "The job facing the four of us is to remind your father of his dreams. Only then will he accept the possibility of yours."

"That's enough for tonight," Nancy chimed in. "Tomorrow you three men can go shopping. You know how I hate to shop."

She tried to hide her grin.

The two old men laughed.

Galen lay in bed, staring at the wall. Was it all that simple? Why couldn't he have seen this back then? His thoughts were interrupted by a knock on his door.

"Come in, whoever it is."

The door opened slowly, and Jacob entered, wearing Tonio's spare pajamas and robe.

"Tio Galen, I'm sorry to disturb you but ... I wonder if, before we went into town ... could we visit the Garden of Remembrance? I never had a chance to do so when Betty died, and I'd like to do it while I'm here, for Tonio's sake as well as my own."

Galen nodded. He, too, needed that visit.

Morning broke with the unique crisp, cool clarity of a mountain spring day. The four had delayed breakfast, until they could trudge down the mountain trail at dawn, their steps accompanied by the chirping of nestling birds seeking sustenance from their parents.

"Here we are, Jacob."

Edison indicated the small clearing, where only the early daffodils were in bloom, their white petals bonnet-like around their central cones.

Jacob carried the sandalwood case. He took off his coat, spread it on the ground, and set the case on top of it. He carefully opened the case and placed one of the *Tefillin* on his left arm, the other on his head. He unfolded the time-worn *Tallit* and carefully draped his shoulders. The *Tzizilts* moved in time with the early morning breeze, tassels of belief in God's wisdom.

Nancy, Edison, and Galen watched the young man step forward and recite the *Kaddish*, the ancient prayer of mourning.

"*Yisgadal yiskadash sh'may rabo. . .*"

Glorified and sanctified be God's great name throughout the world, which He has created according to His will.

The three knew that Jacob had found himself.

It was a long drive by car for the old friends—a long time since any of them had ventured to New York. They had discussed many options for travel, but considering what Nancy had in mind, Edison's Subaru seemed the most practical. And, given the length of the trip, Edison even allowed Galen to share in the driving. He often said it was "white-knuckle travel" when Galen took the wheel.

"You realize, young man, that this car stops for all bathroom breaks. It is one of the joys of surviving as long as we have. The bathroom is a holy shrine for the three of us," Edison solemnly intoned.

Galen and Nancy completed the doxology.

"Praise be the bathroom. Amen!"

Jacob tried relieving his nervous tension by joking, "Are we there yet? Are we there yet?"

The trio smiled in recognition.

As they approached their destination, Edison and Nancy thanked the Fates for their escape from metropolitan New York twenty years ago. Neither had thought the area could get more congested, but during their absence the area had seen an astounding growth in buildings and traffic.

It was Sunday. The *Shabbat* restrictions had ended in the residential neighborhood of old brownstones, where Jacob's parents lived. With his knowledge of the area, they were able to find parking just a short distance away.

Following the instruction of the three, the young man dressed in muted dark clothing—not quite the outfit he was used to, but comfortable. His hair and beard were still short, because he now kept it all trimmed.

"Let us go in first," Nancy warned. "We need to size up the situation. If the police show up, stay in the car."

She tried to laugh at her remark but couldn't. She knew police intervention was always a possibility in family disputes.

Slowly she climbed the worn, stone steps to the heavy, wood door.

We're both relics of a bygone time, aren't we, house?

She lifted the cast-iron knocker. Three times she struck the metal anvil. A minute later the door opened on its intruder chain, and a late-middle-aged woman peered out, her face distinctly lined by stress.

"Mrs. Geltmacher?"

"Yes?"

"My name is Nancy Edison. This is my husband, Robert, and our friend, Dr. Galen. We'd like to talk with you about Jacob. Is your husband home?"

"My husband cannot come to the door. He sits *Shiva.*"

"I'm sorry, have you lost a relative?"

"He sits *Shiva* for Jacob."

Nancy stood impassively but mentally shook her head. Isaac Geltmacher was going to be *one of those*. She tried again.

"Jacob is not dead, Mrs. Geltmacher. He is here with us. We'd like to talk to you and your husband."

The woman's face lit up with relief at the news of her son. Jacob was well! Then her somber expression returned, as she remembered her husband.

"I do not think that would be wise."

Galen moved forward. "We've come a long way, Mrs. Geltmacher. At least give us the opportunity to try."

Rebekah Geltmacher thought a moment then nodded, released the chain, and led the three into the parlor. The diminutive woman, dressed in simple, dark dress—no jewelry, no makeup to sully her natural good looks—moved hesitantly toward a back room.

As they waited, they saw the spinet piano sitting in the corner of the room, and a worn, violin case rested on top of it. There were no paintings or photos on the walls. The furniture had that heavy, stuffed look favored at the beginning of World War I.

Isaac Geltmacher, dressed in a black, broad-cut suit, heavily bearded and locked, entered, followed by his wife. She drew back, her hands clutched in front of her. He wasn't tall but was imposing none the less, in the way he stood and in the angulation of his jaw.

Galen immediately saw the boy in the father. Jacob had inherited that not-quite-stocky build and strong jaw line. He also shared his mother's sensitive brown eyes and delicate lips. And when Isaac spoke, Galen recognized the young man's mannerisms mirrored in the father.

"You come to speak with me about my son? My son is dead! I sit *Shiva* for him. I have no son!"

The words hit Galen head-on like an arrow, wrenching him to the core.

Edison took a step forward, and Isaac involuntarily stepped back.

"Why do you say this? On what basis do you reject your own son?"

Again the arrow pierced Galen, as he heard the words Geltmacher spoke in controlled anger.

"A son must obey his father's wishes."

"No, Isaac Geltmacher," Nancy interjected, a subtle fierceness tingeing her voice. "A son must respect his father. Nowhere is it written that a son must live his father's life."

"Since when is a *shiksa* a *rebbe*?"

Nancy tried to keep her voice gentle, but she felt hard-pressed to do so at the man's reply. Fire now burned in her eyes as she faced him.

"Mr. Geltmacher, my name is Nancy Seligman Edison. My father, Ira Seligman, and his ancestors came from the same village as your family. He fought the ones who made it necessary for your father to be brought here and adopted. Do not insult me, young man!"

Rebekah stood in the shadows nodding agreement.

Galen took up the charge. He could barely resist choking the man.

"Mr. Geltmacher, you are Isaac, son of Abraham. If the God of Abraham Himself had commanded your father to kill you in sacrifice, would Abraham Geltmacher have done so?"

"So now the goy is the *rebbe*."

Galen pushed on.

"Has God commanded you to sacrifice your son?"

Isaac lowered his head.

"No."

"Then why have you done so?"

Isaac slumped into one of the chairs and began to sob.

Rebekah placed her hands on her husband's shoulders. She was smiling.

Nancy turned to Edison and whispered, "Get Jacob, and make sure he brings the thing."

Edison left the apartment and headed to his car. Jacob saw him coming and got out.

"Come on, and remember what we told you—and bring that with you. Did you get it ready?"

Jacob nodded, grabbed the case, and followed Edison back up the familiar steps. He felt strange, both feverish and chilled at the same time. His mouth was dry, as he crossed under the *Mezuzah*-marked lintel and entered the home of his youth. He stood as he had been instructed, until his father and mother looked up at him.

Rebekah's eyes filled with joy. Isaac's eyebrows rose questioningly. The three elders looked at their young friend expectantly, their mental fingers crossed. Jacob took a deep breath, stepped forward, and faced his father directly.

"Papa, Mama, I'm sorry."

Isaac grumbled to conceal his own emotion. He looked at his son and said in quiet tones, "As well you should be."

Then he stood and embraced him.

The tension broken, the six had sat down for tea. Afterward, Jacob opened the case and took out Nancy's violin. Eyes twinkling, he looked at his father and began to bow the opening to Mendelssohn's "Concerto for Violin and Piano in D Minor." His mother went to the piano. His father hesitated then opened his own violin case, lovingly removed the heirloom instrument, tested it, and began to play.

Galen watched with pleasure, as the mother's fingers moved over the keyboard, her body emphasizing the beauty of the sound in motion. Father and son, playing in synchrony, each bow, each nod of the head seemingly choreographed.

Galen's thoughts drifted to a long-ago day, when his old friend and classmate Dave Nash sat next to his father on their Virginia farm. The same thought that had occurred to him then echoed in his mind now:

Twins, not father and son, but twins——one older than the other

They left hearing promises and words of understanding exchanged between parents and son. Each of them silently hoped the identical temperaments of Jacob and his father would remain buffered by Rebekah's conciliatory presence.

Galen had taken Isaac's hand and looked him in the eye.

"Remember, you are an artist, and so is your son. Allow him the privilege of developing his art. I have a feeling there is greatness there."

"Thank you, *Rebbe* Galen."

"Are you sure you don't mean *Reb*?"

"No, truly."

Edison headed the Subaru—now carrying only three—back to Pennsylvania. It was a peaceful trip in the aftermath of the father-son conflict. The episode had exhausted Nancy, and she dozed most of the way home. She was sure the skipping in her chest signified only a letdown from all the excitement. No need to bother Bob or Galen with it.

Edison's eyes focused on the road, his hands gripping the steering wheel. He wondered at how close Isaac had come to sacrificing his own son on the altar of pride.

Galen played and replayed Jacob's situation and compared it with his own past.

Why couldn't someone have interceded for me?

The trio went to bed as soon as they arrived home and slept the deep, comforting sleep of the righteous.

All three had ravenous appetites the next day. They slept in late, only to be awakened by the phone ringing. Nancy answered it.

"Missus Edison, it's me, Lem. You wanted me to let you know. Well, they're back. Your birds are back."

"Who called earlier, Nancy?"

"Lem Caddler. He wanted to let me know the birds are back."

"The sparrows, the Henslow sparrows?"

"Yes, Galen. Bob, do you remember when we first came here, the State Wildlife Commission wanted to make this place a preserve, because we had the only known flock of Henslows in Pennsylvania on our property?"

Edison nodded, mouth full of pancakes.

"I'm going to take a walk later and check them out."

He gulped down the last piece as he gurgled, "Be careful, honey."

It had warmed up by late afternoon. A simple sweater was all Nancy needed, as she walked down the path, a broad straw hat protecting her skin from the increasingly direct rays of the sun, climbing higher in the sky as it approached the summer solstice. But that wouldn't happen for another month and a half. Spring was still her favorite time of year. It carried the promise of resurrection and rebirth to fruition. The dead earth appears to return to life, as solar radiation triggers the photo-synthetic reflex in plants. For Nancy's aging joints, the warmth triggered new energy and optimism.

Pleased with the apparent outcome of Jacob's dilemma, she hoped the truce would remain in effect between him and his parents, and they would allow him to pursue his career freely. She made a mental note to call Diana and Faisal when she got back to the house.

She thought of her birds. Agape Mountain held the ideal, meadow nesting sites for the rare sparrows. Each year the little birds would take their thousand-mile migratory trek north and return to the untouched, tall grassy meadow. They nested low to the ground, fed on berries, small insects, and the tall grass seeds abundant in that one particular field.

Nancy loved her "little friends," as she had come to call them, with their distinctive olive, double-whiskered face with conical bill and rust-colored wings, which caused them to stand out from the more common sparrow varieties.

This time she brought a surprise: a bag of wild bird seed she would spread near their nesting sites.

She approached the edge of the meadow from under the coniferous tree border and took out her birding glasses. The powerful binoculars quickly picked up the nesting sites, and a few of the birds were airborne. Most likely male, she thought. The females would be in brood pattern now, warming the clutches of three-to-five eggs for their eleven-day incubation period.

Suddenly the little birds began to scatter. She scanned the sky and saw the reason: hawks, the marauders of the bird kingdom!

She watched in horror as three Accipiters suddenly dove toward her precious sparrows. She dropped her binoculars and ran toward the birds, waving her hands and shouting. She hardly stopped to think about what she would do if the hawks came after her.

The Fates, hearing her question, decided to find out for themselves.

She didn't see the small stone jutting out of the ground and felt herself falling forward, sprawling face down in the early grass. Her hands went out reflexively, and she felt the impact pain radiating from her wrists to her elbows.

She was stunned. She lay there, not moving, afraid of what she would feel when she did. She tried to roll over and felt knifelike pain in her right ankle. Then she looked up. The sun was in its presetting stage, and the temperature was dropping. She saw the hawks, initially scared by her scarecrow noise. Now they had soared and were beginning their downward dive—heading straight for her!

She rolled over onto her stomach again, gritting her teeth against the pain. She tried to pull the large straw hat farther down onto her head.

She waited and prayed.

Then she heard three shrieks. What was it, their attack cry? She felt no raking of talons, no sharp beak pecking. She rolled over to see what was happening.

What am I doing? Isn't this what got Lot's wife into trouble?

Her eyes took in a scene from Armageddon. Three Great Horned Owls had taloned the three hawks in midair and shredded them. She saw their blood-soaked body parts fall from the sky and land scant yards away. One of the owls, the smallest of the three, landed nearby. It cocked its head then looked straight at her.

"Chk?"

"Baby! You did remember!"

"Chk."

"Are these your mama and papa?"

"Chk."

She felt a sudden flutter in her chest. Her head buzzed and her vision spiraled inward to black.

She didn't hear sounds of multiple paws and flapping wings surrounding her unconscious body.

"Careful with her. Looks like she's got a pretty bad ankle sprain."

She had regained consciousness and heard Galen muttering, as he knelt down beside her and manipulated her right foot. She also heard the unraveling of elastic wrapping and the increasing support and snugness, as he figure-eighted the dressing in a herring-bone pattern around her leg and ankle. Then he took out his stethoscope and listened. He heard the skipping beats and shook his head. She heard him mutter again.

"How long have you known about this, old girl? Why didn't you tell us?"

"Doc, I don't think the Subaru can get in here. I think we'll need to make a stretcher or a litter, or something."

"Yes, Lem. Call Edison on the cell. He can figure it out and get it down here, and we'll all three get her back to the house. She's going to need hospitalization. I'd call in the Medevac unit, but knowing how she feels about her birds, and how that chopper would disturb their habitat, I'd rather avoid World War III by carrying her up to the house the old-fashioned way."

He paused and looked at the other man.

"How did you find her, Lem?"

"Just walkin', Doc, just walkin'."

Galen noticed a sheet of drawing paper sticking out of Lem's back pocket, and he recognized it as one of Miriam's. The old farmer shrugged and handed it to Galen, who examined it. The drawing showed a woman lying unconscious in a field and surrounded by three Great Horned Owls and a phalanx of wolves.

CHAPTER 10

Honeymooners

"We're losing her!"

She was free-floating in that twilight zone between existence and non-being.

She felt ... happy ... free?

No, this was different.

She could see the scene below.

Below?

Yes, she was definitely looking downward at men and women crowded over a stretcher. They were pounding on something ... no ... someone, lying there.

"It's set as high as it'll go. Shock her again. Clear!"

Looks like ye're in a bit a' a pickle, Lassie.

Angus ... Angus Urquhart of the Clan Urquhart? Is that me, Angus?

Aye, Lassie. Ye shoulda told 'em aboot yer heartbeats.

Am I dying, Angus?

Na yet, Lassie. Tha' big man there won' let ya go.

She watched the bear-sized old man moving faster and faster ... faster than she had ever seen him move before. Suddenly he took a large syringe with a long needle on it. He raised his right hand.

What was he doing?

She felt the sudden hot stabbing pain, as he plunged the needle into the chest of the person below.

Now she felt herself being pulled toward that figure on the stretcher. As the vortex coned downward she heard the Scotsman's parting words:

I'll be there when yer time comes, Lassie.

Goodbye, Angus!

"Okay, she's out of V tach. It's coarse, but she's in sinus rhythm. Let's get her prepped. She's gonna need a twofer."

Galen turned to Edison, who had been peering through the small window of the emergency-room cubicle. The carnage of the successful resuscitation lay scattered on the floor around the stretcher where Nancy still lay. The sounds of the heart monitor echoed the now-efficient rhythm that sustained her.

Galen nodded, and Edison burst through the door toward his wife.

"Why didn't you tell me?" he asked through tear-clouded eyes. His body shook as he held her hands in his. The IV tubing in her forearms moved like marionette strings, as he laid his head on her chest and sobbed.

Nancy, still groggy, smiled, as she rubbed the back of his neck.

"Did you see what that brute did to me?"

She turned to the old doctor now slumped exhausted in one of the metal side chairs.

"I didn't know you could move so quickly, Galen."

He looked up.

"How much did you see?"

"Everything."

He nodded weakly and closed his eyes.

Another doctor entered the room, a tall man of athletic build and infectious smile.

"Mrs. Edison, I'm Dr. Crescenzi. We're taking you to the special-procedures OR. You won't be there very long."

Galen rose from his chair.

"Sal, make sure she gets the latest unit put in. This cardiac-resuscitation stuff is tiring for an old fart like me."

"For an old fart you did just fine."

Both doctors laughed, the older to relieve his tension, the younger to reassure his colleague.

Salvatore Crescenzi was head of cardiology now, but he remembered Galen's lectures as a student, and he still felt great respect.

"Mr. Edison, we're going to put in a gadget to keep your wife's heart in regular rhythm. Are you familiar with pacemakers and defibrillators?"

Galen and Edison both burst out laughing.

Galen winked at his friend.

"Sal, some day Edison and I will tell you about an incident that happened before your father was born."

Edison chimed in.

"Let's just hope you guys never need to use a car battery in your work."

The young doctor just stared in puzzlement at the men. Then he followed the orderly, who pushed Nancy's stretcher down the hallway.

Galen sat down again, his face drawn with fatigue.

"Edison, I'll never forgive myself for not calling in the Medevac 'copter. It was just sheer luck that nothing happened before we got here."

"Look at it this way—nothing did happen until we got here. Besides, can you imagine the battle royal that would have ensued if a copter had disturbed her birds?"

Edison paused, reluctant to say what he was thinking. He swallowed, and then he looked his friend in the eyes.

"Didn't you see anything, any signs or symptoms that might have warned you about Nancy?"

Galen looked up at his friend. He was too tired to reply.

They sat and waited.

"Mrs. Edison, we'll use mild sedation and local anesthesia to hook you up. You'll be aware of what's going on. Let us know if you feel any discomfort."

Crescenzi and his resident assistant began their prep, as the nurse-anesthetist administered the combination of conscious-sedation medications to Nancy. She felt relaxed but remained alert enough to watch the monitor screen above her, as the doctors threaded the electrodes and placed the small, under-the-skin pouch just below her left collar bone.

"There. Now let's see how she paces."

They activated the unit, and Nancy felt a sudden, slight jolt, as the defibrillator/pacemaker started to time her heart. Soon it became unnoticeable.

"Okay, Mary. Let's lighten up on the meds."

The anesthetist slowly titrated back on the midazolam drip, and the light fog lifted in Nancy's mind.

"Let's watch her in recovery for awhile, then we'll get her up to a monitor bed in the intermediate CCU.

"You did just fine, Mrs. Edison."

She nodded at the young woman peering down at her and smiled. "Thanks... uh..."

The nurse noticed that she was squinting at her name badge.

"It's Mary, Mrs. Edison. Now just rest in the unit for awhile, and then we'll see if Dr. Crescenzi wants you moved to a regular bed."

She smiled and resumed pushing Nancy's gurney. They reached the observation unit, and Mary efficiently positioned Nancy's stretcher and monitor units for easy visibility. Then she turned to the nurse on duty and gave her the OR records and post-op order sheet.

"I'll check on you later, Mrs. Edison."

"Thanks, Mary."

Nancy lay there, hearing the muted sounds of the heart monitor. The steady-paced beats did not relieve her uneasy feeling. Something was definitely not right between Bob and Galen. Her husband's words echoed in her head: "Didn't you see anything...?"

"Mr. Edison, we're going to keep Mrs. Edison at least overnight to make sure everything remains stable. So far her pacemaker is doing a fine job."

"That's routine, Edison," Galen added, as his friend's eyes started to widen in fear.

"Can I see her, Doctor?"

"Certainly. Come on, I'll take you in."

"Do you want me to come with you?"

Galen hesitated to follow. He knew how traumatic and personal this whole situation was to his friend.

"Yes."

The three men walked down the hall to the intermediate-care unit, but Edison didn't wait for the other two. As soon as he saw Nancy he ran to her gurney.

"Nancy ... I ... uh ... I..."

He couldn't speak. He just laid his head against her cheek and kissed her repeatedly. She wrapped her arm around him.

"Honey, I think we're going to have guests," Nancy said gently, as she spotted Galen and Crescenzi standing in the hallway.

Her husband of almost fifty-five years lifted his head and wiped his eyes then nodded. He stood by her bedside, as the old and young doctor approached.

"Everything is going well … so far, Mrs. Edison. I told Mr. Edison that I'd like to keep you here at least overnight to monitor for any irregularities in your heart beat. The pacer is doing its job well, but I always like to be sure. Is that all right with you?"

"Can't I go home today? I feel fine. Besides, I don't want Norton and Kramden here messing up the house while I'm not there."

Crescenzi raised an eyebrow.

"You're too young to remember, Sal. Maybe 'The Odd Couple' is a better reference."

Crescenzi seemed startled.

"You don't mean…?"

"No, no, Sal, not that way. Let's just say that neither Edison nor I should be trusted alone in a well-kept kitchen or house."

The young doctor blushed and smiled, as a knowing look passed between him and Galen.

"Mrs. Edison, let's just see how things go. We'll take it day by day."

"Can't I stay with her?"

"Go home, Bob. One of us in the hospital is enough." Nancy clasped his hand, and he bent over and kissed hers.

A few minutes later, after more hand-kissing from Edison and reassurances from Crescenzi, the two men walked slowly down the hall. One kept turning around to look back at the room they had just left. The other kept steering him gently toward the hospital exit. It was one of the few times Edison allowed Galen to drive him home.

"Stop pacing, Edison. That won't help."

His friend of over sixty years was wearing a hole in the living room carpet. Edison sat down, fidgeted a few minutes, and stood up again.

"She's not here. She's not here!"

"But she will be, and soon. What you're doing won't help, little brother."

"Stop calling me that!"

He moved closer to the bear-sized man, shook his fist in Galen's face and snarled, "I'm not your little brother, and, for that matter, what gives you the right to tell me what to do in my own home?"

Galen stood stunned for a moment.

"What are you talking about?"

"Yeah, right, go ahead—play the innocent bystander. If you're so smart, you quack, how come you didn't pick up on her heart thing, huh? You're supposed to know everything—right? This might not have happened if ..."

"Edison, that's unfair. I know you're distraught over Nancy, but..."

"You big jerk, you don't understand. I almost lost her once. If I lost her again ... how could you possibly unders...?"

The sudden look on Galen's face sent a chill through him.

"Uh ... I ...uh..."

Galen turned without a word and went to his room, slamming the door behind him.

Leni, Cathy, he doesn't know how lucky he is.

Each man spent an anguished, sleepless night—Edison frightened at the prospect of losing his beloved wife, and Galen feeling alone and lonelier than he had in years. He sat on the edge of his bed, clutching Leni's stuffed toy dog to his chest.

Neither man spoke, as each fixed a quick breakfast of toast and marmalade then headed to the car. They exchanged no words, as Edison took the driver's seat, and they headed down the mountain road leading to the hospital. They walked separately to the intermediate ICU, and they waited separately, while the unit nurse called Crescenzi.

"Mr. Edison, your timing is perfect. Your wife had a good night, so I'm sending her home this morning."

They followed the cardiologist into the small, glass-enclosed room, Edison moving quickly to his wife's side and planting a kiss on her forehead. He smiled for the first time in two days, but his voice trembled, as he said, "Nancy, we're taking you home today!"

Crescenzi turned to Galen then back at Nancy.

"Now, young lady, you're not to do anything around the house, until your resident quack says you can. Understand?"

She looked at her husband, her face glowing. Then she noted the silence. She looked at Galen.

Neither man was looking at the other.

"What's going on, you two?"

Silence.

Crescenzi wisely stepped outside.

"What's going on?"

She knew, as women always do, and she shot an exasperated frown at the pouting, geriatric little boys.

A few more moments of silence then Edison and Galen turned to each other. The old engineer started to speak then stopped. He looked at his friend and nodded. Almost in unison both mumbled, "I'm sorry."

Then Edison leered at Galen.

"Heeey, Ralphie boy, you are so fat!"

A rare smile crossed Galen's face. He cleared his throat, made a fist with his right hand, and struck his left palm, as he roared out, "So help me, Norton, one of these days, POW! Right in the kisser!"

The three old friends, two walking and one in a wheelchair, headed for the hospital exit.

CHAPTER II

Elegy for Aaron

It was said of Galen that his mind was sharp as a tack, even to the day he died. And that was not far from the truth. Indeed, the retired doctor's proverbial steel-trap memory of things, people, places, dates, and times endured. But what few realized, and only two really understood, was how the old man managed to store those bits of data that clutter the intellect to the point of confusion and distraction.

He awoke earlier than usual that day. He lay in bed, underneath the same quilt that had covered him and Leni their first night together. He stared nearsightedly at the still-night-darkened window.

His joints ached even after his usual four hours of rest. Maybe it was just the events of the previous evening. He quietly shook his head and touched the pillow that Cathy had made for him, when they had moved into their first house.

He reached for his glasses, slid them over his nose, and looked at the calendar on the opposite wall. The numerals stood out bleakly in heavy black, not just in print but in his heart.

He shook his head again and sat up on the edge of the bed.

Another day.

He stood up, put on the Beacon bathrobe that June had insisted he wear when he turned fifty-five, and headed to the bathroom.

He dressed warmly. His beloved Leni's sweater, a gift more than a half-century old now and still bright in its variegated fall colors, protected his seven-plus-decades-old chest. The sheepskin-lined leather gloves, Cathy's reminder that he needed to keep his then late-forty-something hands warm, still fit, even over the arthritic knobs on the ends of his fingers. The gloves matched the woolen scarf he carefully wrapped around his neck before putting on June's London Fog coat. She had jokingly told him that his late-fifties body needed the extra protection, and that he could be sure of her advice, because she was a doctor, too.

He carefully protected these and a few other, tangible reminders of shattered dreams as holy relics of his bygone youth.

As he tried to slip out of the house, he caught his reflection in the mirror hanging in the foyer.

So, Galen, who would have thought you'd be spending your last days living with friends and shepherding children, wolves, bears, and assorted other creatures on the top of a mountain in Pennsylvania?

He opened the heavy oak door of the house and stared out into the night.

His destination, even at this early hour, was deep into the woods. His two friends were still soundly asleep, and breakfast was several hours away. But old habits die hard. Ever since he had retired, he still managed to take his solitary, predawn walks, barring the inclement weather the altitude frequently would bring.

His walking stick, a whittled down maple branch Edison had run through his router as a surprise for him a few birthdays ago, tapped lightly on the gravel, as he stood outside deciding in which direction to turn.

The bird pond . . . yes, that should do it.

He headed down the path still covered by last autumn's dried leaves. He moved past the old blind, where they all had first studied the wolves and other mountain fauna. Soon he reached what he always had considered his own private little beach.

The winter snows and spring rains had filled the pond almost past capacity, and its shoreline became a pit stop for the thirsty denizens of the forest.

Spring had only declared itself by the calendar. The overnight mountain temperatures still dropped to the low thirties. He pulled the knee-length coat—June's parting gift before that fateful flight to Colombia—close to his neck. His large ears supported the old pith helmet hat he had worn in the past while planting his Virginia gardens—memorials to his past loves.

He came to the seat-high, glacier-strewn boulder not far from the pond edge and sat to catch his breath. It had been a while since he had been able to walk that far without stopping. He liked to think it was because he was more introspective and not in physical disarray.

Dawn was casting its fireplace glow over the horizon.

They watched the large, two-legged one. Definitely a male to their keen senses, he was well known to them, and they accepted his position of dominance. They didn't fear him. He and the other two-legged ones had never threatened them, and they often left food.

They moved forward, some on four legs, others by wing, and sat in council with him.

His ears, the only sense that had actually improved with age, picked up the leaf rustling and changing air currents. He turned toward the rock outcropping and cave formations that comprised the wolf den and saw emerald-green eyes returning his gaze. They formed the dominance phalanx with the alpha male and its littermate consiglieres at the fore.

The stirring of dried leaves beneath the nearby, still-bare oak tree brought the young owl into view. Its bowling-pin form with folded wings sat on a low limb. The old man's laughter broke the stillness, and the wind-rippled waves on the small pond provided soft accompaniment.

"Where is my Baloo? Come on, old bear. Come sit with your brother!"

Galen laughed even louder then put his hands to his face to hide the tears.

If they knew how much I still cried, they would've dispatched me long ago.

He didn't look up until he heard the low-groaning growl and heavy-padding footsteps approach.

Only the Great Horned Owl showed none of the effects of over-wintering, while *Lupus* and *Ursus* displayed the matting and early shedding of their seasonal, thick fur.

"You look as bad as I feel, Baloo. You're a young bear, not like me."

The black bear waddled slowly to the pond edge, lapped at the water, then moved to within twenty feet of Galen and sat back comfortably on its haunches. It stretched then let out a loud yawn.

The old doctor looked at each of the forest creatures. He raised himself from his sitting position, turned to the rippling pond water, and returned to his audience.

"If this were a vaudeville routine, I'd start off with a joke, but I don't feel like making jokes. I know I'm probably crazy for even standing here and talking like this, speaking to a group of wild mammals and birds. But I sense this strange affinity for all of you."

He felt their keen eyes fixed on him. Okay, he was an old fool, but who else could he talk to? Edison and Nancy would tolerate it, but would they truly understand?

Lem, Ben, Lachlan, the kids? No, he had to remain an image of wisdom and fortitude in their presence. They depended on him.

"My friends, do you know what today is? It's my birthday."

The bear rolled over on its back, large tufts of fur falling out as it scratched itself on the ground. The "tchk-tchk" of the owl kept pace.

The alpha wolf moved forward and sniffed the old man's hand. He looked at its piercing eyes, reached over, and stroked the canine's head.

He began crying again, but it wasn't because he was a year older. He sat back down on the boulder, tapped the ground with his stick, and cleared his throat.

"My friends, let me tell you a story. Would you like to hear a story?"

Maybe it was his imagination, or maybe it was just poor eyesight, but the animals seemed to grunt and chirp in agreement.

"Okay, since you asked, I'll tell you a story about a past time, long before the years when your great, great, great, great grandparents roamed this forest. I was just a boy then ... and full of hope."

The old man stared ahead, his mind leaping over the mountains of memory.

.   .   .

"Edison, are you sure your Mom and Dad won't mind? I can still catch the bus home."

He hadn't even visited another kid's house in years, much less stay for dinner. But he had told his parents that Edison and he were working on a school science project, so the bases were covered.

Hours had passed, as they worked on the circuit for the muscle stimulator, tweaking the controls to get it just right, when a car horn beeped in the driveway in front of Edison's father's garage/workshop.

"It's my Dad. He had to go into work today. They're designing some new type of light fixtures, and he's their top man."

Robert Edison was proud of his old man, and Ron Edison was just as proud of his son. The sailor boy who had courted Gloria and then gone off to war was still tall and lean, with just a touch of gray toward the back of his russet-brown hair. He walked easily, just a hint of ship-board sailor's roll left after a fifteen-year hiatus from his navy service.

"What are you two guys up to now?"

He grinned at his son and the big, quiet kid standing next to him.

"It's a muscle stimulator, Dad. We've designed the circuit so the current and the frequency of pulsation can be varied."

Edison the younger proudly held up the unit that he and Galen had built into a piece of bent-aluminum sheeting.

The older man looked it over, still smiling, and turned to the boys.

"May I make a suggestion?"

"Sure," they said in unison.

Galen wasn't certain how to act around Edison's parents. They were the friendliest people he had ever met, and they lived in a pretty house in the suburbs, not in the drab middle of town.

"Well, if you position the controls this way..."

Ron Edison went on to point out some changes that, as soon as the boys heard them, made perfect sense. Then he wisely added, "But it's your gadget. Change it only if you think it will help."

The three turned at the sound of the workshop door opening.

"Ron, dinner will be ready soon. Bobby, would your friend like to stay?"

Gloria Edison, floral aproned, smiled from the doorway at her husband and son—and Galen.

The senior Edison saw the confused look in the young man's face. His son spoke up to fill the silence.

"That's great, Mom. You can stay for dinner, can't you, Galen? I haven't showed you that old radio I fixed up yet."

·   ·   ·

Oh, yes, Edison, I do remember that old, cathedral-shaped radio. You still keep it squirreled away somewhere, more than sixty years later, don't you?

His forest audience kept watching, as if waiting for him to continue.

"You know, after high school, I didn't see Edison or his father for over forty years. That's a long time, isn't it?"

The bear stretched and yawned again.

"Well, it wasn't too long after Edison and I got back together that I became a medical sounding board for him and his wife Nancy. It certainly gave my ego a boost to realize that two very bright people respected my medical opinion and advice.

"But let me tell you something. There is always another edge to the sword of pride. The Greeks would call it 'hubris.'"

He stopped to catch his breath. The wolves were sitting down on all fours now. Had the owl fallen asleep?

"Edison phoned me one evening shortly after my trip to Florida. I had gone there to give the eulogy at my friend Dave's funeral."

"'Galen, the World War II Memorial is having a special celebration for the surviving vets,' he said, 'and Mom and Dad have been invited. Mind if we stop by your place?'

"It startled me to hear those words, 'Mom and Dad.' I hadn't even asked Edison about them. I had assumed that they were long gone, just like my own parents. After all, Edison was almost sixty, but still younger than I.

"I heard his old Subaru pull into my parking lot the next day. It was covered with mountain and highway dust. As I watched, an elderly couple got out, and in slow shuffling gait they followed their son and Nancy up the walk to my office entrance.

"I was staring at them, noting the various infirmities each displayed. And yet ... and yet ... I could still see the bright, smiling faces shining behind the decay of time, overcoming the inevitability of physical entropy. Ron and Gloria Edison were still there.

"The old man was no longer straight. His shoulders were stooped by the weight of years. The slightly wide stance and minor tremors of Parkinsonism had replaced the sailor-boy's confidant walk. The facial creases magnified his grin of welcome remembrance, and his still-firm grip encompassed my hand in greeting.

"Gloria, shorter than I had remembered her, stood by her partner of over sixty years, her once-linear features now softened by creased cheeks. She, too, was less steady in motion, but her effusive personality and easy way of speaking had not diminished.

"It was one of those rare, quiet weekend afternoons for me. Soon the five of us were in the throes of reminiscence. It continued during a drive down the George Washington Memorial Parkway past the District of Columbia and into Old Town Alexandria to a restaurant I had recommended.

"Over dinner, the W-W-Two vet and his wife told of how they first met, and how his young Gloria had braved the wartime travel restrictions to be with her sailor, before he left for distant shores.

"Memories of my schooldays overwhelmed me..."

Galen noticed he had begun to shake. Was it from the moist chill breeze of the early mountain morning?

"It's almost daylight, my friends. I'd better get back to the house pretty soon. Let me just end my story at this point. Maybe I'll tell you more tomorrow."

He stood up from his rock chair and steadied himself with his walking stick. He hadn't meant to ramble in front of the forest denizens like this, but they didn't seem to mind.

Who'd have thought it?

As he turned to leave, they seemed to object with a cacophony of grunts, chirps, and moaning barks. Was it his imagination, or was Baloo the bear shaking his head no?

Was the whimpering of the wolf pack and the sound of multiple tails striking the floor of the forest grotto a protest against his leaving?

Even the owl added its cherhoots to the feral chorus.

"Okay, okay, I must be crazy after all. I'd swear you want me to finish my story. Am I right?"

Maybe he had finally lost touch with reality, but the animal contingent gave guttural approval.

"Well, you might ask, why am I talking about these people? You never knew them, and I had only that one limited adult contact since the four decades after high school.

"Do you remember my saying that my friends, the other two-legged ones, had come to rely on my advice when things weren't right with their health?"

He paused. The owl opened one eye and nodded its clock-shaped head.

"See, that's when I got involved, when I began to see how the Three Fates were going to deal with these two old people who had befriended me when I was young.

"Each time Edison would tell me about something that went wrong with his parents' health, I saw the pattern evolving, the inexorable slippery slope that ultimately takes all of us—even you, my friends.

"That is where you are blessed. You live, you hunt and kill to survive, and then you die. But unlike us upright apes, you do not ruminate about that time when you no longer exist. For you, death is either the finding of food, or the end of the hunt. There is no such thing as a good death, if you are the participant. It is the end of the wonderful and amazing process we call Life. And, with the very little that our human conceit allows us to understand, we can follow the signs that tell us death is imminent and inescapable.

"My friend called me one day to tell me that his father had been diagnosed with colon cancer. It appeared to have been found early, and his doctors had removed it promptly. But just as you will experience when you are older and cannot run, fly, or chase your prey, so Ron

Edison's body was no longer resilient. If you want to know what that is called ... well ... it's encompassed by one word: homeostasis.

"The man who had helped to defeat the great villains of Europe could not defeat death. When my friend told me how his father was doing, I had to tell him what the signs portended."

"Chk hoot?"

"Yes, owl—or should I call you Baby, like Nancy does? There came a time when I had to tell my friend that his father's death was imminent—probably that very day. Now maybe it helped Edison; I don't know for sure. What I do know is that he made the right decision. He told his father's doctors not to do anything further. It was time for a warrior—husband and father—to enter Valhalla."

The alpha wolf let out a low howl, and the other Moonsingers of the mountain joined in.

Galen waited for the wolves to settle down.

"So, you ask, why have you told us this story?"

The bear let out a belch.

"Yes, that's it exactly, Baloo! It was years ago, but I still remember it as clearly as I see all of you now—because it happened on this day. My friend's father died on my birthday."

This time Galen rose as quickly as his joints would allow from the cold rock.

"Story time's over. I'd best get back to my own den."

He turned and slowly made his way up the incline, a more difficult return trip. As he reached the fork in the path, he made a detour. It was only a small detour, he thought, but an appropriate one.

His steps were steadier now, the fluids in his joints warmed by the climbing exercise. Carefully, walking stick now a pendulum keeping pace as he moved, he entered the Garden of Remembrance.

It was a deliberately peaceful place. Nancy was first to propose it, when she saw how much Galen missed tending his Virginia garden.

It became a way for him to remember and, maybe, communicate with the loves he had lost: Leni to a drunk driver, Cathy to pancreatic cancer, and June in the crossfire of a war.

The three friends, younger then, had planned its shape and best location on the eastern slope of Agape Mountain. Edison had suggested the circle within a triangle, and Galen himself completed the motif with an outer circle. He only half-jokingly commented that it was a representation of life: Circles within circles, each chord, each dimension, yielding flowers from earliest spring to first day of frost. And outside the largest circle, its outline was completed by winter-blooming Christmas roses and snowbells.

The old man approached the outer diameter. This time he ignored the rustlings from the forest edge and the early-morning luminescent eyes of its inhabitants. As he bowed his head and closed his eyes, he remembered the words of Ecclesiastes 3:

For every thing there is a season.

He remembered the old woman, too frail, too overcome at the loss of her life partner, sitting in the car as the remains of her husband were lowered into the earth, and as voices rose in harmony that day, singing the Navy Hymn:

Eternal Father, strong to save,
Whose arm hath bound the restless wave,
Who biddest the mighty ocean deep
Its own appointed limits keep;
Oh, hear us when we cry to Thee,
For those in peril on the sea!

Galen stood at attention and saluted. Then he turned and walked back to the house on the mountain crest. He passed the wooden sign proclaiming SAFEHAVEN and slowly walked up the steps. As he reached for the doorknob, the door swung open, and Nancy and Edison stood there.

"Happy Birthday, Galen!"

In Memoriam
Aaron "Ron" K.
09/28/1924 – 03/26/2005

CHAPTER 12

Transitions

Mountain breezes herded clouds across a strawberry-jam sky.

It was that kind of day. They felt it in their bones—rising tension and the excitement of anticipation. Each of the trio, in his or her own way, had awakened with a renewed sense of purpose and vitality.

The kids were coming home again!

"Now, listen, you two, you're not to tell them anything about my pacemaker ... understand?"

Nancy had brought out a light breakfast of multigrain waffles and homemade fruit preserves. Edison and Galen could barely restrain themselves, but being gentlemen they waited until the lady of the house had taken her seat before stuffing their faces.

"Why not?" Edison gurgled through a mouthful of waffle and Nancy's special, "allberry" preserve.

Galen watched the interplay and understood. He had felt enough difficulty making it through his birthday and could well appreciate Nancy's desire to minimize that episode in her life. He just nodded.

"Little brother..." and he hesitated a moment, to see if the moniker would upset Edison again—it didn't. "How would you feel if you had undergone prostate surgery, and we hung a sign on your neck describing the event for all to see?"

Nancy demurely took a bite of her waffle to stifle a laugh. Meanwhile Edison cleared his throat, took a sip of bi lo chun tea, and tried to think of a suitable retort.

"What's so bad about having a pacemaker?"

"Nothing. It's not the pacemaker. It's what it represents."

"What's that supposed to mean?"

"Mother Time."

Years of listening through headphones to various radio signals had begun to take its toll on Edison's hearing. Only Galen and Nancy heard the sound of two cars pulling into the gravel driveway. But when the old engineer saw his wife's face light up in anticipation, he knew the excitement was about to begin. He led the race to the foyer and pulled open the front door just in time to see his now-vintage Subaru roll to a stop, followed by a red and equally disreputable-looking Ford station wagon.

Was it possible? Carmelita and Antonio, and Freddie, now escorting Lilly Daumier, looked taller and more mature than just a few months earlier.

As the sta wag disgorged its passengers, a taller Faisal stepped out of the passenger side, opened the right rear door, and a muscular Akela bounded out and began rolling on the yellow-white pebbles. Then the driver's door opened, and Jacob smiled and stretched. His face showed a confidence and movements that had not existed when the elder trio had intervened for him in New Jersey.

For all of them—five sighted, one not—the impressive magic and energy of young adulthood dominated the scene.

Carmelita reached the door first, her cheeks in full flush, as she now had to bend down slightly to hug her tia and tios. Galen was first to notice the diamond-solitaire ring on her left hand, third finger. She turned even more crimson, as she noticed his notice and stuttered, "It's a friendship ring. Michael gave it to me."

Freddie and Lilly, twins in mindset and height, arrived next and double-hugged each of the oldsters.

"Our little brother has some big news for us, but he said he wouldn't tell us until we were all together," Freddie said. "As soon as I use the restroom, I want to hear what it is."

He turned and smirked, as Antonio brought up the rear. Lilly punched her beau on the shoulder—and then she kissed him full on the lips.

Edison surveyed the six young people and noticed they all were wearing sneakers, khaki trousers and blue shirts—including Carmelita. Even Akela sported a blue-and-tan harness. Before he could ask, Faisal and Jacob bounded up the steps and stood by Tonio. The three were now only an inch shorter than Freddie.

"It was Jacob's idea, Tio Eddie," Faisal said. "He wanted us to visibly demonstrate the spirit of Safehaven."

Galen looked admiringly at the sightless young man, who saw more than most.

How did he know what we were thinking?

Jacob waved a high-definition, digital camera in his hand.

"I've brought plenty of memory cards. While I'm here we're going to have a big recording session. You guys are going to help make me a famous movie producer someday, and Faisal will write the musical score for my masterpiece!"

Nancy gave the young man a startled look.

Who would want to see a bunch of over-the-hill old people and their humdrum existence?

Still, she had to ask.

"Do you have a title in mind for your future cinematic triumph, Jacob?"

Does he ever, Tia Nancy," Faisal interjected. "He's going to call it 'The Safehaven Chronicles!'"

Edison perked up.

"Listen, boy, I expect some top movie stars to play me and Nancy. For old Galen here, any bit actor will do."

"Ah, that's the beauty of my idea, Tio Eddie. There are no movie stars—or maybe I should say you all will be the stars. Tell them, Freddie."

Very rarely did Federico Edison Hidalgo blush, and those previous times usually occurred when he was alone with Lilly. But now his Castilian good looks turned amber, and he felt tongue-tied, so Lilly took over.

"It's an idea Freddie and I are working on for our doctoral dissertations. It involves AI—artificial intelligence—along with holography and computer graphics. Basically, we're proposing to take anyone's image and make it younger or older very accurately and then project lifelike, fully three-dimensional holograms in motion. Even more exciting, we have an idea how to generate an actual feeling of substance to the images."

"Yep, once I get enough recording data on all of us, the movie will make itself," Jacob said, waving the camera in the air like a magic wand. "And, as for the spirit of Safehaven, well, isn't this really where heaven meets earth and grants sanctuary to all who live here? That's why I chose blue and tan."

Faisal chimed in again.

"Don't believe him. His girlfriend, Rachel, came up with the idea, after we told her about you guys."

Now Jacob's face turned crimson, as he blurted out, "Well, your little Shania added her two cents, too."

The old ones noted the next generation's process of choosing life paths and partners. Galen observed that Tonio did not join in, and he surmised that Betty's memory was still shrouding his soul.

Don't worry, boy, you'll find someone who'll fill that void in your heart.

Edison's eyes seemed suddenly brighter and full of mischief behind their bottle-glass lenses.

"Come on, guys and gals, let's go to my workshop. I want to hear more about this."

The old man was a pied piper, leading his two protégé engineers down to his basement lair, and he chuckled to himself as he walked.

I just might have a surprise for you all.

Tonio moved closer to Galen, tilted his head down, and whispered into the old man's ear, "Tio, can we talk privately?"

Galen peered into the young man's eyes.

Yes, he's definitely taller, no doubt about it.

"Stow your stuff in your room, then we'll talk."

Faisal's sharp hearing had picked up the words, but he said nothing. He pretty much knew what his friend was going to say to his guardian, so he just smiled to himself, as he followed the descending sound of footsteps to Edison's lab, Akela walking beside him.

That left Carmelita and Nancy, who held up the young woman's left hand.

"Friendship ring, huh? With everyone else taking off, I guess you and I will be the only ones eating the fresh brownies I made."

Carmelita hugged her again then pulled back a little—she felt the small, hard lump in Nancy's left upper chest.

"Tia, I'm almost done with my course work. I've got so much to tell you. Next month, if my adviser and committee accept it, I'll be defending my dissertation!"

The two women continued talking as they headed to the kitchen.

Galen followed Antonio to his room and sat on the edge of the bed, watching for signs of what might be coming. The young man didn't seem upset, but he was finding it difficult to contain himself.

Must be good news.

Galen braced himself, as Antonio set his gear in the corner, pulled out the desk chair, and straddled it. He was grinning now, dark-brown eyes reflecting the afternoon light from the side window. The cowlick curl on top of his head vibrated visibly from his excitement.

"Tio, what's your greatest wish?"

"You mean right now, or in the past?"

He could be coy, too.

"You know, right now."

"That you all..." *and you especially* he silently added, "that you all achieve your dreams and goals in life."

Tonio's grin widened.

"I've received early acceptance into medical school!"

Galen involuntarily rose from the edge of the bed then sat back down, as Antonio quickly moved beside him. At first the young man worried that the news had shocked his tio, but he relaxed when he saw Galen's face break out into a broad grin of his own.

"There's more, Tio—I've been accepted at your alma mater."

Now he saw something he had never seen before: tears in the old man's eyes.

"Okay, Carm, spill it—and don't leave out the juicy parts."

They sat in the kitchen, the older woman carefully watching the younger. How far had Carmelita committed herself to Mike? Nancy felt no uneasiness about her adopted niece's choice of boyfriend and possible husband, but she wanted to know that Carmelita was sure. The diamond solitaire on her hand spoke of more than friendship.

"I can't believe it!" Freddie exclaimed.

He and Lilly and Jacob stared at the parade of miniature holographic images—bear, owl, and wolves—parading across the top of Edison's workbench. Even Akela stood on his hind legs, front paws on the table, and began to bark at what appeared on the screens. His nasal openings kept twitching in an attempt to pick up the scent of the miniature beasts.

"What did you do, Tio? Are the other animals simulations?"

"Where did they come from?" Lilly asked.

"Don't you know, girl? Everybody comes to Safehaven!"

The old man grinned then took hold of Faisal's hand.

"There's more. Here, boy, let me put your fingers on something. What do you feel?"

The musical prodigy extended his right hand. The others saw him flinch then grin, as his fingers moved over each of the animal images.

"Tio Eddie, I feel fur ... feathers ... movement!"

Each of the others in turn touched the tiny animals then gasped and laughed in delight.

Freddie stared at Edison, who was now beaming.

"Tio, do you know what you have here? This is brilliant!"

Brilliant.

That word elicited a memory flash that struck Edison's forehead like a two-by-four. His smile instantly erased, as he recalled that day in the distant past, when he had presented his dissertation on the possibility of a worldwide information network, only to be told by Professor Baker that The Powers That Be regarded his concept as brilliant but enough of a danger to national security that it would have to be suppressed.

He sat at his workbench chair and cast a melancholy gaze at the images, flanked by four youngsters just beginning to test their professional waters. The old engineer's mind played back that first taste of reality— that first icy-cold dousing the world pours on youthful expectations.

Everything I had worked for turned instantly to ashes. I had to cave in to government pressure and conceal my design. And what did they accomplish by stifling me? Nothing! They delayed its start for decades, until so many others began recognizing its potential that they couldn't block its development anymore.

What he had dreamed of—conceived to the point of practical application—now had become a staple, an indispensable facet of everyday life. He thought about Galen's frequent remarks about the cynical Fates playing with everyone's lives.

If he only knew how much despair I felt, how if I hadn't met Nancy, well, who knows what I would have done?

Then his smile returned.

Sonofagun! The old geezer was right!

"Tio Eddie, are you okay?"

"Omigod, is he having a stroke?"

Lilly touched Edison's shoulder and felt relieved when he looked up at her. He seemed dazed at first, then he laughed and barked, "'Course I am, girl! I'm not senile like your Tio Bear upstairs."

He turned off the gadget and rose from his chair.

"Tell you what, maybe after dinner we can talk some more about my contraption."

He looked at Freddie and Lilly.

"And, come to think of it, I might just have some suggestions for your project. See, I haven't been able to perfect this little toy of mine. It was sheer luck that it worked just now. It's got more bugs than a college dorm room. If you two want to take it on, you'll have got your work cut out for you."

Lilly, her feminine intuition in gear, understood immediately what Edison had just done. She threw her arms around him in a hug then whispered in his good ear, "You're number one, Tio!"

As the quartet-plus-wolf-dog climbed the stairs, Edison disconnected the device and locked it in the cabinet—old habits die hard.

His offer had been genuine. He essentially had built the device they only conceived of, but he didn't want to discourage them. He wouldn't become what Galen often called a "dream eater." If they thought he had already perfected what they were just setting out to do, well, that would be just as bad as what those government idiots—his own dream eaters and soul stealers—had done to him.

"Tia, we have so many plans. They even involve Freddie and Tonio and the rest of you. Michael figures that after we all finish school we'll start our own company. With the different skills we have, it could do so many things. I even thought of the logo."

She took a paper napkin from the table and drew a stylized picture of three wolves on haunches, muzzles pointed upward, with the capital letters HDE forming a rock cropping beneath them.

"What do you think, Tia? We're going to call it Hidalgo-Dimitri-ades Enterprises. We've even included Faisal and Jacob. Freddie and Lilly are working on a special visual projection system, kind of like holograms, but much more lifelike, and I'm going to work on the language algorithms after I finish school. Faisal and Jacob would be the artistic side of the group."

Nancy noticed the even-larger letters forming the foundation: GES.

"And what are these?" she asked, having guessed the answer.

"It stands for Galen, Edison, and Seligman-Edison. Everything we've done we've accomplished because of what you three did for us. So we want you and Tio Eddie and Tio Galen to be board members and advisers to our family corporation. How's that sound?"

Nancy was stunned at the casual manner in which Carmelita had just laid out an amazing combination of scientific and business concepts.

Maybe something of me has rubbed off on you after all, Carm. Now, how can I introduce an element of planning and common sense without becoming one of Galen's soul stealers?

Carmelita's forehead creased, as she thought about broaching the subject of the object in Nancy's chest. She had become familiar with implanted devices, including pacemakers, from her hospital job, and that's what it felt like. She took a deep breath and blurted out, "Tia Nancy, has something happened?"

Nancy likewise took a breath and related the incident with the owls and the hawks on the mountain.

"What can I say? Even now, when he doesn't think I'm awake, my Bob lays his head on my chest, listening to my heartbeat with his good ear."

She explained how she would pretend to be asleep, knowing how devastated he was when she was hospitalized, and would let him listen—and fall asleep to the machine-steady rhythm of her pacemaker heart.

"Now I've told you, girl. I need you to promise you won't tell your brothers or the others."

"Of course, Tia."

"Not even Mike?"

She hesitated.

"No, Tia, I will keep your confidence."

The two women, one at life's beginning, the other approaching completion, sat and held hands.

CHAPTER 13

Tears

The entire pack sensed it, their ears on full point. An indefinable Something was approaching. It was not right. They did not understand, but they knew.

The three old ones rose and exited the den. They paused outside, while the young alpha male and his two cohorts led the pack to follow and encircle their elders. The graying muzzles pointed upward toward the cloud-filled sky. Their triple-toned howl rose above the trees, soon followed by an orchestra of ten.

Edison and Nancy gazed out the window at the mountain vista and valley below, their clasped hands now roughened by time. Their skin had grown mottled, their cheeks not as firm, but the love between then had only deepened in the nearly sixty years since an awkward young engineer stuttered a marriage proposal on the shores of Lake Michigan, and a young banker accepted. Tomorrow would be that anniversary.

Edison turned to his wife and saw the beautiful young girl with auburn-red tresses in that moment when he had instantly fallen in love.

Nancy turned to her myopic husband, he of the sagging jowls, and she beheld the defurred, rabbity young man, who had audaciously boarded her canoe. She rose on arthritic toes and kissed him.

"Hard to believe, isn't it?" she whispered. "And then we rescued the three kids on the same day thirty-eight years later. Maybe Galen's right. Maybe we're all just pawns of the Fates."

"Maybe, but you're still one beautiful pawn!"

He kissed her again then looked up suddenly. Even with diminished hearing he detected it.

"What the dickens is that?"

She joined his stare out the window.

"It's the wolves. They never sing in the daytime."

"Watch your step, sir."

Galen nodded as he descended the stairway ramp now protruding from the small charter aircraft. It had been ages since he attended a national medical conference. He didn't recognize anyone there in California—all of his cohorts were dead, senile, or happily retired and playing shuffleboard in Florida. But it thrilled the old man to see and hear the young medical leaders describing the latest discoveries in the field. The surprise inclusion of another passenger had made the return flight even more enjoyable.

As they walked across the tarmac, a raindrop struck the tip of Galen's nose.

Lem hung up the phone and turned to his housemate.

"That was Lachlan. Said there's a spell of real bad weather heading in. I'm gonna check the yard and windows. Might even be a good idea to head up to the big house."

Ben nodded. Miri sat on the rug next to her canine guardian and stared at the wall, her normally busy hands unusually calm. Her autistic universe did not recognize changes in the weather.

Lem headed outside and looked around for loose yard items to store. As he bent over to pick up a flowerpot, a raindrop landed on the back of his neck.

The ICOM 7100 emergency-weather receiver that Edison kept permanently switched on suddenly blared, the announcer's voice interrupted several times by the soft crackle of distant lightning interfering with the signal.

"This is a severe-weather alert for Scranton and surrounding vicinities. Expect thunderstorms with strong sustained winds and gusts, heavy downpours, and hail. Beware flash-flooding in low-lying areas. Stay tuned for further bulletins."

"I'd better go outside and move all the loose stuff into the garage," he said.

Nancy watched him walk away.

He looks drawn.

He was getting too old for the heavy work, she thought, especially in the torpid heat and humidity of summer. And she knew he was worried about Galen, who was due back from his conference on the West Coast today. Would the weather affect his flight? She worried about herself as well. Could she handle the work if Lea Ann, the local Red Cross chapter coordinator, put her on call? The kids had taken a road trip to Scranton. Would they get hung up by the storm and not be back in time to celebrate the anniversary of their rescue?

She prayed everyone would arrive safely, before the storm hit.

Outside, a drop of rain spattered Edison's glasses, as he moved the last loose item from the yard into the garage. Wiping it with his handkerchief, he reentered the house and turned on the classical music station to relax his nerves.

"Freddie, slow down!"

Carmelita and the other three human passengers in the car were nervously gripping their seats. And the canine was whimpering.

Mountain roads were not conducive to Freddie's idea of speed limits: ignoring them. Besides, it was starting to rain, creating a dangerous mix of water and detritic oil on the pavement that could make driving treacherous.

"Oh, all right. I just thought you'd all want to get home," Freddie grumped.

"Sure, but all in one..."

"Don't say it, Sis."

He slowed to a reasonable speed, as raindrops dotted the thin film of road dust on the windshield.

It had started gradually, with intermittent but unusually large wads of water striking the gravel drive and kissing the glass of the picture window—splut, splut, splut. Soon it became a steady splatter, still benign, and accompanied by the growing noise of the ancient red Jeep ascending the long driveway and pulling up in front of the mountaintop home.

"Galen's back," Edison announced.

The front door burst open, and in poured the old doctor, accompanied by a lightning flash along the horizon and a delayed rumble of thunder. The rain was picking up now, becoming wind-blown. It slewed across the front yard in sheets, as more cloud-concealed lightning flashes lit up the valley vista.

A second person, taller and younger, followed him in.

"Mike!"

Nancy hugged Carmelita's sweetheart and let out a sigh of relief. She even threw Galen a welcoming smile.

Edison grinned.

"I think a certain young lady is going to be surprised. She's been in a funk ever since you told her you couldn't make it."

The big, handsome aerospace engineer returned the smile.

"Yeah, thank God I came to my senses."

Edison winked.

"Now you're learning, kid."

"Speaking of which, where are the kids?" Galen asked.

"Tonio should be here soon," Edison answered. "He called and said he was going to stop by the nursing home."

"The rest of them are heading back from Scranton," Nancy added, "but they haven't checked in yet."

The rain beat a sustained drum-roll on the roof.

Jesse Orth quickly read through the document on his desk. St. Ignatius Home, like all healthcare facilities, had drawn up contingency plans in the event of emergencies, including severe weather, and he wanted to refresh his understanding of the procedures before meeting with the staff.

He heard footsteps approaching his open office door, and he smiled as he saw Tonio standing in the doorway.

Jesse had aged visibly in the four years since Betty's death from leukemia. The mildly salt-and-pepper hair he had sported when Tonio and Betty were courting in high school now fully reflected the white of the fluorescent ceiling lights.

"Hello, Mr. Orth."

Tonio felt glad to see the older man, but he retained that pit-of-the-stomach heaviness he knew all too well. Even now, everything here reminded him of Betty. But he had wanted to stop by and let her father know that next week he would be leaving for freshman orientation at medical school. He had kept in touch with Hisayo and Jesse since Betty's passing, even while at university. They, in turn, had treated him like the son they never had.

Jesse rose to greet him.

"It's good to see you, Tony," he said, as he took the young man's hand.

"I wanted to stop by for a moment before I headed home."

Jesse could see it in Tonio's eyes—ever the sadness.

"I'm glad you did—only I have some preparations to make and a staff meeting in a few minutes. There's a storm coming. But walk with me."

The two headed down the corridor, Jesse's trained eyes spotting areas needing attention.

"You know, Tony, it might not be a bad idea if you get back up to your folks before it hits us."

"Yes, sir, I've already called home. They're expecting me. Anything I can do to help here?"

"No, we'll be fine. Send my regards to Dr. Galen and the Edisons."

A few minutes later Tonio ran through the rain shower across the parking lot and climbed into the used, yellow Toyota Corolla his guardians had given him as a graduation present. They decided Galen's Jeep was not up to being a hand-me-down.

As he headed down the road, a torrent of raindrops sheeted across the windshield.

They were old now, the progenitors of the pack, so they preferred huddling together in the den even in the summer, the warm bodies of the younger wolves giving some relief from the twinges of arthritis afflicting their hip joints. They licked each other's muzzles, as their ears flicked in response to the nearby flashes and thunder claps.

Water gushed across the stone outcropping above and poured down in front of the den opening.

"Oh, dang, I forgot to batten down the sheds," Edison said. "Come on, it won't hurt you to get wet."

He grabbed an old Bell Labs rain slicker and tossed an umbrella at Galen.

Solid sheets of rain pelted the ground.

Ahmed al-Yusef sat hypnotized by the illuminated display unfolding before him on the Doppler radar. The repetitive forecasts of hot and humid days earlier in the week had been lulling him into a kind of torpor. Not today.

"Want a Coke, Ahmed?"

Seymour Cohen held up a frosty can for his co-worker. They got along well, often sharing lunch breaks and double dates.

"What's on the screen? I hear those heavy storms're still movin' across Ohio and Pennsylvania. Lotsa people gonna get a real soaking and…"

"Holy shit! Sy, look at this!"

In the lower-left-hand quadrant of the screen, the Doppler was now producing red and yellow and white zones of data the two men had rarely seen, particularly over Wyoming County, Pennsylvania. They knew the technicalities: Rising hot winds from the southwest and west were converging with cold jets from the northwest. Like water beginning to corkscrew down a drain—only in reverse—those winds spiraled upward in ever-increasing velocities, moving counterclockwise and approaching a hundred miles an hour at the storm's center. Massive downpours of rain and large-size hail fell out of the gigantic cloud, which accompanied the whirling dervish along its path of imminent destruction. Meteorologists called it a supercell, the rarest and most powerful kind of thunderstorm. Inside it were the makings of a monster tornado.

Each man uttered a silent prayer to the God of Ibrahim and Abraham.

Ahmed hit the alert button on his console to relay the data to police, emergency-response teams, and the radio and TV stations in the area, while Seymour picked up the microphone connected to the emergency channel.

"National Weather Service radio WXM95 broadcasting on a frequency of 162.525 megahertz from Towanda, Pennsylvania. Doppler radar has picked up cyclonic wind shears forming over Wyoming County. This is a tornado warning. All persons in the involved area are advised to seek shelter immediately. Repeat, this is a tornado warning!"

Two phones rang at Safehaven, as the weather-alert alarm sounded once more, and the voice blared out the warning message. Nancy picked up the wall receiver in the kitchen, and a water-soaked Edison pulled out his cordless unit under cover of the storage shed.

"Tio Eddie, Tia Nancy, it's me, Tonio..."

He had been driving the Toyota along the country road, when the rain that had been steadily beating down suddenly was replaced by bursts of golf-ball-sized hail hammering the roof and windshield. Visibility dropped to near zero, as dense, cumulonimbus clouds formed above. Tonio slowed the car to a crawl just in time to see the swirling waters of Sugar Hollow Creek spilling over and washing out the road.

In a few moments the pavement was breached.

"Tio, the road's gone! I can try coming the back way, but..."

The silence on the line scared Edison. Galen put his ear next to the phone. Both could hear Nancy on the line.

"Tonio, what's wrong, are you all right?"

"I just felt the weirdest sensation. My ears suddenly started to pop, and ... geez ... the sky looks green!"

"Tonio, get out of the car, now!" Edison yelled.

"What's wrong, Tio ...oh, my God, the sky, it's now pitch black!"

Galen joined Edison in a frantic chorus.

"Get out! Get out! Take cover in a ditch!"

The excitement had attracted Mike to the kitchen phone. He and Nancy stood breathless, as they heard the car door open and close. In the background, the locomotive noise rose in intensity, even as Tonio's running footsteps punctuated the chugging wind. His "unhh," as he threw himself to the ground, elicited gasps from the two pairs inside and outside the house. The howling wind became a banshee shriek for what seemed like an eternity … and then it Dopplered away.

"Tonio, can you hear me?"

Galen kept repeating the words, straining his ears for the slightest sound. He relaxed slightly as heavy, tremulous breathing on the other end became a weak voice calling out "yes."

"Tio, the trees, my car … they're all gone!" The young man's voice dissolved in tears.

In the background the rain played a drum roll on the forest floor.

"Ben, looka this."

Lem held a wad of drawings in his hand. Miri was rocking back and forth on the living room rug near the little brick fireplace, hands moving like a sewing machine bobbin, charcoal drawing sticks casting image after image on loose stacks of drawing paper.

Ben's eyes widened at the depictions on the paper.

"Lem, we've all got to get out of here!"

Miri's she-wolf stood up, its head and ears pointed toward the front door, and emitted a bone-chilling, ululating howl.

The farmer and the retired state trooper each took an arm and guided Miri out the door and up the lane toward Safehaven. The downpour had subsided but wind gusts blew against their faces. Then suddenly the female wolf began to bark, and Miri emitted a guttural reply. Both performed a howling duet.

"What's that child doing now?" Lem asked.

"I don't know," Ben replied, feeling a mild tightness in his chest. He popped a nitroglycerin tablet, as Lem held on to his daughter.

"Reckon I know. Look!"

The two old men stared in disbelief then dropped to the forest floor and tried to shield the girl. Miri's cry could not be heard above the whirling black dervish of destruction climbing the mountain only two-hundred yards away.

Edison and Galen stood inside the storage shed, as the rising wind gusts shook the structure. Galen tried to yell above the rumble.

"Tonio, hang on, were coming to get you ... oh, sweet Jesus!"

Tonio, struggling to his feet, felt a white-hot bolt of fear, as he heard the blare from Edison's weather-alert radio through the phone Nancy was holding in her shaking hand. He heard her gasp and Mike exclaim, "Holy shit!"

"This is an emergency bulletin from the National Weather Service. A tornado has been spotted in the vicinity of Agape Mountain. All residents take shelter immediately. Repeat. All residents take shelter immediately!"

He heard the all-too-familiar chugging howl, followed by the sounds of cracking wood and the shattering of glass. Then he heard Nancy screaming and calling out, "Bob! Galen!"

Then ... silence.

They emerged from the shelter of their den. The strange violence had passed by, and now their instincts drew them out. Their muzzles rose to catch the scents in the air, their lime-green eyes cautiously scanned the sky. Their cone-shaped ears twitched and turned, detecting distant, unfamiliar sounds.

The three elders gathered their progeny and herded them into the forest and up toward the summit.

The wind gone, only steady rain caressed the forest floor.

Must get home!

Tonio stumbled as he attempted to cross a fallen tree trunk

spanning the still-swollen stream. He felt a twinge in his right ankle as he landed after jumping the last few feet to safety.

Ow! Have to go on. No time to waste. It's not far, I can do it.

Mike rose from the floor where his body had surrounded the older woman's. He helped her to her feet.

"Tia Nancy, are you all right?"

Dazed, she went to the picture window in the living room, now just an opened maw festooned with sharp glass shards, and looked down across the driveway.

"Mike, they're in there!"

"I know…"

"Galen, can you hear me? Galen?

"I can't move, Galen…"

Tonio limped toward the entrance to Vista Drive.

I'm almost there.

Their ears still ringing and popping, Lem stood up first and helped Ben and Miri to their feet. He looked at the swath of destruction that ran up the side of the mountain.

Their little cottage was gone.

"Come on," Ben said. "We've got to get to the big house."

Lem nodded and took hold of Miri's hand.

The pack headed first toward the two-legged ones' small den, their paw strokes on the rain-wet forest floor muted by the saturated ground. Their sharp hearing registered the call of their sister, and they knew she was near.

"What the hell is that?" Ben said, amazed at the canine procession approaching.

"By golly, we got us an escort!" Lem replied.

"Freddie, look!"

He stopped the car. Four sighted, one blind—all turned in the direction of the black funnel cloud howling in the distance.

"My God, that's near the house! Carm, call Safehaven!"

"I'm trying, Freddie. No one's answering."

The car leaped forward. No one complained about Freddie's driving speed now.

Tonio turned as he heard the car horn behind him. The big, Crown Victoria police cruiser pulled up, and Lachlan stuck his head out the window.

"Get in, kid."

"Lach, I think Safehaven's been hit."

He was shaking uncontrollably.

The state trooper put his hand on Tonio's shoulder.

"That's where I'm headed."

"Looka that!"

Lem couldn't believe it. Neither could Ben.

"The big house is safe! Damned tornado only took out a bunch o' trees and those two storage sheds."

"Who's that standing out there?"

They saw Mike pulling away barehanded at the scattered, twisted pieces of sheet metal, lumber, and other debris. Nancy knelt close by. Neither seemed to notice the footsteps and padding paws approaching.

"What's wrong, Missus?"

Mike didn't miss a beat.

"Edison and Galen were in one of the sheds!"

The younger pack members stood by at a distance, as Zeus and Mercury pushed forward and began circling and sniffing at the rubble. Just then the police cruiser, followed by Freddie's car, rolled up the driveway. Both slid to a halt, and their occupants spilled out and ran toward the site of the destruction.

"Michael!" Carmelita squealed with relief and delight, as she ran to him. "What are you doing?"

She and the others saw the look on his face and Nancy's. They said no more and immediately pitched in alongside Mike and Lem, as Ben held Miri.

Faisal whistled for his guide dog.

"Akela, find!"

The wolf let out a sharp bark and ran toward his fellow canines. Miri's guardian instinctively joined them as well. Four muzzles sniffed and huffed, and then Zeus stopped and let out a wavering howl.

Faisal yelled out, "They're over there!"

"I hear something, Galen," Edison uttered weakly.

"Galen...?"

It didn't take long for the men to peel away most of the wreckage. The storm had imploded the shed and flung one of the walls—and Edison and Galen with it—nearly 100 feet into the woods. Fortunately, it had landed between two large boulders, which gave enough support to keep the men from being crushed under its weight.

"Tio?"

Edison looked up into the eyes of a wolf then turned his head weakly toward the voice above him.

"I can't move, boy. I'm pinned. Where's Galen?"

They heard the faint voice.

"Underneath you, little brother ... Tonio ... black bag ... brown bottle ... pills."

Ben heard the old doctor's gasping words.

"Here, give him one o' mine."

Tonio snatched the tiny pill from the other man's hand and, lying down flat across the fallen beams, he reached through the opening to Galen's face.

"Open your mouth, Tio."

He was barely audible now.

"Under my tongue, Tonio."

Jacob looked at Carmelita.

"What'd he just give him?"

Her eyes moistened, as she replied "nitroglycerin."

"Are you all right now, Tio?"

Tonio was close to tears himself.

Galen, though still weak, tried his usual gruff humor.

"Still here, despite Edison's attempt to squash me."

Tonio turned to the rest, all looking down. Their expressions betrayed the worry.

Twenty minutes later they had extricated Edison and Galen from the wreckage, and the Medevac helicopter had arrived to transport them to the hospital. Nancy's Red Cross training had come in handy. She had checked her husband and was satisfied that all he had sustained were some pretty big bruises, though the EMTs advised taking him along for observation.

As the 'copter lifted off, Edison first looked at Nancy, sitting beside him and holding his hand, and then over at his old friend, who was barely conscious, an IV needle stuck in his arm and oxygen flowing to a clear-plastic mask.

"You okay, big brother?"

Galen's eyes shifted in his direction, but he made no response.

The living room was nearly silent, as young and old alike tried to suppress their worry and recover their strength after the post-adrenalin letdown. Lachlan leaned against the fireplace then flipped on his communications receiver, as a voice came through the Bluetooth in his ear.

"Douglass, the town's been hit!"

He hit the send button.

"What's the status?"

"Bad. Better get over there. Reports of a nursing home and a day-care center..."

The tornado did what tornadoes sometimes do. After shearing off the top of the mountain it had made a sudden turn to the south and plowed through town.

Jesse Orth had heard the sirens.

"That's a tornado warning," he called out to the staff. "Get the patients moved to the sub-basement!"

The well-trained nursing-home workers had guided the ambulatory patients down hallways to stairways and wheeled the bed-ridden to the large freight elevator. In less than five minutes they had moved the entire complement of patients to the underground shelter.

Thirty seconds later most of the surface structure was gone.

The rain spattered the debris where once stood St. Ignatius Home.

Kim Thu Nguyen had just graduated from Penn State University with a degree in elementary education. She was slated to begin fulltime in the Wyoming County school system that fall. But like many young people between their school years and the start of their careers, she needed a summer job. So she had jumped at the offer of the Happy Valley Day Care Center.

"Come on Bobby, leave Samantha alone. Timmy, Tommy, quit shoving. Jane, you're not supposed to put gum in Sally's ears!"

Oh yes, she loved kids and loved this job.

The rain had driven them inside, and they were playing musical chairs, six preschoolers marching around miniature chairs and tables.

"Listen, children, listen to the rain. It's going pitter-patter, pitter-patter."

Then Kim noticed the suddenly darkened sky outside and heard the low but growing rumble. It reminded her of the waterspout skies of her coastal Vietnam village.

Realizing, she quickly herded the children together.

"Now we're going to play a special game. Everyone hold hands."

She led them out into the hall and down the stairs to the basement. There she found blankets and spread them out on the concrete floor, one for each child, one for herself. There were no windows, but the kids' sharp hearing picked up the chugging shriek above. She could see the alarm in their eyes.

"Quickly now, let's pretend we're all going camping. I've made tents for each of you."

Her voice was shaking as she laid a second blanket over each child then grabbed the last one for herself. She pulled it over her head and body just as the sky opened up over the building. Thirty seconds later, what had been the Happy Valley Day Care Center was no more.

The rain pitter-pattered on the rubble.

Lachlan's face had turned pale, as he addressed the group now looking up at him from their exhaustion.

"Bad news, folks. The tornado took St. Ignatius and a daycare center nearby. I don't know if anyone's still alive."

Tonio immediately jumped up.

"St Ignatius? No, no! They're in there, they're in there!"

Lachlan held up both hands in a calming gesture.

"They're going to need all the help they can get. My sergeant says the center of town looks like matchsticks. He says the governor has called in the National Guard, but they won't get here near quick enough."

He took a breath.

"There were kids in the center."

Momentary silence, then it was as though everyone in the room suddenly had the same thought.

"C'mon, we can all go in two cars."

Freddie grabbed his keys and headed toward the door.

"What the hell. . .?"

His jaw dropped. The two elders, Zeus and Mercury, sat at the bottom of the stairs, while the rest of the pack watched from the edge of the woods. Lem reached the doorway and muttered.

"I'll be damned."

"What do we do now?"

Faisal had joined them.

"I know . . . Akela!"

The animal bounded out of the house and stood before the canines. Miri's guardian she-wolf soon followed.

Faisal turned to Lachlan.

"We've got to get ahead of them and lead them."

The strange caravan—two vehicles in front, the animals trailing—worked its way slowly down the mountain and took a circuitous route around roads that had been washed out by local creeks. As they entered the little town, it became hard for the group hold back the tears.

"Good God!" Lachlan muttered.

"My God," Lem echoed.

Familiar homes and stores lay in ruin, mute testimony to Nature's destructive power.

The two vehicles snaked around debris scattered across the roads, coming to a stop halfway down the block, where a nursing home and a daycare center once stood. The occupants got out in stunned silence.

Three ambulances and a Red Cross command-and-communications van were parked in front of the wreckage.

Lea Ann called the young adults over and quickly got them outfitted with hard hats, work boots, and gloves. Then the disaster-team leader took them aside for a quick briefing, but when she saw the four animals standing nearby, she stood back with a start.

"What are they doing here?"

Lachlan said quietly, "We need them."

As if on cue, Akela returned to Faisal's side, and the nameless she-wolf rejoined Miri, while Zeus and Mercury split apart, each heading to one of the fallen buildings. They roamed quickly over the wreckage, muzzles low, nasal alars flaring in large, inhaling gulps. Soon Zeus had zeroed in on a part of the daycare center and howled.

"Come on, Freddie," Mike called. "Let's get moving. That's where we need to be."

He gave Carmelita a quick kiss and joined her brother. The two young men began using pry bars and brute force to lift the debris away. More volunteers had arrived and joined them. Soon they had uncovered the stairway to the basement storage room, now lit by streams of sunlight. Down they went but found their way blocked by a heavy, wooden door.

"It's jammed," Freddie said. "We need fire axes!" he yelled up to the surface.

Soon Lem came running with the tools.

The young men were sweating profusely as each, in turn, swung the pointed ax tips at the door. The wood finally splintered, and the two were able to pass through the opening. Inside, beams lay half-broken and dust swirled, as air currents penetrated the enclosed area.

Then Mike spotted the blankets outlined by tiny forms beneath and held his breath. He rushed over and began to carefully pull the blankets back.

Tiny voices piped up: "Is the game over yet? Can I see my mommy? Is Miss Kim here?"

Freddie saw the blanket with the larger outline and pulled it back. The young woman moaned and reached for her forehead then opened her eyes.

"Are you God?"

Mike laughed. "He probably thinks he is, ma'am."

"Guys, help me over the debris."

Tonio, Jacob, and Akela guided Faisal over the nursing-home rubble, as Mercury continued his olfactory sweep of the pile.

"Jesse was preparing emergency plans when I left. He probably moved everyone into the sub-basement shelter. Betty and I ..."

He quickly changed the subject.

"We're not gonna be able to move much of this. We're gonna need a mini-dozer."

He was becoming discouraged.

"There's a John Deere farm equipment store down the road a piece."

Tonio turned to see Lem surveying the scene.

"I'll see what I c'n get."

The old farmer hustled over to Lachlan.

"Lach, c'n you get me to the John Deere store? We're gonna need some brute force."

Fifteen minutes later the sound of a diesel engine echoed down the debris-strewn street, as Lem drove a small excavator into view. Slowly he moved the treads to within ten feet of the young men, who had cleared away a small zone of rubble.

"Show me what you want."

By now, Mike and Freddie had rejoined Tonio, Jacob and Faisal.

Tonio called out, "Start here—go slowly!"

Lem lowered the excavator blade in a surprisingly expert manner and began shoving a path through the heavy rubble. Then he backed the machine off and raised the scoop.

"That enough?"

Faisal stepped in, shouting, "Lem, turn off the excavator, please."

The blind young man turned his head, moving radar-like ears in a circle, as Tonio guided his steps.

"Okay, clear away this section—and go deeper."

Once more the excavator moved, this time creating a dish-like depression. Lem carefully piled up more debris at the back of the machine.

"Look, it's the elevator shaft!" Tonio exclaimed.

Jacob peered down. "If we can get down through the top of the elevator we'd have a direct access to the shelter, wouldn't we?"

Tonio nodded.

"Mike, Freddie, you're the tech guys. Any ideas?"

Freddie turned to Lem.

"If we tie some cables on the blade, can you haul out some of the stuff that's still there on top?"

"Yep."

Jacob walked around to the side of the machine.

"Where did you learn to do this, Lem?"

"Back in 'Nam."

Freddie and Mike found cables in the excavator's tool box, tied their ends to the scoop, and dropped their lengths down the shaft. Then they gripped the cables tightly with their heavy gloves and slid themselves down.

"Lower us some crowbars, guys," Mike yelled.

After each remaining piece of concrete had been tied to the cable,

Lem backed up the excavator and slowly pulled it off the top of the elevator cab, revealing the roof.

Within minutes Freddie and Mike had pried open the access panel and climbed inside. They wedged the pry bars between the doors. Sounds of pounding and squealing metal rose up the shaft, but soon they stopped.

"We can't get them open," Freddie yelled.

"Hang on, guys, I'm coming down!" Tonio responded.

He strapped on a backpack with high intensity lights and another pry bar and lowered himself down the shaft and into the elevator. Soon the three young men together strained their muscles against the steel levers, and the screeching of metal announced success.

Faisal let out a high-pitched whistle. Akela and the she-wolf, followed by Zeus and Mercury, ran to the open pit. One by one they carefully descended the sloping mound created by Lem's excavator scoop and leaped down from the open roof of the elevator into the cab. Once inside, they moved through the open doors into the eerie darkness, their sniffing easily audible to Mike, Freddie, and Tonio.

Soon barking and yelps arose.

"Little brother, you don't need to go in there," Freddie said.

He had always been overprotective of Tonio, and despite their apparent sibling friction, he had shared his brother's loss of Betty. He saw the conflicting emotions on Tonio's face.

"Look, Freddie, I'm the only one here who knows this building."

He handed out the lights and led the way into the sub-basement. Memories of his trysts with Betty in this space tore at his soul—every corner, every pillar silent witness to the love of his life. He heard her voice in every footstep, every wisp of air current.

You'll do it, Tony, I know you will.

He stumbled over a fallen ceiling tile.

Be careful, my love.

The footsteps of his brother and Mike echoed behind him, as he followed the four canines deeper into the sub-basement cavern. They barked, and he saw the faint illumination of a penlight. He shone his lantern at the source and spotted them, some lying on the floor, some in wheelchairs, others leaning against the wall.

"Jesse, it's me, Tonio."

A shaky voice in the darkness replied, "She told me you would come."

One by one the rescue workers lifted the nursing home occupants by harnesses to the surface. Jesse remained behind, until all his staff and patients had made it out. Then he turned and hugged Tonio before being lifted from the underground tomb.

"Let's get our doggie friends out, then it's our turn," Freddie said to his brother, as he playfully wiped soot from Tonio's face. "You're a regular coal miner now, kid."

The wolves would not tolerate being handled, so the team assembled a ladder of debris for them to climb to the roof of the cab. Once there, they easily ascended the piled up rubble to the surface. That left the three rescuers.

"You first, Mike. Carmelita would never forgive us if a hair of your head was harmed."

The brothers laughed, as they saw the big Greek guy blush even in the limited light.

"Freddie, you're next. I'm sure Lilly has some suitable reward awaiting you."

"Watch your tongue, little brother. I know your secret. You've got *cojones*, too."

He watched as Freddie was raised up. He turned toward the darkness.

"I love you, Betty."

As he felt himself being lifted out, the chilled basement air whispered back, *I love you, Tony.*

And then it was over. Men, women, and canines stood and sat in exhaustion.

Ben had kept an eye on Miri while helping out at the nursing stations. He needn't have worried. She spent the whole time sitting on the blanket Lea Ann had placed on the ground for her, making charcoal drawings and manipulating her modeling clay.

Holding a bottle of water, Ben walked over to his daughter and scanned the paper and clay laying there, all vivid scenes of children and patients as they appeared in their underground shelters. Clay figures of rescuers and children and wolves locating other storm victims stood in mute testimony.

Then he noticed one drawing in particular, and he started to tremble. He attempted to yell to Lem, when the chest pain hit him, and he had to stop for another nitroglycerin pill.

Lem sat in the excavator cab. He was used to hard work, but manipulating the machine's controls for so long had made his entire body ache. He smiled, as he saw Zeus and Mercury walk slowly across the debris field and sit a few feet away. They were old, too, and their endurance had been stretched by the run to the town.

"Hey, guys, I know how you feel."

The old farmer started to stretch his arms when he felt the vibration. The sole remaining, above-ground wall fragment that had once been St. Ignatius was beginning to shift forward.

They sensed it before he did. Their canine ears had pricked, and Zeus and Mercury started to whine.

Must be some settling down below.

Lem started to reach for the starter key when the wall fell toward the cab.

Was it reflex?

The two male canines, once beaten and abused by the two-legged one before them, their energies all but spent, nevertheless leapt to the open side of the cab, their forepaws forcing the startled Lem out the other side and to the ground.

As he rolled to a stop his eyes recorded in slow motion a sight that would burn forever in his heart and soul. The two old dogs sat in the cab and looked across at him, as the rubble pile on which the excavator had been sitting collapsed downward, the cavity beneath swallowing machine and beasts, while the massive wall fragment slammed down on top of where it had stood a moment ago.

Lem knew that look, even in the grayed muzzles and filmy eyes of the two aged ones who had willingly sacrificed themselves.

It was love.

The others rushed to the site, as Lem knelt and wept openly over the debris-filled grave. He didn't stop, as Ben gently lifted him to his feet and led him away.

Back on the mountain, the wolf pack gathered around Athena, who stood alone, gazing at her children. The young alpha male and his two cohorts flanked her, as the remaining pack members sat back in deference.

The mother of them all raised her graying muzzle. Her solitary, grief-filled howl carried across the town. Then the pack encircling the mound raised their heads to heaven and joined in.

It was their duty.

They were the Moonsingers of Safehaven.

CHAPTER 14

Reflections

Nancy sat silently, staring at the cardiac-intensive-care-unit door, as the haunting notes of Grieg's "The Last Spring" drifted through the hospital sound system.

"Mrs. Edison, may I speak with you?"

She had grown to know the tall, handsome, athletic, Mediterranean doctor well.

"Dr. Crescenzi, are they all right?"

Salvatore Crescenzi, director of cardiology and cardiovascular inter-ventional procedures, looked at the woman he had treated so recently.

How much do I tell her? Even that pacemaker/defibrillator I put in can't protect her from a double whammy like this.

"Your husband's blood pressure started to spike in the emergency room. We got it stabilized, but because of his heart failure, we're try-ing to diurese him to get the fluid out of his chest."

She didn't quite take in the full import of his remarks.

"Dr. Galen is not my husband, Dr. Crescenzi."

"Yes, I know. Mr. Edison..."

"Has he broken something? I know he had those large bruises, doc-tor, so I..."

"That may be what set this off, Mrs. Edison. When a lot of muscle gets bruised, certain chemicals get released into the blood stream, and they gum up the kidneys. When that happens in a ... uh ... older adult, it puts a strain on the heart. How long has he had high blood pressure?"

"High blood pressure?"

Her facial expression changed.

"He won't go to doctors, Dr. Crescenzi. He won't even let Galen look at him..."

Then, finally realizing, she looked directly into the cardiologist's eyes.

"What are you telling me?"

Crescenzi's brow creased.

She's too smart. Best to go with the truth.

"Your husband has had a serious heart attack. I was able to cath him and lyse the clot but..."

"Code Blue, Code Blue! CCU Three."

Crescenzi whirled around and rushed back into the intensive-care unit.

The music had stopped.

"Can't you go any faster, Freddie?"

Tonio sat on the edge of the back seat with Jacob and Faisal, the seeing-eye wolf Akela at Faisal's feet. Carmelita, wedged between Freddie and Mike, pleaded for common sense.

"Come on. Tio Eddie and Tio Galen are in the best possible place, and Lachlan got Tia Nancy to the hospital in the cruiser. Everything will be all right. You don't have to break any records!"

Nancy stood at the door to the ICU, stepping back as staff members rushed in and out, catching glimpses of multiple medical personnel engaged in the shamanistic ritual of cardiac resuscitation on a patient. She heard the priestly utterances of Crescenzi, as he held the all-too-familiar paddles and called out "up it to 400 joules." Nurses and house staff continued pumping assorted drugs into plastic IV tubes swaying above the patient like spider webs.

Then she heard Crescenzi yell, "Yes! We got him back!"

She remembered what had happened to her not long ago.

Did this unknown patient also watch over what was happening to him?

Six young adults and one canine ran through the hospital waiting room and up the stairs to the intensive-care-unit floor.

"Tia Nancy, what's happening?"

Carmelita embraced her, feeling the tension in her body.

"I don't know for sure. Dr. Crescenzi had to handle a code blue before he could finish and…"

The cardiologist was sweat-soaked as he entered the hallway once more. He looked at the group protectively surrounding Nancy.

Good, this helps.

He took her hands in his.

"We were lucky. Dr. Galen went into cardiac arrest, but we got him back. He's a tough old bird."

"Tonio, wait!"

Freddie tried to stop his younger brother, but Tonio yanked his arm away from his restraining hand and rushed through the ICU door. He didn't ask, as he ran past startled nursing staff.

"Tio, Tio, can you hear me?"

He had never seen his guardian this way: pale, gaunt, eyes closed, shallow breathing.

The old man opened his eyes, and a faint smile crossed his face. His tongue tried to moisten his dried lips. The endotracheal tube had been removed, but his vocal cords were swollen, and he could barely croak out, "I knew you'd come, boy."

He hesitated then, in a barely audible voice asked, "How's Edison?"

Tonio bent forward and kissed the old man's forehead.

The group surrounded Edison in ICU. His breathing was still labored, but the fluid was draining out of him and filling the catheter-fed collection bag strapped to the side of the hospital bed.

Nancy embraced her partner of nearly six decades. She couldn't say anything. He slowly raised his right arm and placed it on her shoulder. She could barely hear him from behind his oxygen mask.

"How's Galen?"

Mama, Papa, is that you?

Si, Berto we are here.

Never thought I'd see myself like that. Strange, isn't it?

Posso venire con voi?

Can I come with you?

Non ancora, figlio mio.

Not yet, my son.

Perché non posso venire con voi?

Why can't I come with you?

Ci sono ancora più affinchè facciano.

There is still more for you to do.

Two wheelchairs sat side-by-side in the intermediate-coronary-care unit viewing room.

Two old men stared out the large picture window overlooking the mountain vista surrounding the hospital. Both men's voices were still a bit hoarse from the various tubes that had been stuck in them.

The bear-sized man smiled, as he croaked out, "Well, Stanley, this is another fine mess you've gotten us into."

His less-stocky companion returned the smile and squeaked back, "I'm sorry, Ollie."

Both started to laugh, but quickly suppressed the urge, as the pain in their chests ruined the moment.

"Bob, Galen, all set?"

Nancy stood next to Crescenzi, as he made final entry and discharge notes on two charts. He looked down at the two geriatric patients watching him expectantly and smiled.

"So, would you two like to stay a bit longer, or should I call your entourage?"

They moved down the hall, one wheelchair pushed by Freddie, the other by Tonio. As the procession of old timers, young adults and wolf-dog approached the Loading Doc, Tonio bent forward and whispered in Galen's ear.

"We're going home, Tio, we're going home."

Galen closed his eyes and sighed.

Home!

R.A. Comunale is a semi-retired physician in family practice and specialist in aviation medicine who lives and works out of his home office in McLean, Virginia. He enjoys writing, gardening, electronics, pounding on a piano, and yelling at his dimwitted cat. He describes himself as an eccentric and iconoclast.

The cat has taken out a restraining order.